POTTER'S FIELD BLUES

By
Michael Tyree

To Gemma

I hope you dig it!

Mic J

Cover art by Jon Young
Cover layout by Kevin Massie
Edited by M.B. Slaughter
Photography by Dreaming Wolf Photography

Printed in the United States of America

Second Printing: March 2021
Michael Tyree

ISBN 9798716973749

Be yourself; everyone else is already taken.
— OSCAR WILDE

Below is a QR code for the Potter's Field Blues Spotify soundtrack. These songs were hand picked by the author to go hand in hand with the book. Scan it and give it a listen.

For Keith.

CONTENTS

FOREWORD

It's 10:31 on a Wednesday night and I'm sitting here wondering where to begin the introduction to this book. I guess this is as good of a jumping off point as any, so here goes.

My name is Michael Tyree (not to be confused with that other Michael Tyree who doesn't pay his Rent-A-Center bill). I'm 37 years old and only a few years away from my first prostate exam and first mid-life crisis (which will most likely be about the prostate exam). I'm a firm believer in solid creative outlets. We as humans are inherently fucked and broken and thus need creative outlets in order to unfuck ourselves. Don't be fooled by the shiny things. Everyone is going through something. Some of us are simply better at hiding it with Instagram filters. The truth is, we all need a positive way to work through our own bullshit. Some people turn to creation like fixing up old cars, painting, knitting, rebuilding homes, writing songs or poetry, maybe some performance art to the Cheers theme music. Others channel themselves into bettering their communities through building homes for the less fortunate or serving food to those who would otherwise not know when or where their next meal would come from. Regardless, everyone needs a *thing*, at least one avenue to better themselves and stave off the existential doom. Writing is my channel, my avenue. I had others when I was younger, and those things and their creations still have a place in my heart.

I wore a lot of masks over the years; tried to be like a lot of strange people other than myself. But as I've grown older, I began burying the men that wore those masks until I found who I really

1

am. Writing, especially writing about dark things has given me the tools to cut myself open to the core and let out all the bile and venom. In here I've created characters with tiny pieces of me woven into their souls. And writing about them and those attributes has helped me talk about things that I wish I had the balls to discuss with a therapist.

There was a point in my life where I had put writing to the wayside. The notion of getting published melted into one of those fairy tale dreams like being a pro skater or porn star. I did what I was told after high school and went after more obtainable lucrative paths that had nothing to do with writing let alone chasing dreams. I put on my marathon runners' tag and joined the rat race full of hate and regret. Almost a decade later I dropped down near rock bottom when my checked-out indifference caused me to lose my job. For the first time in a long time I had no idea what to do with my life, no idea where to go or what I even wanted. I had become so disconnected from all of my childhood dreams while I focused on a career I hated that it felt like being lost at sea in total darkness.

One evening while I was still looking for work, my wife took me to the local bookstore to cheer me up. At the time I didn't read as much outside of a little non-fiction. I didn't have a favorite author and had forgotten what it felt like to get lost in that world. Morgan bought a copy of *The Hellbound Heart* by Clive Barker to cheer me up. I didn't realize it then, but that would be the catalyst to me sitting here right now typing this introduction. That book sat on multiple shelves, acquired four years of dust, and moved with us to two more town houses and then eventually our current home before I opened it up. That tiny 164-page novella reignited something in my heart I thought had long since atrophied. I fell in love with horror again. I fell in love with reading fiction again, but most importantly, I felt inspired to start writing my own macabre chapters again. That moment I decided for the first time in almost a decade and a half I would shoot for something other than my 9 to 5.

This book is the culmination of long nights with a pen and a dirty notepad working through the graveyard shift. It's from early mornings watching the sun creep up over the horizon before passing out over my keyboard. It's from every spare moment I once had for other hobbies, now dedicated to weaving together my own universe.

So, if you are reading this now, I want to say thank you for picking up this book. I don't care if you paid full price for it, half price, or unearthed it in a thrift store bin. I couldn't care less if you borrowed it from your weird friend at work or even stole it for that matter. All I really care about is that you took the moment to put down your cell phone and pick up this book (unless of course you're reading this on your cell phone. In that case…you know what I mean).

Hopefully, there is something for you in here. Maybe you'll get a chuckle from something so dark you'll feel the need to say a few Hail Marys or visit your local clergyman. Maybe you think you've read it all and you can predict the end before it begins. Or maybe something peeks around the corner of your peripheral, and now you're checking under your bed before you turn out the light. If all goes well, something in these stories will tug at your security and leave you reluctant to visit the kitchen by yourself after dark, and so uneasy that you sprint upstairs for fear that some nasty thing is at your heels, ready to drag you to hell. Either way, I dare you. I dare you to turn your phone off and keep reading this (unless you really are reading this on your phone, then don't do that). I dare you to peek around the page at what I have in store for you.

-Mike

POTTER'S FIELD BLUES

114th Street was busy for a Thursday night. Taxis loaded and unloaded with the resonating cadence of car horns firing off from frustration and impatience. Humans from polar-opposite walks of life crossed paths like shooting stars across a barren night sky. Young couples made their way to bars and parties, while older couples were on their way to long, resentful silences. Callused workers sought a modicum of peace after twelve hours of hard labor, while lone businessmen leading the ploy of long nights at the office searched for the company of strangers behind a filthy dumpster. Pushers and hustlers traded fleeting refuge for a few dollars, while addicts and winos crawled on an infinite trek for release. And then there were the working girls and rent boys, back to the wall, nothing else to trade but themselves. Some were runaways, refugees from broken and abusive homes. Or sometimes just lost souls that fell through the cracks of a failed system, ricocheting back and forth between foster families like a deteriorated shuttlecock, losing its feathers and definition with every blow. Finally, there were young dreamers who waited their whole lives to chase the big city lights, only to find them burned out and faded away.

It was 8:53 PM and Monica's night had only begun. She pulled a heavy drag from her cigarette while stepping out onto the fragmented sidewalk. Her jet-black bob haircut curled underneath her jawline veiling all but the oval silhouette of her face. The humid summer climate gave her no quarter as her bangs became cemented to her forehead. She let out a slow exhale

5

from the base of her lungs as the second-hand menthol smoke ascended toward the lemon tinted streetlamp, so much like the steam that roared with violence from the storm drains and manhole covers. The aroma of muggy humid air and wet asphalt painted a landscape across an all too familiar canvas. Other acquainted fragrances filled nights such as these: vending machine cologne, grain whiskey, pay-by-the-hour suites soaked in concentrated bleach, old cigarettes burnt to the filter, stale cum, and the occasional smell of regret.

The accustomed tone of the evening wore off as Monica's attention pulled elsewhere. It was impossible to miss the sweaty, overweight man emerging from an adjacent alleyway. He stumbled over the sidewalk on his way to a champagne-colored Buick in almost worse shape than its owner. The ogre released deep breaths with every stride, as if a spotter had relieved his chest of a barbell at the last moment. His shoulders sagged as he fumbled to produce keys from the pocket of an oversized pair of navy-blue work slacks. At four sizes too large for his torso, it was all his worn, braided belt could do to hold them at attention. The quest for his key ring made the man inspect himself further. He stopped in mid stride, and mid search, so he would guarantee the closure of his fly. Once he reassured himself of that, the man did not miss a beat making his exit from 114th Street.

Another figure appeared from the same dim passage. This one much frailer in comparison and engulfed with ease by the coarse shadows weaving across the storefronts. The thin figure treaded with the tired composure of a soul unable to discern what was worse between staying and going. Splashes of light from the few working streetlamps gave varying clues to the identity of this weary creature: the outline of a faded red spaghetti strap tank top, the shoulder length auburn blonde hair, the frayed Daisy Duke jean shorts. After a more refined look, Monica realized this mysterious figure wiping her mouth clean was her dear friend, Chloe.

Chloe lacked the stamina required to conceal the unease of this evening from her face. The grief, disgust, and hopelessness were all painted across her expression at once in the vein of a melancholy Jackson Pollock. She composed herself with a short lived, obligatory smile.

"Hey."

"Hey yourself there, sweetie," Monica replied with a smile.

Chloe looked back over her shoulder one last time toward the alley, and then to the rusty sedan passing by as it coasted back up the street.

"I need a cigarette," Chloe said with an anxious tone as she searched her purse. She tore through every corner of the handbag, excavating anything but a single cancer stick. "Perfect," Chloe exclaimed with clenched teeth.

"Easy, easy. Here, you can have one of mine. What's got you so worked up?" Monica inquired as she procured a slim menthol and handed it over to Chloe.

"Thanks. I'm fine. I just…I've been on edge for days." Chloe rummaged through her purse once more in hope she had better luck with finding her lighter. "I can't stop thinking about Jess," replied Chloe as she acquired the lighter with a sigh of relief.

"Jess? So, they found her? Is she ok?" Monica asked.

"You haven't heard?" Chloe said.

"Heard what?"

Chloe paused as she put the cigarette to her lips and fumbled with the lighter until it served its purpose.

"You haven't heard?" Chloe exclaimed.

"For fuck's sake, heard what?"

A sudden stillness washed over Chloe's face as she stopped to pull a drag from her cigarette. Her eyes narrowed into defensive slants, stout like tiny dams holding bank any inkling of a tear.

She gazed off into the endless pitch, probing for something to divert her thought process, but to no avail. "They found Jess. Just not *all* of her." Chloe paused for another hit of nicotine and a short break to further compose herself. "Nobody had heard anything about her for months. I mean months, since like January. And then one day, the cops were trying to catch some psycho out near Fairbank, and when they caught up to him, they found this mass grave. They talk about it like there were dozens and dozens of bodies in there, cut up and tossed in like a landfill. Jess was one of the few they could identify, and that was just cuz of her teeth and a few fingers."

"Jesus…" Monica exclaimed.

"You wanna know what the worst part of it is, though? They weren't even looking for Jess. They probably stopped looking for her six months ago when she went missing. The only reason they found her was because they were out in full force trying to find some rich prick's old lady. Somebody that was more important than a homeless twenty-two-year-old," Chloe let out a bottomless sigh as she released a puff of smoke. "They assume that if some bad shit happens to us, then it ain't a big deal 'cuz we chose this life."

Chloe wiped away the sobbing precursor from the corners of her eyes, smudging eyeliner as she did. She pulled her gaze away from the night sky and inhaled into the base of her lungs as she returned it back onto Monica. This time there were cracks and fissures in the fortitude of her expression. Chloe battled against the tears welling up behind her mask of courage.

"People like us…are disposable."

It was 9:37 PM when the black Lincoln Town Car pulled around the corner of McCormick and 114th. As the icy blue halogen head lamps tore through the steam still emerging from the bowels of the street, it crept down the road with the pace of a snail, somewhere between caution and curiosity. It was difficult to tell if the driver lost his way and fate led him to this degenerate hovel or if he knew where he was and what he wanted.

The sedan veered to the side of the street, inching in front of the corner Monica had laid claim to that evening. As the Town Car came to a complete stop, the immaculate condition was more evident than before. Even under the grimy single streetlight, flaws were near to impossible to find. The exterior was lacking even the most minor blemishes within the paint or accents. The rims formed nine-pointed stars within the wheels and were polished to a mirror finish.

As a few of the other girls approached the front passenger side window of this evening's next client with eagerness, an unidentifiable sense of caution washed over Monica as she stood back. She eased herself against the brick wall and began rifling through her purse for the crumpled soft pack of menthols. As she placed the second to last cigarette to her lips and began striking the lighter over and over until it produced a small flame, she pondered on the identity of this mysterious John. Could he be a senator, or a city council member, or maybe a vice cop flirting with entrapment?

She continued to brood over the situation while her coworkers fluffed themselves and strutted around the window like peacocks, pushing each other to the side to be at the front of the line. One girl was bold enough to rap on the window with her knuckles to get the driver's attention first. To everyone's surprise, it was the rear passenger side window that rolled down instead. And just like that, the context of the situation changed hands like the seasons. A lone man sat in the back seat with his attention drawn to a local newspaper laid out before him. The mystery man put it down and leaned over to address everyone gathered around the car. The John did so with the minimum effort needed to present himself. He seemed to exude a sense of entitlement or arrogance. When he leaned over to speak, he did so without sticking his head all the way out of the window. Perhaps he was seen by the wrong person at the wrong time in this neighborhood, or maybe he desired not to be tainted by the adjoining atmosphere of 114th. Either way, he didn't give much in a way of introductions.

"I'm looking for someone to accompany me to a little get together tonight," said the mystery man.

"Right over here, sugar," replied one girl, as she pushed herself in front of her competitors. "What 'chu lookin' at them for, baby? I got everything you need right here," the girl cooed as she leaned over into the window, pressing her breasts against the remaining glass.

He stared back at her with a cold, calculating gaze as he leaned forward even more. If indifference were an emotion, then he wore it well across his face. The mystery John continued to stare at her, almost as if contemplating her offer. Then he raised his left hand up pointing his index finger to the sky, as if to signal for her and maybe everyone else, to hold on a second. He looked around at all the girls that had huddled around his car, even stopped to inspect a few of them from head to toe. As he made his way around, he halted when he noticed Monica hanging back away from the others. He locked eyes with her and without saying a word, he pointed at her and motioned for her to come up closer to the car.

"Whoa, whoa, whoa baby! You don't want that skinny little bitch," replied the girl still huddled around the window.

This time the mystery John put up his whole hand, palm outstretched to motion for her to stop talking.

"I'll be the judge of that." He replied.

Monica advanced with caution to the front of the pack to address him.

"You lookin' for a date?" asked Monica.

"I am. I need a plus one for a little get together this evening with some old colleagues," replied the mystery man.

"Well, anything having to do with *friends* costs extra," Monica stated with a cold punctuation.

He answered her by unfolding a wad of one hundred-dollar bills one at a time to illustrate his seriousness.

"I mean…a *lot* extra," she reiterated.

He stopped the illustrated example and folded the bills back over into a single wad. Looking straight at Monica with more attention than he had given to anything else this evening, he held up all of it between his index and middle finger.

"Five thousand for whatever is left of the evening," he said as he held the wad of cash inches away from her.

What's the catch? She thought to herself.

"Look it, I don't care what it is. Five thousand dollars? Shit! If little miss flat ass ain't gonna do it, then sign me up!!" Replied the girl still hanging on the window.

"No. Just her."

All Monica heard was Chloe, looping like broken vinyl, *people like us are disposable*. Of all the times she traded a piece of herself to get by, none of them spelled it out like this. Never was there a more blatant example of being a commodity. The sight of all the cash was a tease or maybe a dare. She stopped hesitating and snatched the wad of money from his hand. With a half smirk he popped open the door and slid over to make room for her.

His custom tailored, pinstripe suit fit him like a second skin. Every crease and seam interpreted his upper torso with perfection. Monica had never seen anyone, let alone a man, with a better maintained physical appearance. His almond brown hair was slicked back with a light pomade that smelled of honey. All the extremities of his face were proportioned in meticulous order. Whether by plastic surgeons or by the hand of the creator, his brow, nose, and chin were all aligned in a seraphic order.

The mystery John said all of eight or nine words to her during the sixteen-minute drive out of the city and into the surrounding hills. He may have fancied himself as Richard Gere by throwing unfathomable sums of money at whatever he desired. Maybe he'd prove her wrong this evening, but thus far he had the personality of a damp washcloth.

As they climbed the deserted highway east into the hills, the distant lights of the metropolis twinkled and glimmered like a legion of outlying constellations. The stark magnificence of it all swept her back to a time when she dreamed of the big city. Just like that she was nine years old again, fantasizing about Broadway and Times Square. Or sometimes when she felt a little bolder, she imagined herself living the American dream out West, complete with her own name etched on the Hollywood Walk of Fame. Even in the months leading up to her departure from home, she almost died with anticipation at the idea of leaving the quiet Midwest town she had spent her entire life in and trading it for the glow of something, anything, new and exhilarating.

The Town Car shifting into park interrupted her nostalgia.

"This is our stop, my dear," said the mystery man.

A towering mansion overlooking the city awaited them at the end of their commute. Nestled into the mountain range bordering the metropolis, the house let off a breathtaking glow standing out like a lighthouse in the endless void. The manor itself stretched to the heavens at least four stories with statuesque turrets establishing the skyline on each corner. Eight large Romanesque pillars encapsulated the stairs and landing leading to the front entrance. A gothic four tier water fountain rested in the center of the driveway, transforming the very front of the property into a roundabout. A grand depiction of Adonis and Aphrodite locked in each other's embrace lay atop the exhibit while six jets released water from around their feet and down upon the lower levels. Exquisitely trimmed rose bushes lined the perimeter of the fountain leaving a welcoming fragrance upon exiting the town car. Valets glided about the front of the property with the uninterruptible focus of worker bees as they shuffled around automobiles for the arriving guests.

An older gentleman stood at attention by the front door, waiting to greet them. His salt and pepper hair was pulled back along the top and sides, accented by a trimmed white beard, and a tailored tuxedo adorned his body. He welcomed them both with a warm smile.

"Ah, Mr. Vandenbrook. So glad you could join us," said the doorman with enthusiasm.

"Oh, I wouldn't dream of missing these little get togethers," replied Vandenbrook.

The doorman held the front door open with grace and chivalry while Vandenbrook and Monica made their way inside the foyer then followed in behind them.

"Most of your colleagues are in the banquet hall. Dinner should be served in another half hour."

"Thank you. Since we have some time, my guest could use a change of clothes," replied Vandenbrook.

"Of course. This way ma'am," the doorman motioned for Monica to follow him.

They ascended a tall, curved set of stairs that mirrored an identical flight climbing the opposite side of the foyer. A beautiful wrought iron handrail adorned in intricate filigree ran the length of the stairs to the next floor. He led her down the right side of the adjacent hallway to the very end. There he opened the door to one of several dozen guest bedrooms in the manor. He entered and strolled over to a set of double sliding doors along the left wall. With an effortless push, he cast them both aside and revealed a walk-in closet larger than any bedroom Monica had ever slept in and stocked along all four walls with cocktail dresses and gowns of every size and style, followed by racks of shoes all along the floor.

"Here, I trust you will find something suitable to your palate. When you are ready, we will be waiting downstairs," said the doorman.

"Wait. So, I can pick anything from here? Like...anything?" Monica inquired.

"Yes, my dear. Pick anything you would like for this evening. But try to be quick about it. Dinner will be served shortly," replied the doorman. He then exited the guest room, shutting the door behind him to ensure Monica had privacy.

She was beside herself at the lavish wardrobe engulfing her. The walls lined with outfits in every size and style, every taste of color from the deepest candy apple reds to the most vivacious lavenders and violets. Monica picked up the pace in her search, while convincing herself that this was not a dream. She probed and rummaged through trying to find something in her size when a spaghetti strap, black dress whispered her name from the far corner of the closet. There in the very back, stuck between two long red gowns lay an onyx Marchesa cocktail dress. The low-cut, backless gown spoke to Monica with the intimacy of an old childhood friend.

Monica changed into her new attire which included a pair of polished black pumps to match the dress. She descended back downstairs to the foyer to find Vandenbrook and the doorman waiting for her return. Together they proceeded through grand halls and galleries to the growing melody of cellos and violins ringing out through the manor.

Moments such as these lived with exclusion in Monica's wildest dreams. But even as a child fantasizing about fortune and

fame, she imagined nothing like this. The siren song calling to her originated from a string quartet, strumming and plucking with the grace of cherubim. Men and women hailing from the most elite seats of power all dressed in the poshest attire money could buy filled the banquet hall. Bankers, politicians, CEOs, and their colleagues fluttered about the hall, rubbing elbows with one another. In the center of the hall lay a grand table with more than enough seating for the hundred or more guests in attendance tonight. Polished marble flooring radiated the sheen of the chandeliers like a fresh snow drift burning white under the mid-day sun. The aroma of wine and rose buds filled the atmosphere in contradiction to what Monica had become accustomed to over the years.

The doorman escorted them with minutes to spare before being considered tardy. Guests began seating themselves all around the table in preparation for dinner. As Vandenbrook led Monica around the right side, she began to recognize some patrons already sitting down. Though not through her personal life, she knew their faces from billboards, newspapers and the occasional advertisement stuck to the back of a park bench.

"So, how is the new acquisition coming along?" a statuesque man from across the table inquired of Vandenbrook.

"Excellent. We will draw up the final paperwork next week," Vandenbrook responded with a smile.

A clean-shaven gentleman with short light gray hair combed over to the side nodded in approval of Vandenbrook's response. The two men continued back and forth on inside matters that Monica was not privy to, as she tuned them out from her subconscious and took in her surroundings at the table.

One common denominator stood out to her as she gazed around at the other guests. There was a clear distinction between those invited here and their plus ones. The only people laughing, socializing, and acting in accordance with the party were the

15

members of this club. Almost every plus one sat in silence as the night raged on without them.

It appeared Monica was not the only person brought here from less desirable walks of life. She even recognized some other girls and guys sitting around the table. Seven seats down to her left on the opposite side of the table, sat a young twenty something named Trish. Monica had known her years ago when she first moved to the city. Trish had shared a bed with Monica the first time she took money for "an evening with some friends". The cobalt blue, off the shoulder dress accented Trish's dark complexion well; however, it did little to distract from the distress worn on her face. Her facial expression confirmed the same feelings Monica had been trying to ignore since she arrived. Trish turned around and met Monica's gaze across the table. Laying eyes on Monica again brought a smile to her face, however short lived.

And there were others like her. A young, blue-eyed, blonde rent boy named Josh sat two seats down to the right of Monica. They had placed Josh between two other older gentlemen. On his left sat Clifton Snead, a once prominent defense attorney, now next year's front runner for the mayor's office. To his right, William Bowes, a property tycoon from up North. By their body language and enthusiasm, it was unclear who brought the twenty-three-year-old runaway with them to dinner.

After all the guests claimed their seats at the table, dozens of servants began bringing out a first course of zucchini carpaccio with salt-broiled shrimp, then followed up with a main course of either Chicken Valentine garnished with parsley or a Lamb Tartlet. Glass after glass overflowed with Pinot Noir and top shelf whiskey as the dinner party picked up steam around Monica. The elites and their colleagues rambled on throughout the night about buyouts, campaigns, property deals, and other such topics foreign to her as she kept to herself.

"Are you a vegetarian?" asked Vandenbrook.

"I'm sorry. What?" replied Monica.

"Well, I only assume this isn't to your liking. You've barely touched your plate."

"I um…I'm just not very hungry," replied Monica.

This couldn't have been further from the truth. The small amount of value meal fast food had barely carried her throughout the day, but Chloe's revelation less than a couple hours ago had caused her appetite to vacate.

"Well, that is a shame. The Chicken Valentine is our chef's Magnum Opus. There are very few who rival him at his work," Vandenbrook said as he nodded his head in assurance.

"Actually, I'm not feeling too well. Where is the restroom?"

"I'll have someone show you."

Vandenbrook turned and motioned to one servant standing at attention in the banquet hall. The young man walked over to Vandenbrook's side.

"Please show my guest to the restroom?" Vandenbrook requested.

"Certainly, sir. This way madam," replied the servant.

Monica got up and followed the servant back through the manor on a different course than she had taken upon entry. Through a series of corridors off the main hall, they passed by several other pieces of fine art, hung along the walls.

"Here we are ma'am. I trust you will find your way back without my help?" said the servant.

"Yeah, I think I'll be ok. Thank you," Monica replied.

"My pleasure. Just remember, down the hall to the left, then take a right and straight down till you get back to the main hall," the servant reiterated.

Monica just smiled and nodded as the servant turned and walked back to whatever chores awaited him for the rest of the evening.

Everything about this evening originated from a place disconnected and foreign to the life she knew. The company, the cuisine, the garments, even the air taken into her lungs existed on the other side of a window. And all it allowed her were brief peeks through the glass. The more she grasped at the thought, the more anxiety set in. Her gut fought against her newfound indulgence in an unruly tug of war. It didn't matter how it appeared; she knew the bottom could fall out at any moment. As her gut came out victorious against her lesser judgement, Monica began drowning in an undertow of should haves and would haves.

"Fuck. Get ahold of yourself," she said to her own reflection in the gold-plated bathroom mirror.

Chloe's words lingered in her mind without pause. The image of her dead friend thrown away in pieces akin to rotting garbage still haunted her and set the mood for the evening. The fear that she could go missing any day, and no one would acknowledge it gripped her without mercy. For people like her taking that last breath into her lungs meant slipping through the cracks of society as if she never existed.

Monica rummaged through her purse until she came across the wad of hundreds. She pulled it out and stared at the cash. Cataloging every moment in her life, Monica concluded that she had never held this much money at one time. She calmed herself a bit at a time as taking it all for herself and walking away from this life seemed more relevant. Her fears became pacified with the daydreams of taking a bus as far as it would travel and start over in a new city. She took another long look in the mirror and then back at the cash before folding it back up and stuffing it inside her bra.

"Just get through tonight."

18

POTTER'S FIELD BLUES

Monica returned to the banquet hall, but to her surprise everyone had migrated to another wing of the manor. Everyone was gone except for the servants confiscating plates and silverware with steadfastness, while returning the table to its original glory. No one seemed to notice Monica's overdue return, or maybe that wasn't as pressing as bussing the gargantuan table. The repetitious clicking and clacking of heels on marble resonated with a lingering echo as Monica traversed the grand hall.

It wasn't until that moment she stopped and took in the serenity of the colossal manor. The ornate ceiling climbed upward at least two stories. Hand carved cherry wood beams came together with unrivaled symmetry to create the arches and definition. Like the rib cage of an aged titan, the rafters bridged the width of the hall, separated only by exquisite octagonal glass panes. No two paintings were the same. Depictions of glory laden battles spanning centuries, single portraits of patriarchs and matriarchs, and even the occasional mythology.

A muffled exchanging of words brought Monica's train of thought to a grinding halt. The din came from the same set of double doors the servers had used earlier to bring out tonight's dinner. Unaware of where the other guests had retired to, curiosity pushed her toward the commotion. The conversation still undecipherable regardless of how she approached it, she inched one door far enough to peek through.

Just past the kitchen a pair of servants argued back and forth as one of them pushed a stainless cart over toward what appeared to be a trash chute built into the wall. The one pushing the cart continued cursing his partner as they both started picking up large sacks and putting them through the chute. One by one they tossed their mystery bags through the portal to who knows where. As they neared the end of the task, it became clear the servant that had shown his aggravation struggled with the parcels closer to the bottom of the container. He almost fell in as he teetered on his hips attempting to retrieve the last bag. He heaved it up onto the lip of the cart as he found his footing back on the ground, but that would not be enough to hold it, as the sack toppled down to the floor, breaking open at the seam. Monica couldn't make out what the bag had contained. From that distance it appeared to be just a mass of wasted animal carcasses. The servant who dropped the sack bent down and picked up the pieces with a grudge, placing them back in the bag. As he moved them around to clean his mess, one very odd lump of waste rolled out from the epicenter a little closer into Monica's line of sight revealing a blob about the size of a cantaloupe or larger, and unlike any animal carcass she had ever seen.

"Excuse me, ma'am," came a voice from over her shoulder.

Monica turned around to see the doorman from earlier walking toward her.

"Miss, I believe the other guests have retired to the adjoining ballroom," said the doorman with an assuring nod.

"Oh, I was wondering what happened to everyone else. I had to find the restroom," replied Monica.

"Well, I trust you found one of them?"

"I did," Monica said with a brief smile.

"This way, ma'am," ushered the doorman.

He placed his right palm on her lower back and extended his left arm outward, pointing toward the doors separating them both from the calm of the dining room and whatever lay on the other side. Monica proceeded forward with some reluctance to the cherry wood double doors, looking back over her shoulder one last time.

A dim corridor met them past the banquet hall. Petite chandeliers threw a warm tangerine aura along the hallway leaving shadows dancing about canvas portraits hung along the walls in filigree laden frames. The aroma of the dinner table vacated and thus replaced with the concentrated fragrance of vanilla.

"You look perplexed, my dear," stated the doorman.

"I just...I've never seen anything like this. Everything here is so surreal, and it makes me feel so out of place. That's all."

"I, too, felt that way many, many years ago. Some days I am unable to remember what my life had been like before I arrived here."

"Well, do you at least enjoy what you do? Are you happy?" asked Monica.

"I suppose I've grown very fond of this place, and the people I owe my services to have always shown me the utmost respect, as I return the sentiment to them. So yes, to answer your question, I believe I am happy," the doorman said with a smile.

As Monica and her escort closed in on another set of doors at the end of the hall, the fragrance became more intoxicating. The odor lashed out, stinging the inside of her nostrils like a dozen pin pricks. Monica stood back as the doorman stepped forward and pulled the right door open for her, holding it in place. As he did, a flood of pulsing light breached the threshold, casting tendrils of shadow and radiance.

The entirety of this evening had been filled with ambiguity and lavish distractions, none of which could have been a precursor for what lay ahead. The ballroom owned a heartbeat unlike any other, a rhythm pounding to the beat of its own drum. The resonating sound of the string quartet ejected itself from her mind all together, and yet, supplemented with a choir of gasping exhalations, gratified moans (some fabricated, but a couple honest ones here and there), and the collision of tired flesh against more of the same. Shadows waltzed across the elegant tiles as their doppelgangers coursed over burgundy tapestries. They heaved back and forth like a churning sea of contrast.

In that moment Monica received perfect clarity. They had pulled away the curtain to cast light on what "an evening with some colleagues" necessitated. This was a free for all. As she panned the room, she ran through the mental gymnastics attempting to find a word more concrete than orgy, because that unadorned, two-syllable title could not encompass what she was taking in with all senses at once. Nothing was forbidden here, no appetite unsated, no desire unquenched. Nothing was off the table (not even a sloppy four way mashed together on top of a small table in the corner). This wasn't an afterparty at the Four Seasons or a late-night train running through the frat house. This...this was something different. They had exchanged the small talk about revitalizing downtown for leashes and astroglide. Some members of the club shared their plus ones with others in free spirit, while a few greedy constituents wandered off to more secluded sections of the hall.

Gary Dill, the property tycoon Monica recognized from countless billboards, held a petite brunette off the ground as she straddled his hips. His forearms formed a swing seat under her knees, with his fingers overextended, digging into the posterior of her thighs. She wrapped her hands, one over the other across the back of his skull. The girl's neck and shoulders writhed and contorted as Gary lifted her up and down every inch of his cock. The voyeurism did not go unnoticed. With mouth wide open and teeth clenched, Gary locked eyes with Monica. It gave her gooseflesh as he watched her watching him from across the hall. Monica froze in place as he gazed right through her, but then the strangest thing happened. Another club member stepped into view between them as he made his stride toward Gary and the brunette. It was then Monica realized that Gary was staring at this man and not her. She shrugged it off and started to move toward the less populated side when she looked back over her shoulder at the trio. The second club member sauntered over toward them while stroking himself. He nodded at Gary as he found his place right behind the girl. Gary let her all the way down on his hips as the second man aided in propping her up. In mid gasp the brunette pulled a hand away from Gary and cocked around to wrap it around the second man's neck. The three of them mashed together into a writhing Eiffel tower of sweaty flesh.

An older matriarch with illustrious silver hair running halfway down her back partnered with Mr. Snead and Mr. Bowes in parading Josh around on all fours by a collar and chain. Between the four of them, someone had the desire to play pin the tail on the gimp, as they rammed a donkey tail butt plug all the way into Josh's anus.

Monica panned over the scene unfolding all around her. Every minute that went on led to more depravity, and she couldn't help but wonder what was in store for her. She stacked, categorized, sorted, and justified all the things she had done for cash before. All the beatings, sore muscles, and long nights with no rest. But how many pounds of flesh is worth five thousand dollars? Then, as the surrounding scenes escalated to more raw depravity, she couldn't help but wonder where Vandenbrook was in all of this.

Just as the thought had passed through her mind, she heard a very subtle succession of foot falls creeping up behind her. He made his presence known by pressing his hips into hers. The palm of his left hand found the side of her neck as his fingers rolled from pinky to index across her throat into a gentle, but firm grasp. His right hand slid up her dress and under the waistband of her boy shorts.

"Are you ready for dessert?" he whispered. The question punctuated with teeth snaring the cartilage of her right ear lobe.

Though Monica was there in person, her mind went on vacation a mile away. Her out-of-body experience led her across the hall, away from the unhinged sexual abandon around her, all the way back to 114th Street, where she daydreamed of what tonight could have been behind door number two. She didn't even notice when he began peeling the shorts almost halfway down her thighs.

And just like that, with the resolve of an immediate thunderclap, one lone scream belted out from across the room, jerking Monica back to reality. It rang out from amidst the maelstrom of debauchery. Anonymous at first, but after a few moments the origin of the bellow stumbled out onto the floor. It was Trish. She toppled over, bracing herself with palms and knees. Blood ran rampant from a gaping laceration starting at the base of her neck and continuing in a diagonal slash across her left shoulder blade. Her life spilled out on the tile without restraint. With every hyperventilated release of oxygen, her arm and collarbone became painted vermillion.

The room held its breath as one. Guests and all stopped in mid stroke as Trish took center stage. The shock and terror painted across her face passed through the crowd like a contagion. Those bearing witness wore the same mask of disbelief and primal fear as she did. Everyone froze in place as she pushed and pulled her way in any direction away from her assailant.

"Well, it looks like somebody was an eager beaver," Vandenbrook said with a sneer.

The unthinkable act of Trish crawling across the marble, slick with her own blood, had been the calm before the storm. The tone of the room shifted through the congregation. A few pleas and cries for mercy became audible from the corners of the ballroom before moving all about. Not long after Trish took her last breath face down on the tile did the terror erupt into a pandemic. Screams rang out from every corner of the ballroom in hasty succession. The club members all turned on their guests without hesitation. Even those in need of a few sit-ups moved with the resolve of a starving leopard bringing a lean zebra to the ground.

Incisors gnawed and tore through every ounce of flesh they could latch onto. Once the cat was out of the bag, there was no need to delay the inevitable.

"You should have tried the chicken valentine. Chef Alexandre adds a little something for our honored guests that makes this whole ordeal a little more...tolerable. I've never cared for the aftertaste. If you have a well-seasoned porterhouse, why would you drown it in steak sauce?" Vandenbrook added with a chuckle.

Adrenaline took the wheel and without a second thought Monica cocked her right knee up and back down as she drove the two-inch heel down at a steep angle into the top his right foot. The blow landed in the crook between the tibia and the tarsal bones, sending him into blinding fury.

"AAAH! You cunt!" Vandenbrook screamed as he spun Monica back around behind him.

Monica laid eyes on him for the first time since she excused herself from dinner. The cool, refined composure had melted away and, in its place, left a ravenous animal. The once fair azure blue eyes had now shifted to a neon violet that pulsed with his every breath. A set of jagged barbs replaced his aligned, pearly teeth. Intersections of veins bulged in his hands and neck as he treaded toward her.

Monica pivoted around to flee as best she could in heels, but the boy shorts were still pulled down off her waist, binding her thighs together like a bola. It not only halted her from putting one foot in front of the other but caused her to topple over to the marble floor. Though the adrenaline high caused her to falter, she corrected herself and hiked the shorts back up while scrambling across the floor to distance herself from this thing wearing Vandenbrook's skin. Then, it happened. That moment becoming the prelude to your life flashing before your eyes. Her shoulders found the back wall of the ballroom. This was it. Nowhere else to crawl or run to.

Vandenbrook took a bounding step forward, reached down, and grabbed Monica's left ankle, dragging her back away from the wall, right to him. He squatted down and rested his forearms against his knees as he stared at her with a cold gaze. The sweet honey aroma had abandoned him. Instead, his breath and his pores smelled of copper.

"I take back what I said. I'm glad you passed on the chef's special. I would rather my dinner not be doped to the gills," Vandenbrook said with a crooked smirk. "I think I'll start with your liver," He noted as he sprawled his right hand out like a bird of prey stretching out its talons in preparation to claim a wild salmon. He pinned Monica down by the throat and raised his right hand up over his head with a sneer.

A loud crash left Monica's ears ringing as the chaos of the ballroom interrupted them. Before Vandenbrook could claim his prize, a hurricane of bloodlust collided with him like a freight train, knocking him several yards across the floor. It was Josh. Somehow, he had broken free of his tormentors and was fleeing in whatever direction he could. The path he chose put him on a collision course with Vandenbrook not a second too late.

The instant his hold over her vacated, the drive to fight hit Monica like a tidal wave. She glanced back over her shoulder at the wall to get her bearings aligned and witnessed the very thing she was searching for. Her way out was ten yards away through another set of doors. She flipped back over to her stomach and rushed through the motions of propping herself back up to get on her feet.

"Where are you running off to?" Vandenbrook growled as he latched onto her left ankle.

Monica peered back at her assailant once again, but this time the drive to live took dominion over her muscles. There was no thought process, no hesitation, no bargaining. Just cause and effect. She cocked her right leg back as far as she could, bringing her knee up into her chest. And with every ounce of resolve she thrust out once more to strike him with her heel. This time the wound had been far more critical than a bruised foot. She drove the pump at a harsh angle through his neck, entering the esophagus and exiting beside his spine. Vandenbrook let out a guttural roar as the shoe bottomed out in the side of his throat. Monica struggled to retract it, but Vandenbrook's violent writhing clinched it in place. She contended with it until her foot freed itself from the heel. Upon breaking free, he collapsed over onto his back. Releasing his clamp on her ankle, Vandenbrook held both hands around his throat with desperation as a putrid, lemon-colored fluid spilled from his neck.

She never looked back. Not once did she flirt to gaze over her shoulder for her assailant or any other survivors for that matter. Every willing muscle overextended itself to put miles between Monica and Vandenbrook. She hobbled through the exit and down the hall as fast as the lone heel would allow; her gait thrown into a wild stupor from the adrenaline dump paired with a missing shoe. Frustrated and terrified, Monica kicked the air until the second pump came off. She slung it from her foot with no regard where it would land and with not a moment to spare.

"THIS WAY!" A shrill voice bellowed out from behind her.

Now barefoot, she sprinted up the hall as a pack of them advanced to close the gap between themselves and their prey. The din of chattering molars and smacking lips resounded through the corridor. Every passing breath beat the inside of her ribs without mercy. Her lungs and esophagus caught fire as she pushed every muscle to outrun her attackers. She dared not look back over her shoulder at the men pursuing her. She couldn't even bring herself to judge the distance. They could be a hundred yards away or they could be right at her heels reaching out to drag her back at any moment. Inquiries like that became void as her thought process latched onto one thing. *RUN! Run as fast as you can and do not stop!*

"WHERE ARE YOU GOING OFF TO?" came a second, more guttural voice.

The end of the corridor came into focus as her pursuers closed the gap like a pack of wolves on the brink of starvation. The creatures wearing the skin of the club members bellowed in frustration as their dinner continued to fight the inevitable.

She broke her rule and looked back to see four of them closing in fifty yards behind her.

"Goddamn it!" she screamed as this immovable force closed in on her.

She pushed as hard as she could as her chest throbbed from the unscheduled cardio. Her breath became shorter and shorter as her body fought to keep up with her demands. Seconds turned like eons as the corner of the hall inched closer. Anything and everything lie around it. It could be an abrupt, dead end and the last page of Monica's biography, or it could be the only way out of this prison. This maroon-clad Schrödinger's hall was the only card left to play.

Monica pivoted hard around the corner to face whatever awaited her. There, another hundred yards up the hall, lay ornate glass doors leading to the east garden and a bright stone walkway running the length of the manor. The closer she got the more evidence of the outside world became clear. Monica could see the faint reflection of light posts poised around the perimeter of the manor shimmering on the glass panes. Pale moonlight danced across the windows lining the hall as she passed by them at breakneck speed.

"STOP MAKING THIS HARDER ON YOURSELF!" another voice shouted.

The primal fear of being forced into a corner by an apex predator with no means of escape collided with the adrenaline driving her to keep moving at all costs.

Monica's mind raced at how she would survive this nightmare, even if she made it outside. How would she lose these creatures bent on tearing her apart like wet paper mâché? How would she escape the property without stealing a car? Could she put enough distance between herself and these things to hide somewhere? As the what ifs piled up in her mind, the panic set into place and clouded her vision, so much so that she didn't notice the shadowy figure stepping out into the hall between her and the door. It was a tall skinny man in a well-tailored tuxedo. The doorman. The doorman stood out in the middle of the hall just in front of the doors leading to the garden. His arms were folded behind his lower back as he stood at attention.

"HEEEEEELLP! PLEASE...HELP ME!" Monica screamed as she barreled toward him.

The doorman stood his ground unmoved as he witnessed Monica and the four club members racing up the corridor.

Suddenly, the doorman's arms fell back around his sides. A small, rectangular box protruded from his right hand. Telegraphing no emotion or reasoning, he raised his right hand up and pointed the box at Monica. There was a loud pop as the front of the box split down the middle and broke apart into two halves, and in the same breath Monica froze in place. Not of fear, but because of physical paralysis. Her arms and legs turned to stone as a searing pain shot up and down her spine and through the tips of her nerves. The sound of her own cries for help almost drowned out the crackle of the taser gun as it shot fifty thousand volts into her nervous system. Monica toppled over to the floor as the din of her assailants stampeding up the hall crashed around her.

"WAIT! Not this one," the doorman commanded with the utmost authority.

"What do you mean, not this one?" exclaimed one of the club members.

"Allow me to clarify this for you so that nothing is lost in translation. Mr. Vandenbrook gave clear instructions. This one is to be brought back to the kitchen, *at once*. Under no circumstances is anyone to deviate from those instructions. Do I make myself clear? Or do you wish to speak with our generous host about the matter?" The doorman stated with a calm composure.

A series of frustrated grunts followed as one member picked up Monica and flung her over his shoulder like a rag doll.

A thick haze veiled the space between consciousness and the subconscious imagination. Every few seconds faint flashes of life played out in front of Monica in low definition. Garbled bits of audio came and left with the grayed-out visuals. Three seconds, five seconds maybe thirty, but they cut out all the same, with no transition or warning, just back into darkness, or inside the second act of a dream with no beginning or ending. At first the lack of context dulled her senses and intuition. Maybe this whole evening had been a mere nightmare, and this was Monica returning to life. Her eyes struggled to open wider, let alone stay open. Little blurred images of her bare feet surrounded by a haze and then nothing. Next time she made out the sheen of white tile as the backdrop, then, nothing. Seconds, maybe minutes later, her head rolled back and forth in time to see a large shadow moving around the corner of her left eye, registering as a blob of darker contrast through the lining of her eyelid, then nothing.

"No, no, NO.... NOOOOOO!" Came a piercing, disembodied voice.

POTTER'S FIELD BLUES

Monica drew in a long deep breath as the banshee scream shook her back to consciousness. Like a jigsaw puzzle falling into formation, all the dazed visions fit together. She looked down at her bare feet suspended above the ground, the same bright white marble tile that ran the length of the banquet hall. They hovered six inches above the floor. The same blissful ignorance leaving her mind left her nerve endings in unison. Monica found the bloody welts left from the taser prongs on her left hip and under her left collar bone. Blood still poured from the wounds. She pulled her head back to see the zip tie restraints binding her wrists to a polished stainless-steel hook suspended from the ceiling.

"Noooooo...please no!" the same disembodied voice pleaded.

Unable to see where the cries originated, Monica postured her head forward again, but a third unconscious person suspended between her, and the screams blocked her view.

"AAAAAAAAAAHHH! OH FUCK!"

Monica leaned her head forward just in time to witness one of the other girls writhing with her hands bound to a similar steel hook at the end of the row as a heavy-set man dressed in a chef's uniform peeled flesh from the anterior of her thighs with a large kitchen knife. He removed skin from muscle then muscle from bone with ease and precision and placed the shanks of flesh onto a large cutting board to his right. He cut and sawed away at the girl like a piece of livestock. The butcher pulled another small sliver from the back of her left calf and lifted it up in front of his face as if to inspect it. He looked over his shoulder toward a stainless-steel door leading out of the kitchen then back across the room, ensuring no one could watch him. He held the piece of skin up high as he cocked his head back underneath it. The butcher's jaw sprung open from side to side, splitting down the middle. The two halves unhinged like a serpent's and spread upwards and back, leaving the two points of his mandible that

31

had once formed his chin, flexed like wings, forming an inverted triangle of bones, incisors, and inflamed gums spanning seven or eight inches across. Now unconcealed, the butcher's real mouth lay exposed. Underneath the faux human architecture rested a two and half wide orifice surrounded by hundreds of small barb-like teeth. As he lowered the thin piece of skin down into his mouth, the barbs crawled over one another grasping at the sustenance like tiny worms evacuating the ground after a torrential downpour. A look of utter satisfaction poured over his face as his finished his cheat meal. And just like that, the two halves of his mouth relaxed and returned to a more human appearance.

His moment of indulgence cut short as he noticed his audience, making his posture tighten upright. His stare pierced Monica as she dangled from the hook, helpless. The butcher's eyes glowed an even deeper shade of violet than Vandenbrook's.

"Huh. Wakey, wakey," he said with a smirk and narrowing brows.

"Pleuuuugggh. Oh God, Oh Jesus," exclaimed his most recent victim as she coughed herself back into consciousness.

He turned his attention back toward the girl on the end of the row painted with her own blood.

"Please...please let me go!" the girl continued in protest.

The butcher reached out and caressed her cheek with the palm of his left hand, rubbing his thumb underneath her eye to wipe away tears in a brief faux display of compassion.

"Shhhhhh, hush now," he replied.

"Noooooo, please. Just let me go."

He continued holding his hand to her face as he reached over to the table of instruments. His fingertips strummed over each device from left to right until he stopped on one laid out between several knives. The butcher's posture made it impossible for Monica to see what he was picking until he had brought it up to the girl's face. He held a pair of stainless-steel tongs. His left hand transitioned from a caressing motion to a vice grip along her jaw. The butcher pressed his thumb and index finger into the hollows of her cheeks as he pulled her mouth open. Her screams of protest became muted gags as he slipped the tool halfway into her mouth. He continued to say nothing at all as he twisted and squeezed the instrument until it satisfied him with the clamping force. He released his hold of her cheeks and procured a small scaling knife from the same tray. Still holding onto the tongs with a firm grip he reached in with the knife at an angle and moved it back and forth in a sawing motion while his victim let out half muted wails. As he neared the end of his task, the repetition grew faster until the knife broke through. Through painful gurgled sobs the butcher removed the knife and tongs as well as a sizable portion of the girl's tongue. Plopping the dead muscle onto the pile of dissected viscera and laying the tools back on the table where he had produced them, he returned his attention to her with his index finger held up against his lips so as to signal for her to be quiet (not that she had much of a choice in the matter).

"Apparently, you must be something special," the butcher said as he stepped over to Monica. "They have given me very strict instructions to save you for last." He raised his right hand up, brushing her face as Monica turned her head away in disgust. He grabbed her face along the jaw to ensure she made eye contact with him, smearing blood across her cheek. "Someone else wants to take you apart and play with your insides. Someone higher on the food chain than myself. Pity, we could have had so much fun together." The butcher turned and walked back toward the doors leading out of the kitchen. "Why don't you just hang around for a little while? Hahahaha..." He said as he closed the kitchen door behind himself.

Devastation crashed over her like a wave as the undertow of her life flashing before her eyes pulled Monica under. Her stomach performed backflips as the dread set in. The overwhelming aroma of copper and grease filled the air.

"Oh Jesus. Oh Fuck." Monica whispered to herself as she looked around the kitchen.

Fumbling with the zip ties and struggling to pull herself up off the hook only cemented the notion that fate had punched her ticket. The bindings sawed into her wrists as she writhed back and forth in a desperate bid to free herself. She went through all the motions of every futile escape plan, from tugging on the hook to wriggling from side to side hoping to break free.

"Goddamnit!" She muttered to herself.

Monica swung back and forth hoping that something, anything would give in her favor. Nothing gave but the flesh around her wrists as the bindings cut deeper with every motion. Despite the obvious futility and fruitlessness of her actions, Monica kept at it, not knowing what else to do, or how long she had left until her executioner returned. Then, on a painful return swing backwards, her toes grazed something solid behind her. She tried three more times until both feet caught the cold stainless-steel behind her. Monica wrenched her head as far as she could to see what was behind her. A six-foot-tall stainless-steel industrial shelf sat up against the wall, housing various boxes from top to bottom.

Without having an actual plan to follow, Monica focused on the fixture behind her. She locked her ankles around the side of the shelf and pulled forward as hard as she could. This of course did nothing, as her feet slipped off the shelf, slinging her forward again. So again, she tried her plan. Over and over at least twenty times, each attempt became more desperate, as she realized there weren't a lot of options, and even if she moved it, she hadn't thought through how to even use it or if it would work. Then, after another dozen tries, it gave from the wall and toppled forward pushing her out of the way as it crashed to the ground under her. There the shelf lay amongst the debris of its former contents. Cartons split at their seams, almost revealing their contents. The shelf landed front end down underneath Monica, like a makeshift stepping stool, giving her just enough room to prop up on the tips of her toes hoping to raise the bindings over the hook. Monica's feet agonized as she flexed and strained every tendon to hold herself up.

"Gooooodaammmmnitttt!" she uttered as she overextended every muscle between her toes and fingertips to reach the tip of the hook.

She did so with the grace of a drunken sloth, tipping off the hook and plummeting back first to the ceramic tile. The fall pushed the last breath out of her lungs. She lay there on the floor gasping for air. Though her wrists remained bound, she was at least free of the hook. With her lungs held shut in a vice, she rolled over to her chest. Elbows bent and tucked in under her, she pushed herself up to her feet. Stainless-steel counters, appliances, and islands gave a haunting vignette of the industrial size kitchen. The massive room left space for at least a dozen or more chefs to work without ever crossing paths. The surgical precision of the instruments and stations were laid out like the production line of a slaughterhouse.

A few seconds went by before Monica regained control over her lungs. She wasted no time sprinting over to where the butcher had been dissecting the other guests. An array of tools lay in an ordered fashion on a steel tray. Monica grabbed the first knife she could fit between her wrists, hoping to saw through the binding. Her desperation to cut free caused her grip to lose traction with the tool several times. The posture of the eight-inch blade held toward her and against the zip tie could not have been more awkward. After a minute of duress, a minimal amount of progress began to show with the bindings.

"And what do you think you're doin'?" came a voice from behind her.

She turned to see the butcher had returned from his errand. Appearing as surprised to see her as she was him, he took a bounding leap toward her as she pulled the knife across the zip tie once more. Lashing out just two feet away from her so quickly, her knee jerk reaction caused the blade to slip out of her palms and fall right to the floor. He swung again, just failing to connect. She spun about and ran around the stainless-steel island laying in the center of the kitchen to block his advance.

He didn't even attempt to pursue her around the island. Instead, he faced off across from Monica. The butcher stood there for what felt like an eternity, watching Monica watching him, planning his next move as he anticipated hers.

He vaulted onto the island, lunging at her. In dodging his advance, she stepped away, finding her back against one stove. The heat from the burner danced around her skin as she scuttled away from his advance. He landed on his feet with a loud thud, shaking a couple dozen pots and pans hanging from a rack suspended from the ceiling. With hands still restrained and unarmed, she looked for anything to defend herself with. Like the climax of a Tom and Jerry bit, her attention fixated on a large metal skillet full of sizzling grease burning on the same stovetop. Monica reached out for the handle of the pan just as the butcher did the same for the back of her head. He clutched a thick handful of black hair and balled it up into his fist. With total confidence, the butcher reeled in his catch toward himself.

Monica had gripped both hands around the handle, though unaware of how best to use it in that moment it proved most effective. Upon being pulled back around, she flung the scalding hot contents, sending molten fat flying toward his face like a swarm of hornets, singeing his retinas on contact. The boiling grease splashed over his exterior, seeping into his eyes and mouth. His windpipe burned as the contents of the pan drew inside his nose. The external reaction was instantaneous. Boils and blisters multiplied across the skin of his face and his hands from attempting to block the delivery.

"HRRRRRRRRRAAAAAAAHHH AAAAAAAAHHH! YOU FUUUUUUCKINGGG BITCCH!" He screamed.

The back of his left hand flew away from him in a haymaker, connecting with Monica's temple hard enough to knock her back stumbling to the floor. She fell straight to her back against the tile. The force almost knocked the wind out of her lungs for a second time. Though she kept the breath in her, the drop forced her elbows outward from her sides just enough to snap the rest of the zip tie. Free again, she scrambled to her feet in time to see him pull both hands away from his face. There were blisters upon blisters. The skin on his face and neck puffed up and in seconds turned into a diseased, bloodied crimson. His eyes had become lost under the swelling of his cheekbones and brow. Even upon locating them, they stayed sealed shut. He lurched forward a few steps at a time swinging blind one hundred eighty degrees around him at a time, hoping to get a lucky hit in.

"You…stupid…fuckin'…cow! Do you really think we'll let you leave? You think you can get away?"

Monica reached down and picked the knife back up on her way out of the kitchen. She back tracked to the same exit he had used earlier and prayed that she wouldn't run into any more of his acquaintances.

"DO YOU FUCKING HEAR ME? We own this town! We own this country! We own this WHOLE FUCKING PLANET! WE… ARE…LEGION! And you…are nothing but CATTLE!" He shouted as he continued to swing in frustration.

His threats trailed off in volume as they escalated in violence. Monica could still hear him bellowing from the kitchen as she made her escape. After several wrong turns, Monica realized she had to be close to the dining hall. Down to her right the aroma of garlic began to linger, growing stronger as she approached the end of the hall. She peeked through the double doors and as she had hoped, there lay the banquet table. Now that she knew which end was up, maybe she had a real chance of escape. These doors she hunkered down behind must have been the same ones she peered through earlier when the nosiness in her took notes of the frustrated servants dumping bags of waste into a garbage chute. Monica peered back over her shoulder to find the same compartment just fifty yards behind her. Her concentration was broken as a series of voices and heavy footfalls rang out from the banquet hall. She peeked back through the small crack in the doors to find an entourage of seven armed guards dragging an unconscious person by the shoulders across the tiled floor and toward the doors Monica hid behind. As their proximity closed in on the door, the garbled communications from their individual radios interrupted the intermittent banter between the guards. Monica turned and ran back the way she came. Her mind void of any doubt, she sprinted down the corridor straight to the end. With all the confidence left in her, Monica climbed feet first into the chute and prayed to a God she didn't believe in that this would lead her to safety.

Sliding downward through the darkness made time stand still. For all she knew, Monica could have fallen ten stories into the unknown. As she dropped further and further, the smell of copper and rot enveloped her. The toxic odor lashed out and tested her stomach's resolve. Even in the descent she had to hold her hand over her face to keep the vomit at bay. Monica landed with a thud into a mountain of cloth waste bags. Some had spilled their bloody contents all down the pile. Half broken, and even shattered skulls, lay tossed about with femurs, tibias, and humerus all snapped in half and scattered like scrap wood for a bonfire. Mounds of decaying entrails were spread out all along the floor circling the base of the pile. Sacks of clothes, shoes, purses, and wallets, all belonging to former guests, were arranged around the remains of those same people. The rotten smell that branched out into the chute now settled around the dim room. The stench lay heavier than the oxygen, so heavy it became a labor just to breathe. After a few seconds of resistance, Monica lost the fight with her stomach and retched at the aroma of death and decay. The only source of light came from a large industrial furnace in the center of the room. A hellish orange glow seeped through the seams around the door to the heart of the machine, bleeding out into the room. The tint only further accented the horror scattered about like yesterday's refuse. The gargantuan incinerator stood ten feet tall, with six branches of duct work stretching up into the ceiling. Beads of sweat poured down her whole body as the heat radiated from the blaze roaring inside the machine's core. The atmosphere had a good twenty degrees or more on the mild, climate-controlled mansion.

While her eyes adjusted to the low light, she sidestepped through the viscera with a blind caution. The ambient light from the furnace threw deep and misleading shadows across the machinery and cinder block walls. The perimeter of the basement remained submerged in deep shadows that soon engulfed Monica as she began to stray away from the center of the room. With the kitchen knife still drawn in her hand she fumbled back and forth in search of anything resembling a door handle.

An eardrum shattering explosion went off behind her as the furnace burst into overdrive, almost as if the incinerator's previous state had been a mere idle and now was warming up in preparation for a sacrifice. Along with the furnace screaming to life, three rows of fluorescent tube lights began turning on, one by one, bringing a new definition to her current surroundings.

Michael Tyree

The greenish-blue hue of the bulbs warming up revealed more macabre detail of the former dinner guests lying around her in pieces. She averted her gaze as the death-rattled glances of several mutilated faces stared her down. Some looked almost condescending, as if they would inform her, she will die in this furnace room taking a seat right next to them. Others expressed shock and despair with their death masks, which was more than enough to persuade Monica she had to find a way out so she would not join them.

Now that the lights had almost warmed to full capacity, more features of the basement revealed themselves to her. The far-left wall that had been consumed by darkness now exposed a steel door with a single four-inch wide, vertical glass pane on the right side. She pulled at what she could only hope was a portal back to the outside world. Monica cracked the door open enough to steal a peak of what lay on the other side. For the first time in several hours, a wave of relief washed over her. The exit led out to the west side of the manor, a few hundred yards away from the front of the house. The symphony of crickets carrying on conversations all around the hillside filled her ears the more she separated the door from its threshold.

"Well, *maybe* if you didn't piss off Louie for the thousandth time, you wouldn't get stuck with cleanup duty," came a voice just outside the door.

Monica pushed the door into the frame just as someone from the other side opened it again on their way into the furnace room. Cementing her back to the wall behind the now wide-open door, Monica held her breath as she clutched the kitchen knife with both hands to her chest. The conversation that had started somewhere in route to her location continued just a few feet from where she hid in terror.

"I'm just sayin', if you keep fuckin' up, you'll get stuck on this detail forever."

"It wasn't even my fault this time! That old French twat just has it out for me, that's all."

A brief pause lingered in the exchange leading Monica into a panic. With small quiet breaths, she inched the knife up toward her face and then just over her head as she prepared herself for the inevitable moment when she would have to plunge it into one of these oblivious men.

"Jesus! They sure went at it this week."

"I know, right? It's more than the last two months combi..."

The crackle and static of a walkie talkie interrupted the servant before he could finish his sentence. A distorted voice called out from the radio demanding attention.

Henry? You there?

"What do you want Marcus?"

Is Ron with you?

"Yeah, we're down in the incinerator room."

Don't worry about cleanup right now.

"Aww, but you know how much Ron loves it!" The servant said with a sarcastic tone.

Seriously, the boss wants everyone upstairs. We got a live one on the loose somewhere on the first floor.

There was a short break in the transmission before the man came back over the radio once more.

She fucked Louie up bad. Marcus said with a chuckle. *Burned his face all to shit.*

"All right we're on the way back now."

The radio clicked off again and with audible sighs and mumbled curses, the two men turned around from where they stood in the doorway oblivious that their prey lingered two feet away concealed behind an inch and a half of steel and tempered glass. Hands trembling from trauma and overstimulated nerves, Monica clutched the knife over her head even after the men had both left with the steel door slamming shut behind them. With

41

calculated caution she let out a slow, deep breath and inched her way over to the thin window hoping to confirm the men now hunting her had truly left. With nothing apparent through the looking glass, she cracked the door in small increments putting one eye up to the crack and then both, then sticking her face outside the door with tactful posture.

Her inquiry showed her two young men walking uphill along the perimeter of the mansion with a lazy stride. Time must have pulled a grand illusion on Monica, for in the moment it took her to find the resolve needed to look outside, the young men had already put a couple hundred yards between them. Even as she began watching them, the duo changed course into one of the garden entrances on the first floor.

Monica charged through the door with anticipation. The abrasive, dry summer air brushing her face came as a relief in contrast to the infernal basement. The west side of the property faced a wood line accenting the hills separating her from the lights of the city. For the encore of the evening, Monica ran for her life once more.

Just a little after 5:00 AM, Monica found herself back in the familiar part of town. The last four hours cost her body every ounce of strength. Running on nothing but fumes, she collapsed on the first clean bench at the Park Street station. Exhaustion had nipped at her heels all night, but only now did it find the moment to strike.

"Rough night?" came a strange, disembodied voice.

The phrase jolted her from a dreamless void. It felt as though two seconds ago she closed her eyes to the predawn twilight hanging over the city, and now mid-day sun baked her skin.

POTTER'S FIELD BLUES

She moved for the first time in almost six hours, squinting as she attempted to address the voice. Her eyes adjusted to the daylight as she sat upright. A short, husky man in a Ralph Lauren suit stood in front of her. His worn glasses fought to stay in place on the top of his nose. His stroller luggage and attaché brief case led her to believe he was on his way out of town or just arriving. He stood there waiting for a response with a genuine look of concern on his face.

"Oh, ummm. I'm fine." She said like an automated response.

Monica knew without a doubt that was a lie, and she was not ok. Nothing about last night was ok. But who would even believe her if she tried to explain it?

"Well, you must have had the time of your life last night, because you're missing your shoes," he replied with a chuckle.

Monica looked down at her muddied bare feet and back at the man in front of her. She tried her best to play along and emulate someone who misplaced her shoes on an early morning walk of shame, not someone who just spent the last night fleeing from apex predators in Armani menswear.

He shook his head and smiled at his own remark.

"Well, you take care now," he said as he nodded and continued his way toward the station.

She sat there on that train station bench for most of thirty minutes, contemplating where her life goes from here. She didn't want to move from that bench, because the only place she had left was the rundown room back on 114th. Teetering on the edge of a panic attack, she stood up and walked about the station in a vain attempt to calm down.

This whole time her mind remained in a dozen separate places at once. In doing so she had forgotten all about the wad of cash that was stuffed down into her bra instead of her purse. She surprised herself that a single moment of caution could be her golden ticket. She pulled out the stack of hundred-dollar bills and looked all around her to ensure nobody took notice to what she was about to do. She unfolded the wad and counted it all out for the first time since Vandenbrook handed it to her. It was all there. All five thousand dollars. She rolled the cash back up and clutched it to her breast like a mother duck hovering over her brood.

Monica laid in bed night after night dreaming of the day, she could put this city in her rearview mirror once and for all. Now, despite the circumstances, she had the means to do just that. She carried herself with a fresh sense of weightlessness.

Time lost its definition as she looked over all the possible destinations. She held more than enough in her hands to take her far away from this horror show and all the ghouls and ghosts therein. And with no premeditation her destiny lit up on the board above her. She knew in her heart of hearts where to start over, and with no doubt she put one muddy bare foot in front of the other toward the ticket clerk.

"How may I help ma'am?" said the clerk.

"Yeah, I'd like to buy a one-way ticket to Los Angeles, please."

"Ok, well I can help you with that." The attendee started keying in data as he gazed at his computer screen. "So, you will not need a return ticket?"

"No. Just a one-way ticket."

"Ok, a one-way ticket from here to Los Angeles, scheduled to depart at 12:30 PM. That will be $217.31. Will you be paying with cash or credit?"

"Cash," Monica said as she pulled three hundred-dollar bills from the roll with care and handed them over to the clerk.

"All right, $82.69 is your change, and thank you for traveling with us today," The clerk said with a smile as he handed her the change and ticket.

Monica slouched down in the window seat of the passenger car. She found one void of any other travelers, just as she had

44

hoped. Occasionally the passing scenery lulled her to sleep throughout the first day of her trip. Mountains, fields and then more mountains passed by her window at a hypnotic pace. She only regained consciousness around 8:00 when the dinner cart came around, allowing her to gorge herself on everything it offered. With hundreds of miles between Monica and her past, she breathed with ease. She dozed off once more that evening and without interruption.

"Los Angeles has always fascinated me. *The city of angels, Tinseltown, The city of flowers and sunshine,* etcetera..." came a slight, raspy voice from the other side of the train car.

Monica yawned as the anonymous disembodied voice continued with its monologue about L.A. She awoke to sunlight breaking over the horizon, casting beams of light across an orange grove. Shadows weaved through the fruit trees as the early morning light began dancing about them.

"Have you ever...visited L.A. before?" The raspy voice inquired in between guttural coughs.

Monica sat up straight and turned to address the voice coming across the way.

Monica gazed out onto the passing scenery once more while she pondered about where she would go and what to do now that she once again held the reins of her life.

She focused with such intent on the daydreams that she didn't even see the shadow of her fellow traveler until he was in her peripheral, even as he sat down in the seat across from her and began staring out the same window at the grove sailing past the window, she paid no attention. Monica turned away from the window to see the gentleman with the raspy voice now sitting in front of her gazing at the scenery.

"L.A. is just to die for," said Vandenbrook.

THIS IS NOT AN EXIT

Where did he go off to this time? What blackout daydream edging toward its cliffhanger did David Kingston float through before his eyes anchored in reality and a gasping inhalation returned him to his glaring laptop screen. Nothing concrete traveled with him, no patchwork pieces of a lucid fantasy or useless inventions, only the sudden scene changes lacking any crossfade or theatrical sweep of a divided curtain. The digital clock on his computer taunted him as he laid eyes on the same thought he designed hours ago, accented by a blinking cursor refusing to produce any wittier prose for him. More often than not his writing process fell from the tracks until it collided with rabbit trail ideas like how the McRib is the most overrated sandwich in the history of processed food. Between these side notes dripping with absurdity, he would put down some decent prose, maybe a line here or there that convinced him to stroke his ego more than his own cock. Despite the lies he told himself, he was slow with the pen. His publisher knew it as much as his fans, though the ones who lusted over his mindless dribble made excuses for the delays. He limped through until the last hours of every deadline. The publisher allowed it because unfortunately for them, David Kingston was their biggest cash cow. Even now a few pages a day stood as a milestone for David. Running the empty palms of his hands against his face, he blinked hard and gave in to a deep exhausted sigh. The unblinking computer screen stared back at him with the same paragraph he started two hours and three drinks ago.

Michael Tyree

He looked back once more over his shoulder at the void staying at his heels. Somewhere in the black, his worst mistake waited patiently to correct itself. He held the pedal to the floorboard against the gear and belt driven protests screeching from the engine. When Eddie turned again, the dirt road beneath him melded into debris, leaving broken limbs in its place. In the span of one breath, a congregation of trees sprouted from the darkness, halting his escape. Corrine shared one last exchange with him before the void took her away into its nothingness.

The pale light radiating from his laptop left him blind to the deepening shadows filling his hotel room. A crimson glow seeped through the window from the bar across the street teasing David with promises not kept by the now empty fifth buried in the waste bin. Particles of dust danced like sprites along the bold scarlet beams bleeding through every seam in the blinds.

"Jesus Fuck," David muttered under his breath.

After what seemed like an eternity, David sat up and found his way through the void, with only vague clues left by the cherry, neon light of the bar across the street. His fingertips fumbled across the walls with no more luck than a prepubescent freshman attempting to negotiate a bra clasp for the first time. After a few moments of trial and error, he found his way to the bathroom light switch. The sudden flash of light from the single halogen fixture gave no warning before singeing his retinas with a sharp abruptness. The gold Submariner next to his wallet read 11:37 PM, and that alone was the only cue he needed for a trip across the street. After splashing some water on his face, David changed into something a little more presentable as he refused to let a single minute go to waste chasing the scarlet homing beacon.

The March night bit at every part of his skin uncovered by several layers of clothes as frigid air weighed his lungs down with each breath. A heavy fog lay over the city that night.

POTTER'S FIELD BLUES

Tomorrow is St. Patty's Day, the socially acceptable day of celebration for functioning alcoholics like David Kingston. It was that special time of year when anyone of the Caucasian persuasion pretends for one night, they are more than just one-sixty-fourth Irish. Under normal circumstances David would celebrate it in style, but this time tomorrow he will drag himself back on a plane for his home in Albany, New York.

Only a handful of patrons occupied Harrigan's, all scattered about the darkest corners of the establishment or huddled at the far end of the bar near one of the two working TVs. David claimed a nice vacant spot away from everyone else where he could worship the only way he knew how in his holy of holies, where his absolution came from a steady flow of single-malt whiskey, and always with a price. More often than not his brand of communion left him face down on a bathroom floor in ways that made him question if it was his liver's passive aggressive way of saying, *we should see other people.*

"What'll you have?" came a soft voice from outside his peripheral vision.

He looked over to find a young woman standing behind the bar, bouncing back and forth from the taps to a credit card machine as she closed out someone else's tab. She was tall and fit with long candy apple red hair falling halfway down the back of a bleach faded Ramones shirt.

"I'll have a Jack and Coke."

"Easy enough. I'll be right back with that," she said while returning to the other patrons with two pilsners and a receipt.

A CRT TV tuned into the late-night local news already halfway through a piece about asbestos hung from the ceiling in a black steel cradle in the bar's corner to David's right.

"You wanna open up a tab?" the bartender asked as she mixed David's drink.

"Yeah. Sounds good."

49

Michael Tyree

She placed the highball glass on a red napkin, slid it in front of him and went back about her business tending to other patrons.

David Kingston was a man who wore his arrogance with more fashion than any tailored suit. Whenever David engaged in even the most pedestrian of human interactions, his vanity crawled past his humility and common sense straight to the forefront of his mind. He never missed an opportunity to daydream of a stranger acknowledging him for his fifteen minutes of fame. He imagined that maybe this time his name printed in big bold letters on the front of a hardback would earn him a second glance from anyone.

Breaking News. A hit and run in Catalina County last night has left a seven-year-old dead. Police estimate that sometime after ten o'clock a speeding car struck and killed Andre Sparrow on Crest Street, just a few roads over from his home in the Ventura Heights suburb. No witnesses have come forward yet with information about the car or the driver. If you have any information that would lead to the arrest of...

As the ambient noise played its symphony around him like mid-summer crickets in harmony, he dwelled on the barriers that stood in the way of his current work in progress. *Why was Eddie even there that night? It doesn't make sense.* With his buzz reignited, he slid the smartphone from his pocket and pulled up a series of notes he had made at times when he did not have his computer or notepad handy.

"Change the circumstances so he just doesn't pick up the phone," he said to himself.

Tomorrow begins with opening statements in what is said to be the trial of the century. As new evidence has come to light in recent weeks, the question on everyone's mind isn't whether William Jean Delacroix is guilty or not, but whether or not the prosecution will seek the death penalty.

"Do you think they're gonna give him the needle?"

David looked up from his drunken notes to the bartender now turning her attention to him and anxious for a response. Sipping her own drink behind the bar, she motioned to the TV with her eyes. He looked up at the court room coverage, picking up on the few buzzwords he committed to memory in passing.

"If he did everything they say he did, then yeah, they should fry him."

"One of the regulars here knew a girl he killed. Said she went to work one night and never came back," the bartender said with a sigh before getting back to putting away freshly cleaned glasses. "Haven't seen you around here before. You new in town or just passing through?"

"Oh, I'm just going to be here till tomorrow evening."

"So, what's making you *pass through* Mr...."

"David"

"Mr. David?"

"No, no Kingston. David Kingston."

"So, what does David Kingston do to bring him through our little city on a weeknight?"

"Well, I'm a writer, and I'm finishing up a book tour here in town tomorrow.'"

"Really? That's pretty cool. What kind of stuff do you write?"

"Mostly thrillers and horror."

"Really? I would have pegged you for the craptastic YA scene," the bartender said with a chuckle. "Ya know, blah blah blah ten book series about vampires from New Orleans."

He just shook his head and gave a tiny laugh under his breath that could have been disguised as a hiccup. The few remaining customers got up from the other end and made their way behind David's seat toward the exit. The overpowering stench of booze and motor oil wafted past with them. Like a lesser animal standing before a greater stag, David kept his attention straight

51

ahead, maintaining a smaller profile for reasons he could not explain, except that his gut convinced him it made sense.

"Hey, Tracy, when you gonna let me take ya out sometime? I'll treat cha real nice. Might even let ya polish my knob," one man with a crooked smile full of brown and black tobacco-stained teeth and inflamed gums said.

"Why don't you blow me Tommy," the bartender responded with a chuckle.

The three men glared at David on their way out. Their hateful gazes locked on him until all three exited the building. One even turned back and stared at him through the window, mouthing some mute statement David took for either a threat or a line of insults before turning and following his buddies down the sidewalk.

...missing since yesterday afternoon. She was last seen by her coworkers leaving work around 4:30. If you have seen this woman...

"So, have you done this kind of thing before?" Tracy said as she poured David a refill. "Goin' around the country, signing books, answering questions from your *adoring fans*?"

"Yeah. I've had a few over the years. I've gotten a little tired of them, really."

David knew before the words left his lips how much of a bold-faced lie that last statement was. His ego fed on these little stops from his book tours. He loved the attention more than anything. David only hoped that she didn't see through his faux humility.

"*WHAT*? You are so full of shit," Tracy said, shaking her head and guffawing at the obvious bluff. She took another sip of her drink and set it down on the back counter before pulling a flyer from a stack next to the cash register. She placed it on the bar and slid it over to David.

"What's this?"

"If something happens and you're still in town tomorrow, then you should come by The Basement. My friend's band is playing for a big Saint Patrick's Day party."

"Well, my flight home is tomorrow night, so I doubt I'll make it."

"You never know."

...downtown. Stop by Unknown Worlds tomorrow where author David Kingston will read from his new novel Undercurrent, answer questions, and sign autographs.

The TV caught Tracy's attention sending her into a double take looking at David and then back toward the television.

"That's you, isn't it?"

That single inquiry with all its various evolutions had become David's kryptonite. The vanity he covered with fabricated humility and patchwork unpretentiousness slipped out whenever someone connected his name to his mild celebrity status.

"Yeah, that's me all right. You should come by tomorrow and check it out," David said with the casual suaveness of a middle school virgin.

"Maybe," Tracy said with a subtle smirk and a nod of her head.

Several drinks and two hours later, David pulled his scarf tighter as he stepped back out into the frigid winter air. The gusts scraped the skin of his cheeks and nose like coarse sandpaper. Wasting no time, he picked up his pace to the warm climate-controlled hotel lobby.

Seven paces to the front entrance and David stopped himself. A faint cry for help drifted through the fog. From where he stood on the sidewalk it came as a whisper. He held his ground for a minute, struggling to discern if what he thought he heard had been nothing more than the winter winds casting an illusion.

With no answer he took another few steps toward the lobby entrance. Then, with more definition, it happened again.

"Heeeelp!" came a request just above a whisper in his ear.

David looked all around him. Convinced someone was calling out to him alone for help, he hunted around himself for any clues to no avail. And then, there it was once more.

"Please, God! Help me..." screamed the phantom victim.

"Hello?" David answered back

He back tracked out into the road trying to follow the sound. At this late hour, the busy street felt as abandoned as a dirt crossroads in the heart of a ghost town.

"Where are you?" he reiterated, now standing in the middle of the road.

He labored to get a bearing on the disembodied voice coming from somewhere in the darkness. Then it happened again.

"Please."

It was the voice of a young woman. There was a distressed break in her call. Like the tone of someone at the end of their rope, and with no hope of rescue. And just like that, David noticed a thin silhouette out of the corner of his left eye. Standing down the road where an alleyway joined the darkened street was a young girl in her late teens, maybe mid-twenties. She wore a long grey dress with white ruffles and broken, worn features that lay ripped and dirty as if she just had broken free of a struggle.

"You have to help me. Tell them the truth. They are going to kill me," The young girl pleaded with David, catching her breath between protests.

"Shhhhh, it will be ok. Just calm down and take a deep breath. No one is going to hurt you," David said reassuringly. "Just sit tight, and I'll call the police."

"Please, tell them the truth. Tell them it wasn't me," exclaimed the young girl as her tone began to escalate and become more agitated.

"Ma'am, I'm sorry, but I think you have me mixed up with someone else. Look, no one is going to hurt you. Just stay right here and I'll call the police," he said with a loose reassurance, still not sure what kind of trouble this girl was escaping from.

"Noooooo!" The young girl screamed at the top of her lungs.

David reached out for her shoulder as he protested one more time. "Ma'am, it will be ok." Just as his fingertips grazed her upper arm, she reached out and latched onto David by his jacket with both hands and an almost superhuman strength.

As she brought her grasp around his collar, she pulled him in almost inches away from her face and gave one final protest. "NOOOOOOOOO!" She howled as David stood there frozen like a housefly bound in the spider's web.

This alone should have been enough to shake him to his core, but as the girl howled at him in defiance, her torso combusted into flames leaving the girl's body consumed by the immolation from head to toe. David struggled to liberate himself, but her grip would not falter. A myriad of putrid fumes took siege of his nostrils leaving him with a menagerie of burnt hair, molten bubbling flesh, and singed linen. He could feel the overbearing heat of the flames all around him, lashing at his nerve endings with every passing second. The conflagration that had all but consumed the girl was now dancing upon the sleeve of his jacket. He made every attempt possible to break free from her grip, but with every failed bid she just pulled him in tighter. In his last attempt to flee, he made the mistake of bringing his gaze back upon the face of the young woman holding him hostage. What he witnessed was more unnerving and visceral than anything he had written before. Not his worst nightmare, nor his most depraved literary work could have prepared him for what lay ahead. Her eyes that were once a faint blue like that of a clear mid-day spring sky, disappeared into nothing. They melted away inside of her sockets and ran down her face like under cooked eggs. Her nose fell away like so much pale candle wax, leaving her nasal cavity raw. The girl's jaw loosened with every bellow; as tendons detached and skin stretched paper thin, her mandible flopped in ways once anatomically incorrect.

"You will burn too," she said.

She released him, and David collapsed to the road. Grasping at a parking meter in desperation, he pulled himself upright. His vision blurred into a narrow tunnel as a sharp ringing resonated in his ears. The uninvited taste of Jack and bile hung at the back of his throat until it all came back in a quick and violent burst all along the front of his jacket. In his drunken sensory overload, he still mustered the strength to look up just to find his attacker had vanished as well as any evidence of her being. He remained alone on the sidewalk, swimming inside his own head.

The digital chime of his cellphone alarm screeched at David until he awoke the next day to a throbbing pulse surging between his temples. Last night's events were almost lost in the void of his short-term memory, only returning in small puzzle pieces at a time: that bar across the street, a redheaded bartender, pieces of a conversation about his story no one would publish.

What was her name? Kelley? Stacey? Tracy?

David lay on his stomach with his face buried in the three hundred thread count pillow when the seventh alarm he had set for that morning fired off without warning around 9:35 AM. Every movement put his stomach on edge. Even the act of rolling over to silence his phone once more started a maelstrom of nausea in him. He teetered on the edge of vomiting a few times before transitioning to his stomach to then sitting upright on the edge of the bed. The cold realization set in that David had three hours and twenty-five minutes to get his shit together before his appearance at Unknown Worlds.

POTTER'S FIELD BLUES

The mid-morning luminescence peaked around the blinds in the modest sized hotel room. David kept them tight together for fear that like the vampires in some of his older fiction, he too would turn to dust if exposed to direct sunlight (or at least he would feel that way while the mild alcohol poisoning worked its way out of his system).

The harsh weather dictated that David layer his clothes like a Russian nesting doll. He decided on a grey wool turtleneck sweater underneath a navy-blue sports coat underneath a heavy black leather trench coat, accented with leather gloves and a black wool cap with a red and grey pinstripe around the bottom. Even with several more pounds of armor added, the deep cold penetrated the nooks and crannies, driving straight to his bones. The chill caused David to shiver for a moment as he strolled back around the building to the rear parking lot.

Flashes of memories about last night flirted with his curiosity. Like any other blacked out episode, David pieced it together a little at a time while trying to determine where and when his memory stopped. The deductive process helped him ignore the winter chill bearing down on him.

David prided himself on being early to everything, so in keeping with tradition he gave himself two-and-a-half hours to find some hangover food that would be easy on his stomach before he had to arrive at the bookstore. His plan seemed simple enough for one of these trips; find some hole in the wall mom and pop diner, order a little artery clogging grease with something that resembled food on the side, sober up long enough to read a couple of chapters from the new book, sign some copies for an hour or two, then fly back home with a drink in his hand, easy peasy. There was one major cog in the machine of David's master plan. Those steps required him to have some mode of transportation.

Michael Tyree

A swift revelation hit him like a cold shower, revealing that his plan wouldn't work, when he rounded the corner to find the Buick he had rented from the airport agency missing from the parking lot. There were only two cars behind the hotel, neither of which had been loaned to him for this trip. In a panic he ran back and forth between the back lot and the street out front trying to make any sense of this before convincing himself that someone must have stolen the rental. He called the police first thing and while waiting for the detectives to arrive, he played the unamusing game of phone tag between his insurance company and the rental agency. When the officers arrived, there was little they could do for David. Following a row of questions from him, they interviewed the night manager, pulled the information on CCTV cameras in the area that may or may not have spotted the vehicle leaving the parking lot, and got the insurance and rental agency information. They left David with a bid of good luck for his appearance later, but no reassurance about the property that disappeared with the sedan. Between calling the cops, calling the rental agency, calling his insurance company, and waiting for the police to arrive on scene, David spent most of the time he allotted himself pacing in the parking lot. After the detectives finished taking his statement, he had just over twenty minutes to get to the bookstore on time. Crossing breakfast off his to do list, David sucked it up and hailed a cab to take him to the next stop on his itinerary.

The hustle and commotion of late morning commuters made for an irritating soundtrack to David's hangover. He gazed out from the window at life passing by as the taxi cruised east toward his destination. Office buildings and skyscrapers mounted all around him like a deep valley of steel and glass. It wasn't until they took an exit away from downtown on 705 East toward Silverton Road that the skyline appeared again. The taxi stopped at one final light a block away from David's appointment with less than five minutes to spare. The perpetual tick of his Rolex mocked him with every second lost to midtown congestion. An advertisement on an adjacent billboard reflected the midday sunlight back at his eyes and sent him recoiling back with whispered curses. Under the tagline *Bowes Real Estate* stood an older man in his early fifties dressed in a navy-blue Ralph Lauren suit with his arms crossed in the center of the ad. His synthetic toothy smile told a contradicting alibi than his eyes and brow. Through high dollar veneers his expression begged for the trust of his sincerity, but his eyes held him in a different light. The violet accented blues hissed like the lone copperhead laying in the brush waiting to drive fangs into flesh. The billboard advertisement fueled David's irritation to the cusp of his limit when traffic let up bringing him within reach of Unknown Worlds.

After a nerve-racking stressful commute, the taxi delivered David to the old town district that was currently going through gentrification. Sitting on the corner of a brick and cobblestone street in one of the oldest neighborhoods in the city, Unknown Worlds stood out amongst the other Main Street stores like a titan among lesser deities. The aisles intersected and veered off to form a labyrinth of literature floor to ceiling. From Fitzgerald to Steele, from first edition leather bounds displayed in meticulous climate-controlled glass curios, to comics and graphic novels stacked by customers searching for that one unique variant cover, this store had it all. Their current affairs section reflected that of a city nestled in the polished, long horn buckle of the Bible Belt with new and old releases all tailored for the fine folks who believed in their heart of hearts that Sean Hannity was a prophet of the Lord.

A small table with a few bottles of spring water and an assortment of pens awaited him in the middle of the store. Timothy Chalders, the owner, and general manager of the store stood by the table as fans remained where they had waited for over an hour and a half to meet their favorite author. Fanfare erupted into an ear-splitting cacophony the very second the first-person laid eyes on him walking toward the front of the line. He looked over and gave cursory glances and waves at his adoring followers from time to time. For the next few hours, his remaining strength would be funneled into keeping his cool for all the adoring fans. He would stretch his mouth muscles into fake smiles, erupt into laughter at nothing amusing, and force himself to feign investment in small talk.

"Ladies and gentlemen, patrons of Unknown Worlds, it is my deepest honor to introduce the man of the hour. He is a two-time Bram Stoker award nominee and author of over a dozen well received titles, including his newest novel *Undercurrent*. Please give a warm round of applause for David Kingston," Mr. Chalders said moments before another eruption of ear-shattering fanfare.

"...red...everything red. Every shade...rose, crimson, vermillion, maroon, cherry, burgundy...marrow, marrow, the hue, and consistency of it sets my teeth on fire. The walls, the ceiling, the floor...my hands...my hands. I close my eyes and it is all still a dusky pink membrane. I can't..." David said with a sigh, finishing the last sentence in that passage before closing his book on the podium. His fans held their awe until they knew he had finished reading before blessing their idol with a crashing wave of applause.

Timothy returned to David's side to address the audience.

"Now is the time for the Q&A section. Anyone that would like to ask Mr. Kingston a question can get into line right over there. Thank you," Mr. Chalders said pointing to the right side of the crowd where a store employee stood waiting with a wireless microphone in hand.

The die-hard fans shot up and pushed their way over to get in line first. After a few minutes, something that resembled an orderly single file column assembled, waiting to speak. Some questions had a surprising sense of depth, causing David to weigh his response, while most of the others were the same regurgitated dribble asked of him at every convention or signing. The questions that would irritate a sober version of David Kingston caused a hungover David to devolve into the worst version of himself.

"When do you think we'll see the TV adaptation of *Save the Last One*?" said an underweight teenager with dyed jet-black hair, a red and black lumber jack long sleeve shirt, and ripped black denim pants.

"The studio just brought Alex Nyunne to help pen the screenplay. He was one of the head writers for *Shadow Heart* and *The Last Rites of Mary Denton*. I'm not at liberty to give a specific date, but I would keep a look out for it sometime maybe before the end of next year." David responded with a forced smile.

"Is there a common theme with any of your stories?" a young man with a blonde crew cut and an OSU sweatshirt mumbled at an almost inaudible level with a tense nervous tone.

"Well, regarding my first series, I think the common denominator would have been isolation. Whether it was physical, mental, or any other. I've always found the theme of isolation terrifying. Take that first collection for instance. In one story you have a person who is physically trapped far away from anyone that can help him. There is no foreseeable chance of him getting back to his family alive. As far as he knows, he will die alone, and nobody will ever know. And in another you have a character trapped alone in her own head. She is isolated in this mental limbo where she goes further down the rabbit hole, the more her dreamworld bleeds over into what she assumes is reality. Soon she can't discern between the two. Isolation is a terrifying notion regardless of what form it takes."

"Are there any characters you regretted killing off or vice versa?" a pudgy, older fan whose stomach tested the resolve of almost every button of a royal blue dress shirt, said.

"A few. My first story took a while to complete because I couldn't decide if I should kill the main character off or not. I kept saying to myself that if I did, it might make the story feel like torture porn and that the character deserved better. That one survived, and I'm glad that she did. Maybe it would have been more shocking if I had killed her off. I think that leaving her alive ended the story with an invitation for others to interpret it however they want. Maybe she got away. Maybe she didn't. Who knows? I think that was the only time I struggled with that."

A clean-shaven slim man in olive drab trousers, a white undershirt tucked in, and rounded horn-rimmed glasses stood next in line to ask David a question. The man just stood at the front for a moment and stared at David. After a brief silence he spoke up as he pushed his glasses back against his face with the index finger of his left hand.

"Where were you?" the man asked.

David paused for a moment before responding, not sure if he heard the man correctly or not. "I'm...sorry. What do you mean where was I?"

"Where were you?" He repeated.

David had no answer for the young man addressing him. He could only shake his head in confusion as he looked to other people in the audience for a clue. As he labored to find the right words, another young man wearing identical clothes as the first stood up from his seat amidst the sea of people and, looking at David, said the same thing.

"Where were you?"

Before David could say anything to the second person interrogating him, two more rose up; one from a seat on the right side of the audience, the second from the center of a group of people standing in the back. One after another they all repeated the same mantra over and over with a haunting cadence.

"Where were you?"

"Where were you?"

"Where were you?"

As the chanting picked up its pace, the men all stepped out onto the floor as the rest of the audience remained still as a photograph. Nothing moved except for the four audience members marching toward him, chanting as they did. Within a few seconds they surrounded David. He took a few steps back, tripping on the same chair he was sitting in just over an hour prior. He turned to catch himself from falling and in doing so, put eyes on three more men dressed the same as the first walking toward him from the far-left side.

The seven all repeated the same question over and over again, one after the other in a haunting stanza. Then all at once they became silent again. David peered over the shoulder of the one facing him to see that the crowd remained frozen in place. The young men's faces, and extremities started shedding pounds with every second that went by. Cheeks that had once been tight and full of youthful color regressed into hollow cavities. Muscle mass shriveled away as all seven men withered. Lesions multiplied across the arms and faces of the seven men. As time crept by, these men adopted the motor skills of toddlers. Legs buckled and bent as their muscles rotted away. Arms fell at their sides and swung about like pendulums.

The one in front of David took a few steps forward, bringing himself just a couple feet away. He reached out with labored effort and rested his arms on David's shoulders by the wrists. He peered into David's face with a blank stare.

"Where were you?" He alone asked again.

He repeated himself over and over like a skipping record. His top teeth started dropping out of his rotting mouth with the form of every other syllable. The bottom ones loosened and fell to the side, some dribbling out of his face, others sliding down his throat adding the ambience of a garbage disposal as the words formed with less haste.

He heaved forward again on David as his arms dislocated out of the shoulder sockets, leaving the remains to teeter and slide down the front of David's trembling chest. The man collapsed against him causing the two of them to topple to the floor as the other men swarmed David. Some knelt around him while others collapsed with all their exhausted dead weight piling on the author. Their extremities continued to waste at an accelerated rate until they were nothing more than bones with thin pale skin barely hanging on. The deteriorating, white shirts grew stains and tears. The ripped apparel displayed thin skin covering brittle rib cages. A mass of bony rag doll men pinned him down, blotting his vision. They blocked out the light from David's eyes. All he had was the odor of dried blood and feces racing through his nostrils, bringing the vomit he had held at bay all morning back into his mouth. David slipped an arm from under the pile of bodies and brought his hand over his mouth as he choked back the bile.

The pile shifted again and once more the overhead light breached the separations between shoulders and arms, giving him a clearer view. The one that had stood in front of him struggled to hold his pale eyelids open as he prepared to make his next statement. Each word seemed to ride on the peak of every other exhalation removed from the young man's lungs.

"We…were…counting…on…you…Jake," the young man said with a raspy breath.

As he finished his sentence, a small, black, shiny object about the size of a dime fell from his mouth that was still hanging open. It landed on David's cheek and slid down toward his ear. Soon another and another fell. He pushed the young man up away from his chest until fluorescent light pulled the veil from David's ignorance. The cold light left him with an image that brought his stomach on edge. The young man's mouth hung open wide as small bugs continued their exodus from inside the boy. Beetles and maggots fell from the jaw as it tipped open wide. Worms slithered out of his nose and pushed their way from behind his eyeballs. David could no longer hold himself back. He screamed from the bottom of his gut as he tossed and turned to free himself from his assailants. Their grip loosened just enough, and he scooted on his back toward the door that read employees only.

"GET OFF ME GODDAMNIT!!" David screamed as he put his back to the door with his eyes closed tight and arms out in front of him in a defensive posture.

"Mr. Kingston? Mr. Kingston? David Kingston?" Came a voice overtop of David.

David opened his eyes and looked up to see Mr. Chalders standing over him with a look of genuine concern on his face. He held his hand down to aid David to his feet. David looked behind the store owner, and to his amazement and confusion the seven men had vanished.

"Sir...are you ok?"

David stood up without the help of Mr. Chalders to find everyone in the crowd staring at him with a look of complete bewilderment. Several people throughout the crowd had their cellphones out recording David.

"Where did they go?" David asked Mr. Chalders, hoping no one in ear shot could make out the inquiry.

"Where did...who go?" Mr. Chalders responded.

"The men. There were seven men back here trying to assault me. They came up here and attacked me."

Mr. Chalders took a step closer to David, looked over his shoulder, and then back to David. In a faint voice he responded: "Sir. I have been the only one up here with you."

"No. There was a man in green pants and a white shirt standing in line asking me *Where I was*, and then he and some of his friends came up here and attacked me!"

"Mr. Kingston, I've been up here with you through the whole Q&A. No one approached you. You stared at the crowd and didn't respond for almost a minute and then you fell. Are you ok?"

David let the question linger for a moment until he could compose himself. He stared out onto the crowd once more, watching people watching him. They all looked as shocked as he felt, unable to process the queer spectacle that just took place next to some general fiction. Further back, near the patrons standing up, Tracy had already begun walking away from the crowd. David caught sight of her just as she stopped and looked back over her shoulder in his direction one more time before continuing her exit through the mob.

"Um. Yes. Yes, I'm fine. I just…need to use your restroom."

"Of course."

"Ladies and Gentlemen, that concludes the Q&A portion as well as the rest of the event," Mr. Chalders said as he addressed the crowd.

The late afternoon sun hung low, taking the last rays of amber warmth as David arrived back at the hotel. An hour later his suitcase lay on the edge of the bed stuffed full again. Several missed calls and voicemails waited for him as David stepped out of the shower: one from his agent, and another from his publisher. Both were inquiring about what he had put up his nose before turning a simple Q&A into an embarrassing viral online video. But the last person who called didn't leave a message. Instead, upon returning the call, he got in touch with one detective he had met this morning looking into who stole his rental car. After a brief exchange of small talk, the officer informed David that they found the sedan this afternoon. Whoever took it totaled the front end. The police found the car on the edge of the city wrapped around a tree, with the windshield broken from the inside out. It appeared as if one or more people had not been wearing seatbelts and went straight through upon collision. The immediate reaction that David knew not to confide with the detective was that whoever did this got what they deserved.

With the last few days behind him, David looked through the terminal for a vacant section where he could decompress without interruption. The crowded lobby would not allow him such comforts while he waited to board his plane. Squeezing by three different families congregating in tight proximity, he found one empty seat between them all. His body wanted to rest, but the firm plastic chair did not allow him such leisure. His irritation reached new limits as he could only dwell on being home and not in this city. All around him droves of people flocked in and out. More than a few sat around and across from him having phone conversations that were too important to not have on speaker phone. The involuntary peek into other people's lives left his teeth on edge. Free range toddlers ran amok through the terminal, screaming like stray cats and dogs while their parents remained transfixed by tablets and phones. David looked around at the socially acceptable chaos surrounding him and hung his head down as he hunched over to stare at the navy-blue carpet of the terminal. He did his best to lose himself in a daydream or even determine which came first, the chicken or the egg. It almost worked until the shadow of a small figure flooded the ground in front of him. He looked up to see a young boy not running around with the others screaming. He was dressed in a dark grey hoodie with red accents on the sleeves, and green cargo pants tucked around a pair of tattered Nike shoes. His hair was pulled into tight cornrows that lead into braids falling down to his shoulder. He stood there and looked at David without saying a word while the maelstrom of feral children raged around the two of them. He cracked his mouth as if to begin a sentence but then lost the nerve before he could start. A look of confusion and melancholy lay across the boy's face.

Attention: Flight 307Z to Albany has been delayed until further notice. Flight 307Z to Albany is delayed until further notice.

"What?" David said to himself as the intercom buzzed with static and clicked off.

He stood up from his chair and looked back to a large, computerized LED board near the front of the terminal with flight times and destinations listed. The one for his plane back home to Albany changed from *on time* to *delayed*.

"Fuck! That can't be."

When he turned around, the boy had disappeared, vanished, or maybe swallowed up by the unsupervised hurricane.

"Weird little shit."

David stood in line for twenty minutes before his turn to approach the terminal counter came.

"Yes, how can I help you?" said a middle-aged woman with purple rimless eyeglasses and shoulder length sandy brown hair.

"Yes, did I hear that intercom correctly? Did it just say the 7:45 flight to Albany has been delayed?"

"Let's see here…" the attendant said as she typed away at her keyboard. "Yes. Apparently, there is a severe snowstorm heading that way, and the runway has been temporarily closed."

David shook his head in frustration.

"Well…do you have any idea when the next flight will be?"

"Hmm, it looks as if the next one will be the day after tomorrow."

"I…Fuck!" David said as he gritted his teeth and clenched his fists. Looking around at the circus in full swing all around him. "Fuck this."

"Looks like you're going to be here with us longer than you expected," the attendant said in a low, subtle monotone.

"I'm sorry?"

"I said the next available flight would be the day after tomorrow. Would you like to take that one instead?"

"Well, I don't see where I have much of a choice in the matter," David said with reluctance.

Harrigan's Pub had already begun filling to the brim with St. Patty's Day patrons when David arrived. He pushed his way through the crowd and found the only seat available at the bar. Tracy glanced over at him from the register as she finished up the tab of a group of college kids on the front end of tonight's bar crawl.

"I thought you would have been long gone by now," Tracy said without looking up from the terminal.

"My flight was delayed for a few days. I'm gonna be stuck here 'til day after tomorrow," he said as David pulled up a stool at the bar.

"Well, don't talk about it like it's such a terrible thing, sugar," Tracy added with a sarcastic tone. "So, let me guess…you're bored, and you think your liver should be the one to suffer?"

Without a witty comeback, David just shook his head.

"Look, I'm still planning on leaving early tonight so I can go see my friend's band play," she said while moving in front of him and leaning over on her forearms to put herself eye level with David. "I think it would be in your best interest to pull up your big boy pants and come with me. Who knows, you might actually have some fun."

David looked around at the bar packed with obnoxious twenty somethings all screaming at the top of their lungs, then to his watch, then to Tracy.

"What kind of music do they play?"

Tracy just smiled at him in response.

David and Tracy got in line just as it started to wrap around the block. The crowd waiting to get in was not the usual bunch David associated with. On the contrary, it consisted of people he would have discounted any other day of the week. These were Tracy's people: clad in black leather and spikes, fishnets, high-heel, thigh-high boots, and denim vests with patches stitched all over in varying collages. Tracy stood next to him in a black leather biker jacket with rows of pyramid spikes protruding from the shoulder straps and pockets. Several coats from a sea green paint marker accented the outer edges of the lapels with color. Dozens of round pins filled the spots not scribbled on or covered in metal, all with artwork from various bands, artists, and even some that had political slogans or symbols, like a pale white button with the word *WAR* being crossed out with a bright red circle. Next to that was another larger pin with a stick figure throwing both a swastika and a hammer and sickle into a flaming waste bin with a text underneath it that said *Save the Earth, Dispose of Garbage Properly*. She wore a torn Black Flag shirt with ripped grey jeans and black Doc Martens, also accented in paint.

Her hair was pulled back into a ponytail, while most of her head remained covered in a brown wool cap. The undecipherable language coming from the speakers inside grew louder as they inched their way to the tattered brick threshold overshadowing the entrance to the club.

David slid his way through the crowd lingering in the doorway as Tracy took his hand and led him inside. The scratching of distorted electric guitars and thumping of bass drums poured out of the ceiling-high stacks of speakers. One of the opening bands already halfway through their set worked the crowd up into a rage. A tsunami of grey denim battle vests and plaid jackets collided up front as a wave of vermillion and violet stage lights flooded the crowd. The pulsing luminescence showed an audience crashing into each other in slow motion.

"Why don't you go get us some drinks, hmm?" Tracy said with a smirk.

"What do you want?"

"Surprise me," she answered while disappearing into the crowd between him and some high-top tables.

Pounding industrial metal bombarded David's eardrums in a way all too foreign to his normal sense of adventure. The plucking and crashing of the five-string Ibanez bass forced him to scream his drink order at the bartender over the riffs.

"Jack...and coke, and...a whiskey sour!"

The bartender was dressed in a blue denim shirt with the sleeves cut off into a makeshift vest that was draped over a black Venom shirt and black jeans with almost half of the material cut out of the front of them. He looked at David with a cold dead gaze through the separation in his straight shoulder length black hair. Parted down the middle, it only revealed a minimal portion of his face, just enough to see the look of indifference in his eyes. The bartender looked over David's shoulder at the band without moving his head, then across the club to Tracy. His eyes darted back to David as he nodded his head upwards just before walking away to get the drinks.

David turned his back to the bar and took in the spectacle in the front of the club. Anonymous people were pushing and punching each other without a second thought. Chaos unchained before him. The song ended with a distorted single note from each guitar echoing in the speakers followed by a handful of extra snare crashes, leading the audience to erupt with fanfare and howls.

A young woman in her late twenties sat at the bar to his left. Like a peacock among a murder of crows, she stood out from the others in a skintight, royal blue cocktail dress. Long onyx black hair fell down past her shoulders, and the incandescent light of the bar complimented her olive skin tone.

"You should stay," the woman said still looking toward the back of the bar.

David moved his attention away from the stage and toward the statement he didn't know was aimed at him. The woman turned to face him at the same time as David met her gaze.

"I'm sorry, were you talking to me?" David said at an exaggerated volume to convey that he couldn't hear very well right now.

"You need to stay."

David leaned over toward her, propping himself on the bar with his elbow.

"I still can't hear you. What were you saying?"

"You need to stay," She repeated herself. "You should want to stay."

"Well, this isn't my usual idea of fun, but I think I'll stick around 'til the end of the show."

The woman said nothing in response, just took another long sip of her martini until the glass ran dry. She put it down on the bar and pulled a twenty from her clutch leaving it next to the glass for the bartender. The woman stood up and took a step closer to David, leaning toward him as if to say something she wanted him to hear clearly. He met her halfway and leaned over further as she began to whisper in his ear.

"Don't leave us! Please, you can't!" The woman pleaded with a combined look of worry and sorrow.

David just stood there shaking his head with dumbfounded confusion.

"Please!" she said as the precursor of tears welled up around her caramel eyes. She placed her left hand across her stomach and moved it around in a circular motion. "We both need you to stay."

"Look, I'm not sure who you think I am, but I believe you're mistaken."

David looked back around to inquire where the bartender was with his order. The next song began to play as the stage lights went out again. Only faint diffused blue LEDs displayed behind the band until the first verse which ushered in flashes of white strobes all around the club. He turned to find the woman standing there sobbing and shaking her head. Then in mid sniffle, an invisible force yanked her up off the ground leaving her toes dangling a foot or more above the floor and knocking over the barstool behind her. Her neck folded over to the right almost to the shoulder with a loud snap, breaking over the guitars and drums, then followed up with a series of cracks and pops as she remained suspended in front of him. Her arms drooped at her sides and convulsed with her legs, leaving her entire body spasming under the strain of the phantom force. The woman's tongue flopped from her mouth as she choked on her last pleas. Stumbling back in terror, David fell against the bar as she swayed back and forth in the air. He peered around himself to find everyone else in the club continuing to enjoy themselves without missing a beat. Nobody paid attention to him or the woman hanging next to him. He turned back as she called out once more.

The phantom had been looking at the ground due to how the unseen rope had postured her head, but as she moved side to side, her once deep brown eyes, now gelatinous milky orbs, rolled up to her brow to make eye contact with David once more.

"You...belong with...us," she said in a garbled tone.

The bridge of the song led into a series of long blue and white flashes from the stage lights. The pauses of darkness and light made a slideshow of the woman's decomposition. When the bright white lit her body, she had wilted away further into a corporeal form. Eyes sunken in, jaw hanging low, her once spotless olive skin now a diseased greyish blue sagging away from muscle and tendon.

David fell backward, bumping into a couple standing at the bar watching the band play. The man he collided with pushed him back making David trip and fall to the ground. When he stood back up the woman had vanished leaving an untouched bar stool where she had just hung moments ago. He turned to face the man.

"I...um...look man, I'm sorry! I didn't mean to bump into you."

"You better fuckin' watch yourself, asshole!" The burly man said as he drove his right index finger into David's chest.

David put his hands up in front of him as if to show that he didn't mean the man any harm and it was all just an accident. The man turned back to watch the show as he muttered obscenities to himself while the young girl clung to his chest and tucked under his arm. She continued giving David hateful stares as her partner gazed off in the distance.

The bartender returned with David's drinks holding up one finger, then six. He reached into his wallet and pulled out a twenty and handed it over. He did not hang around long enough to get change back, just took the two drinks and walked away.

In that moment David Kingston's last straw split in two, his remaining fragment of sanity slipped away like the final grain of an hourglass. His true north, lost. The line between his life and those he birthed with the incessant clicking and clacking of his keyboard blurred. Reality and fantasy, calm and horror, interwove together till neither could distinguish itself from its antithesis. Like a fine oil painting left to the elements, the lines that once stood as clear borders and restraints, were now unable to segregate the light from the dark, the defined and the uncured.

"What the fuck? What the fuck? What the fuck?" he muttered to himself as he slipped between strangers holding both drinks with a firm grip.

At safe intervals, when nothing blocked his path to the small tabletop Tracy had claimed for them, David took full swigs of his drink with more haste than he had ever known. Over half of it was gone by the time he handed Tracy hers. The chilled whiskey and cola did nothing for the tremor taking the reins of his muscles. His whole body shook as he closed his eyes and attempted to take in several deep breaths while bracing himself against the table. The stomach acid brought on what felt like an ulcer beginning to burn in the pit of his core.

"What's *wrong* with you?" Tracy asked as she sipped her drink.

David didn't respond. He couldn't. The author felt solely incapable of forming sentences. Instead, he just looked all around himself, then back toward the bar, toward the exit, and then back to Tracy. David just shook his head and finished his drink. David Kingston, self-proclaimed master of the macabre, teetering on the threshold of his sanity. His anchor in the real breaking away from its weakest link, leaving him to float away in the never-ending sea of madness. Dementia maybe? The daytime hallucinations of lunatics? Have the ghouls and goblins of nightmares and fiction past now turned to flesh and taken the first steps into his world?

"HEY!" Tracy said as she poked him in the forehead with her index finger. "The fuck's wrong with you?"

The volume went out in David's head as a loud, sharp ringing replaced it. All the ambient noise from the club died down, almost mute. David tried to respond but found his own words reverberating in his head as if his ears were under pressure. His heart picked up the pace, crashing to the beat of someone else's drum while his head spun, and his stomach sloshed with acid. Beads of sweat formed at the back of his neck and the top of his forehead. His skin became warm to the touch.

"I don't...I feel..."

"Hey, you still with me? Ya know what, just sit down right here, and I'm gonna get you some water," Tracy said in a tone David could only understand by reading her lips while the ringing in his head dampened his auditory system.

David sat at the table with his face buried in his palms, his stomach still tossing and turning, his senses either numb and useless or inflamed. Even with the lightheaded ringing in his ears muffling the world around him, it had become clear to him shortly after Tracy disappeared for a few minutes that the club had grown strangely mute. David looked up from his hands to find the band had not only stopped playing, but all stood still as they fixated on the corner of The Basement where he sat. Most of the audience all turned around and gazed at him. One by one, people emerged from the crowd and walked away from the stage toward him. They slid and sidestepped through the audience from every corner of the club. Everyone approaching him wore garments from different walks of life, different periods of time, different corners of the world, all in contrast to the patrons David had met tonight in leather and denim. Some were in military fatigues last issued over fifty years ago, some in prison jumpsuits, some dressed in nothing, but scraps of animal hide and jewelry made of bone and teeth, while others were adorned in the finest garb of a former aristocracy. The only commonality was their humanity, a diverse tapestry of phantasms.

Even with garbled tunnel vision, David made out the silhouette of the young man that attacked him at the bookstore. Then from the corner of his left eye a shadow blotted out the luminescence from the single halogen light over the entrance to the restrooms. He knew without looking that it wouldn't be pleasant. His gut gave him a preview before his eyes cataloged it, or really, they. He looked over his left shoulder to a couple dozen people appearing from behind him. Soon there were a couple hundred or more packed shoulder to shoulder in attendance in a tight circle all around.

"This is all just a dream, just a bad dream," David whispered to himself.

They all stood in silence, giving David a small circle to occupy at the epicenter of the mob. He made a feeble attempt to escape, but the dizziness and fatigue dropped him to his knees a few feet from the table. They remained in silence watching him with cold dead eyes. After a few moments, the mob started to part into two, leaving a path down the middle. It started in the back with a few people bowing their heads and stepping back or to the sides to form a walkway, the domino effect finished right in front of David. He didn't have the strength to hold his gaze upright for long before sinking back to the floor. But when he did, he witnessed a pair of thin legs in ripped denim jeans moving toward him through the crowd. It was Tracy making her way to the head of the pack.

Tracy squatted down to get eye level with him. She reached out and cupped his chin in her hand like a parent tending to an injured child, lifting his head upward to meet her gaze.

"Oh, Davey."

"What is this?"

"The word that most describes it might be penance, but that's not quite right. The real irony of this is that you're a mildly successful writer; however, you'll never know a word that encapsulates what *this* is," Tracy said as she released his face and stood back up, towering over him. "Every time we do this you have to see it for yourself first," she added.

As David tangled with her riddle, a young girl made her way to his side and bent down to touch him on the shoulder. David looked up in bewilderment. He recognized this girl from somewhere. His memory came and left like a classroom presentation missing half of the slides. Flashes of memory that may or may not have had anything to do with this person taunted him. Then it hit him in the jaw. Last night after he left the bar, there was a girl screaming for help, but that was the only piece of the story he could remember.

The club disappeared, and he found himself transported miles and centuries away in an instant. What played in front of him seemed like a dream at first, but the detail was as a photograph, like a vivid memory where even the smells and nerve endings in his fingers felt as real as anything else. Every detail, every sensation was as genuine as anything he had ever experienced before. He stood in the vision convinced that the moment in The Basement, as well as his entire life prior, was the nightmare and this present iteration was in fact reality.

David was no longer David. In fact, he was no longer male. He looked through the eyes of a twenty-three-year-old German woman named Helena Lasbeken. He was Helena, and she was he. They were both one and the same. He saw through her, not as a lucid dream or some overdone fan fiction, but with the chilling recollection of a memory with perfect historical accuracy. There were no blurred edges in the peripheral, no inaccurate sense of time, no illegible text. Everything replayed as it had so long ago. Like recalling a recent conversation, he watched this point in time through her eyes as he did over three hundred years ago. He breathed the same air as her, felt the coarse fabric of her dress against her body. He felt the familiar sting as the texture of the town square agitated the bruise on her right heel. He remembered how the wind on that particular day pricked her nose, how every shrill *sh* and *ch* sound leaving the priest's mouth hit her ear with a sharp ping, like a snare drum striking out of time.

She stood among others in a crowd gathered in a Würzburg street during the 1626 witch trials. The skyline bled amber as the sun sunk in the west. A frigid wind rattled the bare tree branches, bringing an icy chill against Helena's face. The mob remained silent as one man stood in front and gave an empowered speech about the Devil and his agents. He screamed and ranted while beating his fist on a tattered black copy of the Bible. Behind him a small group of men worked to stack kindle and logs around the base of a single ten-foot-tall wooden pole. Although David knew nothing about the German language, the words flowed through him like a cool stream. As Babel ascended high above David Kingston's soul, he listened while phrases he never knew or could enunciate came to him with a clear and concise understanding in plain English.

"Bring forth the accused!" the priest shouted.

A door opened from a building to the right, and four men armed with muskets escorted a young girl toward her last moments on this earth. Adorned in a grey dress with white ruffled sleeves, the girl inched to the center of town with her captors behind her. She couldn't have been over nineteen or twenty. Her face and hands trembled as the proximity between her, and her executioners closed in. The girl's chest heaved from hyperventilation while her eyes darted over the crowd. Her search stopped when the girl's eyes met Helena's. She stopped moving with the others and took a bounding leap toward the crowd.

"Helena, you must tell them the truth! TELL THEM IT WAS NOT ME! Tell them, please!" the girl screamed in panic.

Two of the men swarmed her, grabbing the girl by the elbows, and dragged her back against her heels to their previous course. Her resistance proved meaningless as her captors forced her before the crowd where a stake surrounded by kindling awaited her. The men bound her to the pole with a generous amount of coarse rope. The knots were tied so tightly around her back that she erupted in a wince of agony when the last bit of slack came out, cutting into her forearms.

Tears welled up in her eyes as she looked upon her accusers. She shook her head in disbelief as she continued her protests to a deaf crowd. The preacher continued rambling on for another five minutes before turning to face the girl awaiting her death sentence.

"Anna Wydmanyn! You have been found guilty of treason and conspiracy to practice witchcraft. The sentence is death," the preacher said.

"I'm not a witch! I was with Helena the whole time! Please, you must believe me!"

Her pleas devolved into more cries of anguish and fear. Snot and tears cascaded down her face as she screamed for mercy. One man that had escorted her from the jail returned to her side with a torch blazing to life. Warmth from the single flame kissed the skin of her face and brought the beginnings of small beads of perspiration to her brow. The preacher nodded his head in approval, signaling the other man to start the pyre.

The conflagration ate the young girl alive in a few moments. Helena held her hand over her mouth and nose to block the smell of burning human flesh. It wasn't until the screams hit their highest notes that she shook to her core. Tears welled up behind her eyes, but she fought them back, for she knew if she showed any sign of remorse for the girl burning alive in the town square the authorities might question and sentence her in the same way for whatever reason they deemed fit. So, she stood in the sea of onlookers as they booed the supposed witch and praised their God, while she mourned her friend in her heart and gagged on the aroma of charred flesh and shit.

David opened his eyes to the familiar crowd surrounding him in the club. The girl holding her hand on his shoulder was now seared black as pitch. Her skin cracked and peeled in places around her joints where the incineration ate the dress from her skin. Her eyes had melted and slid down her cheeks like runny eggs.

"What is this?" David said as he first addressed the burnt girl, then the crowd, then back to Tracy. "What is this? Am I dead? Is this Hell?" He blurted out between pants of exhaustion.

"You can name it whatever you like, honey. Everyone has their own mythology. Hell, Purgatory, Limbo, whatever you need to call it to wrap your brain around this current predicament," Tracy said as she walked around and took a knee behind David, whispering in his ear. "I prefer to call it this: *The Lives and Crimes of David Kingston.*"

"I...don't..."

"That title is starting to grow on me. After all the thousands of times we've had this conversation, that little snippet always had a ring to it. Maybe one day I'll write your story myself, and that's what I'll call it. *The Lives and Crimes of David Kingston.*"

"This isn't real. This is just a dream."

Tracy ran her nails up the back of his neck and through his hair as she stood up and stepped out in front of him.

"Who are these people? I don't understand!" David pleaded.

"Every soul goes through dozens, if not hundreds of lives. Every life you live is a chance for you to learn from the mistakes you made previously, and find nirvana, enlightenment, etcetera. However, in every life you crawled through, you managed to fuck it up not just for you, but for the people closest to you, and in turn impact the lives of others with your selfishness, cowardice, and indifference."

David closed his eyes as tears began seeping from the corners of his lids. He just shook his head and muttered to himself.

"This is just a dream. It's all a dream. It's not real."

"Open your eyes, David. Look at the fruits of your labor."

Upon hearing the gentle commands, he dug his heels in and squinted even harder, refusing to look.

"I SAID, OPEN YOUR EYES!"

The voice that addressed him once before had transformed into something else altogether. The gentle sweet tone he had known that day mutated into a thunderous, androgynous scream, transcending anything male, female, or human for that matter. Her every syllable deafened him and shook the walls surrounding them.

Two sets of ice-cold hands crawled over his face holding his head forward and peeling his upper eyelids open. Tracy, the smartass bartender melted away and ascended into a whole new being. She hovered there before him a few inches over the floor with arms outstretched to her sides. Her clothes had burnt away to nothing leaving her body in all its nakedness glowing like living magma. The cherry red hair now blazed like a Californian wildfire. From her toes to the top of her head, her whole being existed as a newborn star. Bright white orbs blazed in her eye sockets. The radiance from her form chased away every shadow in the building. Nothing hid from her light. She hovered with the grace of an angel and the fortitude of a goddess of fire and retribution.

Tracy looked down at David with the stern scrutiny of a parent contemplating an unruly child.

"Every soul reaches a point where they either transcend or they do not. If that person finds themselves with the latter, their tab needs to be settled. These people? They come from your worst nightmares, but they are nothing you could have ever created with a pen and paper. No David, these are the people that cried out for death long before it released them. All thanks to your choices."

Unable to blink, the roaring open flame that was once Tracy made tears cascade down his cheeks. He witnessed a final page to his story that he couldn't have known existed. Defiant to the end, David called out to a God he didn't even believe in, hoping it would save him if he couldn't wake himself.

"Oh God PLEASE...HELP Me! Jesus..."

"Just know this is the end of the line. There are no more chances for redemption, no avenues for atonement. No purchasing fire insurance with a few magic words. This is simple cause and effect. Your score is being settled."

Tracy descended to the floor and stepped toward David. She bent down just enough to caress his cheek with the back of her hand. The other phantoms formed lines around David, placing their hands on him. One by one he relived centuries as if they were only memories of yesterday; lives from five continents and dozens of countries.

The seven young men from the bookstore approached him at once. They laid hands on him at the same time, taking him back almost fifty years when he was a young army recruit named Jake Campbell. Jake never intended to join the armed services, however found himself drafted into it. Five months into his first tour in Vietnam, his squad had been sleeping while he had first watch like so many other nights before. He alone sat by a tree with his M16 and waited for his four-hour guard shift to end.

He daydreamed about what he would do if he found himself in danger on a night like this. His fantastical delusions of stopping the entire Viet Cong army by himself made him smile. Playing and replaying the fantasy in his head lulled Jake into a shallow sleep where he dozed off in intervals of ten or twenty minutes without even registering it. He hadn't realized what he had done until he opened his eyes once more to noises coming from the dense jungle foliage a couple hundred yards to his left. Subtle at first, the rustling grew louder as it approached their location. Jake positioned himself near the tree between him and the noise. He knelt and held his rifle at the ready, aiming its bore at the mysterious shapes in the darkness. Five, maybe ten minutes passed, and his dominant arm began to get weak with fatigue. He dropped lower into a prone position and propped the gun up by the magazine against a piece of tree root. His nerves caught fire as the acid rolled over in his stomach. The sound began tapering off, leading Jake to believe that whoever or whatever had been trampling through the jungle turned in another direction. He remained in that position for a little while longer until he had convinced himself they were in the clear again. Jake let his rifle lay sideways against the tree so he could prop himself back up on his feet.

"Phew," he said to himself.

Then the nighttime silence broke once more, this time far closer than he had expected in any of his egotistical daydreams. Several men rambled back and forth to one another in Vietnamese within ten yards of his post. Jake hunkered down again, this time darting sideways into some foliage without grabbing his rifle. There he laid still, hoping his concealment would keep him undetected. The clouds began to part leaving an unrestrained moon to glare down on the areas of the jungle not under the canopy of trees. Jake took quick short breaths as one Viet Cong soldier stepped within a couple yards of his hiding spot and lit a cigarette. He stood there while the soldier bickered back and forth with another. A series of loud screams and orders rang out in Vietnamese. Jake turned his head just enough to see the enemy platoon had surrounded his squad while they slept. Two shots from a Kalashnikov rang out through the night as an enemy soldier executed someone. The Viet Cong soldiers brought the rest of his friends up to their feet and bound them together with rope. The man in proximity to Jake finished his cigarette and moved on to join his comrades. Jake never flinched, never made a move to retrieve his rifle, not even after the enemy had all passed him. He froze in terror and watched as the Viet Cong marched his friends off to die in a P.O.W. camp.

For what felt like an eternity, angry phantoms took turns showing David their pain and his shame. Each one took a piece of his soul, leaving him a husk of his former self. Then after they made their peace, the crowd parted once more making a path for someone else.

"Don't worry, we saved the best for last," Tracy said as she stood behind him, putting both her hands on his shoulders.

The crowd opened further, letting two figures walk side by side down the aisle. A young woman with shoulder length golden blonde hair wearing a green parka jacket over top of a blue cocktail dress and a young boy about seven or eight with woven cornrows transitioning into braids almost to his shoulder tied off with white shells walked toward him. The boy wore olive green cargo pants with a grey and red hooded sweatshirt. They both had the same look of sorrow and disappointment on their faces. It remained unclear who was leading who as they clasped hands walking toward David.

"Wait...No...No, Michelle?" David said as he cupped his hand over his mouth. "Oh...Fuck!"

"Do you recognize her?"

"...yes..."

Michelle and the young boy walked over to David and, without letting go of each other, they placed their free hands on him.

David blinked and found himself at the moment he arrived here yesterday. Just a little after five in the afternoon he picked up the keys from the rental agency and set out for his hotel. He was then planning to catch up with an old college girlfriend of his who lived just outside the city. The hours flew by in front of David's eyes until he stood in the door of a high-end bistro Michelle had picked out in uptown.

"Hey you!" Michelle said as she walked over and wrapped her arms around him.

"Hey there yourself!"

The atmosphere in the restaurant Michelle had chosen was loud for a weeknight. It was an hour and a half wait for a table, so Michelle suggested they get a spot at the bar instead. They found two unoccupied seats near the end and started in with a drink order.

"So how have you been?" Michelle asked. "I mean you can't be doing too bad, with the book tours and all."

"I've been doing good. Really busy on the road and back home."

"The publisher keeping you in line?"

"Hahaha. Yeah, I guess so."

"As if anyone could keep you on a leash," Michelle said with a grin.

The two went on for over an hour sharing small talk about old college friends, hometowns, family, even some mild politics. David attempted to restrain himself as he nursed his second Jack and Coke, while Michelle finished her fourth martini.

"So, how's Don?" David asked.

"Oh…well he's good. He stays pretty busy with work. A lot of late nights."

"What does he do for a living again?"

"He works for Carlyle and Finn in their downtown office. He handles some of their higher profile accounts."

David just nodded his head as he took a swig of his drink.

"Or at least, that's what he's doing when he isn't balls deep in his secretary's face," Michelle added.

The comment came so abruptly David almost spit his drink out. He held the back of his hand to his mouth to help restrain himself.

"He thinks I don't know about it, but I do. I've known for a long time now, actually."

Not knowing what to say, David just shook his head and remained silent.

"I'm sorry. I didn't mean to blurt that out."

"It's ok, really."

"No, no it's not. It's just…I'm leaving him."

She cleared her throat and finished her drink before motioning to the bartender to close out her tab.

"I'll be right back. I need to find the little girl's room," Michelle said as she excused herself.

After about fifteen minutes Michelle returned to her seat. David tried not to let on that he noticed the small amount of white powder residue still clinging to the bottom of her nose.

"You wanna get out of here? Don is gonna be gone all weekend and I have the house to myself."

"This is pretty nice for a rental," Michelle said as she leaned the passenger seat back.

"Yeah, this is one of the better ones I've had."

87

"Well, I'm glad we took this. The heat in my car has been acting screwy and the repair shop can't figure out what's wrong with it."

The conversation devolved into more sporadic bursts of questions from Michelle about random topics until she got back on the subject of her husband, Don.

"...he's such a piece of shit. You know? I mean you met him when we were in college. You remember him, right?"

"I mean...yeah I remember Don. We had a lot of the same friends."

"Friends...that prick doesn't have friends. Never did."

"Well, I mean we knew each other."

"I just don't...don't know why I ever married him. I don't know what I was thinking. Buuuuuut...I'm gonna get him back, though."

About ten minutes away from Michelle's house, David stopped at a light near a new subdivision when suddenly Michelle unclipped her seatbelt, twisting her body to put herself face down in David's lap. Still sniffling from the coke, she unhinged his belt, lowered his zipper, and slid his cock into her mouth. Other than a surprised *Oh*, David didn't argue. The light had been green for almost ten seconds before he realized it. He coasted through the neighborhood just under the limit while she worked him over. The slight buzz he still had coursing through his head slowed his reaction time. He caught himself looking down at her from time to time watching her blonde mop bob up and down on his lap while his cock rubbed the inside of her cheek. He watched her so intently that he never saw the boy hit the front end of the rental until he had rolled off the windshield.

The kid had been skateboarding home that night from a friend's house. Coasting along the sidewalks, he came to a corner where a few of the neighborhood roads intersected and had tried to kickflip this little grassy section between the sidewalk and the street. He had been trying it all week but never could stick the landing. This time he pushed up on it a little faster than he had before. He popped the tail, flicked it, caught it, everything seemed perfect, but when he landed his weight was too far back and the board shot out from under him into the road. He chased it into the street, but before he could catch it a black sedan came rolling through and struck him in the hip, sending him rolling onto the windshield and then straight to the pavement.

"Ughhh," Michelle gagged as she shot up and sat back in her seat, strands of saliva still hanging off her chin and lower lip. "What the fuck was that?"

David stopped the car a few yards up the street and looked hard into the rear view and side mirrors. He couldn't believe what he had done. He rolled down the window and stuck his head out to peer behind them. The boy lay bleeding and broken in the middle of the road. His arms and legs were contorted out of place, and his chest rose and plunged as he took in hyperventilated breaths. The blunt trauma had turned his head toward the car and his eyes met David's for a moment as blood trickled down his brow.

David slammed his foot on the gas and whipped out of the neighborhood without even rolling up the window. Not knowing the area, he took several random roads through other neighborhoods and side streets until he found himself near the outskirts of the city. The whole time he drove, Michelle screamed and shook David, slapping him in the face and chest.

"What the FUCK have you done? What the FUCK have you done? You killed that kid! We have to go back! You need to turn around right now and go back!"

Frosty winter air roared through the open window as he pushed the rental past seventy-five on a windy mountain highway. The shrill whistle blowing past his left ear muted some of Michelle's screams.

"We can't go back! Ok? We just can't," David said as he turned to face her for the last time.

When he faced the road ahead of him once more, fate had left him with enough time to utter one last… *shit* before plowing the rental into an enormous sycamore on the right side of the road. He collided into it head on, sending Michelle soaring through the windshield and out over the side of the road, into the black void of the night.

Where did he go off to this time? What blackout daydream edging toward its cliffhanger did David Kingston float through before eyes anchored in reality and a gasping inhalation returned him to his glaring laptop screen. Nothing concrete traveled with him, no patchwork pieces of a lucid fantasy or useless inventions, only the sudden scene changes lacking any crossfade or theatrical sweep of a divided curtain. The digital clock on his computer taunted him as he laid eyes on the same thought he designed hours ago, accented by a blinking cursor refusing to produce any wittier prose for him. More often than not his writing process fell from the tracks until it collided with rabbit trail ideas like how the McRib is the most overrated sandwich in the history of processed food. Between these side notes dripping with absurdity, he would put down some decent prose, maybe a line here or there that convinced him to stroke his ego more than his own cock. Despite the lies he told himself, he was slow with the pen. His publisher knew it as much as his fans, though the ones who lusted over his mindless dribble made excuses for the delays. He limped through until the last hours of every deadline. The publisher allowed it because unfortunately for them, David Kingston was their biggest cash cow. Even now a few pages a day stood as a milestone for David. Running the empty palms of his hands against his face, he blinked hard and gave in to a deep exhausted sigh. The unblinking computer screen stared back at him with the same paragraph he started two hours and three drinks ago.

He looked back once more over his shoulder at the void staying at his heels. Somewhere in the black, his worst mistake waited patiently to correct itself. He held the pedal to the floorboard against the gear and belt driven protests screeching from the engine. When Eddie turned again, the dirt road beneath him melded into debris, leaving broken limbs in its place. In the span of one breath a congregation of trees sprouted from the darkness, halting his escape. Corrine shared one last exchange with him before the void took her away into its nothingness.

The pale light radiating from his laptop left him blind to the deepening shadows filling his hotel room. A crimson glow seeped through the window from the bar across the street teasing David with promises not kept by the now empty fifth buried in the waste bin. Particles of dust danced like sprites along the bold scarlet beams bleeding through every seam in the blinds.

"Jesus Fuck," David muttered under his breath.

After what seemed like an eternity, David sat up and found his way through the void, with only vague clues left by the cherry, neon light of the bar across the street. His fingertips fumbled across the walls with no more luck than a prepubescent freshman attempting to negotiate a bra clasp for the first time. After a few moments of trial and error, he found his way to the bathroom light switch. The sudden flash of light from the single halogen fixture gave no warning before singeing his retinas with a sharp abruptness. He braced himself on the bathroom countertop and stared into the mirror as a person he couldn't recognize stared back at him. The rose tint from the neon sign across the street danced among the hotel blinds and their reflection caught David's eye in the mirror as he realized he wouldn't be sleeping again soon tonight. His Rolex read 11:37 PM when he finished layering himself to prepare for the harsh sub-freezing temperature outside.

The chilled wind hit his skin harder than expected. David tucked his scarf tighter around his neck and popped the collar of his trench coat in a vain attempt to shield his neck. Being the night owl David was, he figured he would try to get some work done while he was up. He ran by the rental to grab a notebook he forgot to bring in earlier that contained the rough draft of his next book. He turned down the driveway to the main parking lot behind the hotel. A few lampposts in need of service forced him to walk around in some large shadows as he made his way across. He stopped in the middle and took in the nighttime skyline he had neglected before.

"Beautiful."

A low clicking sound brought his attention over to the corner of the building beside the hotel. A tall, thin, feminine silhouette stood in a pale shadow. He made out the vague shape of a leather jacket with stainless steel accents reflecting tiny amounts of light as well as dark pants and boots. The sound repeated and on the third time he realized it was a cigarette lighter striking until it produced a flame. The figure brought the flame up to her face and the tangerine glow revealed long bright red hair flowing down the back of her jacket. She lit a cigarette held up to her lips with her other hand. Once lit, she disappeared back into the shadow on the corner. The curious nature in him wouldn't let David look away. The woman took a long drag and as she did, the ember at the tip made her gold nose ring stud sparkle in the lowlight. She gazed at David like a game of chicken, not giving in until he turned away. Even when he continued his detour, he could feel her eyes on him.

He crossed row after row until he reached the back of the lot where he had parked the rental. David stopped and rubbed his eyes to make sure he wasn't still half asleep as he searched up and down the parking lot.

"Where the fuck is my car?"

DAYDREAMERS

Every day like the clockwork ascension and descension of the sun over the horizon, Marc Bellman walked out to the abyss and stared down into its infinite nothing, listening for the siren song. *It will be ok. It will all be ok if you jump.* His soul lingered on the tipping point waiting, waiting for that last mild inconvenience, that last word or thought taken far outside of its literal context. He waited for permission to be granted to fall over the edge into the black. Every day he stepped back was a small victory in itself. One more day without kissing his veins with the sharp end of anything, one more day without stepping out into the freeway, one more day trying to feel something concrete through nerves permeated with Novocain.

He tried to experience what others held in their hearts. He poked and prodded at the sensitive subjects in his head in hope of igniting the characteristics of his being that he lacked. After a couple years of ineffective, if not detrimental anti-depressants, Marc's core organ atrophied to nothing. Great disappointment lashed out with its worst and he could not find a deeper pit of sorrow. People close to him gave their last breath and he could not mourn them. Like a grand mechanism that, despite all its bells and whistles, had one feature fail in tandem with the rest. Maybe due to a small, chipped tooth on a minor gear or a lack of oil, but he continued to operate despite his dysfunction to feel love in his heart.

It was one year to the day since his mother's body had been committed to a crematorium furnace, and yet he felt nothing. He loved his mother, that could never be argued. However, somewhere between adolescence and now, a piece of him stopped working, then another, and then another. Even at eighteen with the world and his future on the horizon, Marc drifted through his days hollow and numb to the touch.

As a young man he learned early on what it meant to internalize. Marc kept his demons locked in a tiny box inside his very core. He never wore things on his sleeve other than cotton shirts and winter coats. On the surface he appeared as a normal teenager, but on the inside, he lived one day at a time holding himself together at the seams. Marc's parents gave him every material thing he needed: clothes, food, medicine. But what they made up for in basic needs, they lacked in delicate touch. When Marc started to come of age and questions about himself and others lurked around the corner, his parents did not give him *the talk*. Instead, when he turned sixteen (years after Marc had exhumed his dad's porno stash and answered most of his own questions with sticky VHS tapes) his mother gave him a cartoon book with no pretext that, in the most innocent and vanilla way possible, explained the human body and sex. The content of the book, although aimed at a teenager, read as though the author meant it for a five-year-old. It was like a mash up of a Gary Larson "Far Side" strip and a Cialis commercial where two bloated middle-aged people pretend to enjoy Great Value brand missionary sex with the lights off before sharing their own separate bathtubs. His father, on the other hand, came around to mentioning something related to the birds and bees just a few months ago. It was something comprised of two sentences and went to the effect of, *well…you shouldn't…you know…have sex until you're married. But if you…just make sure you wrap it up.* And like that, most of the difficult moments in his life came and went with painful trial and error.

His awkward day by day journey through adolescence brought him to this very moment, just months away from graduation and the freedom to go out in the world to carve his path or fuck it up entirely. Either way, he did not care. The only friends he had joined him with the money they had all scraped together with part time jobs or had been bestowed with by parents or relatives for graduation. They put what they had together and scored two small beach front motel rooms for spring break. This week stood as a milestone for the five teenagers. After this week, the sand sifted through the glass as they all prepared to go their separate ways across the country.

A birdshit stained railing held Marc back from experiencing the warm concrete beneath him. From four stories up, the early morning tourists marched across the beach like ants without purpose. Sunlight jutted above the Atlantic, glimmering over crashing waves. Lost again inside his mind, Marc fell to the hypnotic ambient soundtrack around him and wandered into the deep end of thoughts he never escaped. The void whispered his name once more. It called out with sweet words, tempting him with release. For a few moments he contemplated it. Marc thought *what if…what if I were to go down to the beach, step out into the tide, and swim until I could swim no longer…until the sea pulled me into oblivion.* As his body remained motionless, his mind began filling with taunts. Dripping with venom, the abyss hissed in his ear as it reminded him of what he already believed. *These people pity you. They tolerate you. You're a burden to be around. You shouldn't be here.* The haunting cadence of saltwater crashing along the sand made the fantasy that much easier to pursue. Like a statue, he stood frozen in his depression for twenty minutes. Loneliness and unpredictable melancholy brought the precursor of tears to the corners of Marc's eyes.

"Hey!" Kelly whispered as if to not disturb the hypothetical people still asleep at this hour. "I was looking for you."

She slid the glass door behind her shut and found a spot next to Marc on the railing. Kelly's platinum blonde hair caught fire in the flaring sunrise. Tiny yellow glimmers danced around her locks.

"We're probably gonna leave soon, once Kyle finally wakes up."

The early morning episode left a catch in his throat. He choked back his melancholy and placed his normal mask for Kelly.

"I just hope it's worth the trip. Kyle just took their word for it about this place?" Marc replied after clearing his throat. "What if it's a bust and there isn't anything out there?"

"I dunno, Marc. Then I guess we'll find something to do. This is our only spring break. You need to just enjoy the time we have."

"I hope this isn't some prank the local kids pull on the tourists. Like sending us out to a swamp or something."

Warm rays of early morning sunlight caressed Marc's face through the rear passenger window of Kyle's Honda Civic.

Slowly he peeled his eyelids open to find a thick haze over his pupils left from dried out contact lenses. Marc squinted as the rising sun warmed his face. That morning, Marc and his four friends left their beach front budget inn and set out for their own personal El Dorado. The journey to the clandestine shoreline prophesied by locals they met last night took them down back roads through the marshlands and across strips of coastline so flat no one could decipher where the earth ended, and the heavens began. Emma's red, white, and green patchwork Honda Civic led the convoy with sketchy directions from their new resident friends. Kyle followed close behind with no desire to become lost, while Kelly sat up front with her head stuck in a Twitter thread between a Kardashian and some other faux internet celebrity.

"So, Emma doesn't know yet?" Kelly asked with a timid curiosity. Her voice fluttered in volume as the gossipy subject had been readdressed that morning.

"I think Hashi is just scared of what she'll say," Kyle added after drawing a long-winded yawn.

"Well, yeah, I bet she is scared. I thought they were both set on going to State?" Kelly added.

"Hashi just told me about it yesterday, so I can't imagine she'll keep it a secret much longer. Maybe she's waiting until after graduation," Kyle replied as he flipped through playlists on his phone.

Unamused at their current soundtrack, Kyle scanned through what was available until settling on a current pop station. Marc recoiled in his seat as the first notes of repetitive snare drums and EDM shook the speakers behind him. In that moment he regretted being conscious, and his body reacted of its own accord to show how displeased he was by his head shaking from side to side in irritation.

"What's wrong with you? It's not *that* bad!" Kelly said.

"I mean...I don't think Maroon 5 would be *that* bad if Adam Levine didn't sing like an auto-tuned French police siren," Marc replied.

"Pfft. You're not right," Kelly added with a scoff.

The rolling landscape lulled Marc into a relaxed state as he lounged in the back seat. A small piece of roadkill caught his eye and Marc's pitch-black sense of humor forced out an involuntary chuckle as they passed by.

"What's so funny?" Kelly asked.

"Oh, nothing. Just something stupid."

She didn't prod him any further, and he was glad of it. Marc had noticed a small squirrel dead on the side of the road. It lay stretched out on its back and the last moments of rigor mortis had left the animal with its front legs strained outward and to the sky like tiny arms. Marc thought it appeared as though in the squirrel's last moments on this earth it reached out as if to tell squirrel Jesus, *I'm ready*. He shook his head at his own pitch-black humor and drifted back to the relief of this little vacation.

Thirty minutes into their adventure, the state-maintained roads ended before transitioning into narrow loose gravel. The path twisted and slithered upwards with such frequency that one or both compact cars almost found their way off the side and into a ditch. Sometime before eleven the anxious teens arrived at a plateau overlooking a section of shoreline untouched by wayward tourists. The warm coastal air rolled in from the Atlantic saturated in salt, sending the aroma of it wafting through the air vents as they closed in on their utopia. The warm April climate engulfed the quintet as they stepped out onto a foliage overgrown cliff side. And for a moment, all was still. No one dared say a word. Every phone was put away or set down as they just listened.

The five walked to the rocky lip of the plateau they had parked on and gazed out over to the wonders beyond it. The crashing and recession of wild ocean waves roared below the cliff. Pure and unmolested, the beach in front of them existed with no human influence. Golden sand and clean blue water stretched as far as their vision limited them. Down the coast to their right, waves beat against a peninsula of bare rock jutting out into the ocean like a naturally formed pier.

The teens gathered their chairs, towels, and bags before taking a narrow, overgrown path from the plateau down to the beach. Tall grass and wild shrubbery welcomed them down to their paradise while seagulls let off a fanfare of caws. Searing golden sand flaunted its heat against the soles of their sandals as they marched across the beach. The teens found their little corner of the world waiting for them over virgin sand free of debris and human contact. As far as the five of them were concerned the beach was theirs for the taking. Like the first explorers on an uncharted island, the spring breakers drove their flag into the sand and declared it in their name.

Marc stretched out his lawn chair in the perfect spot atop a little mound. Rifling through his bag he retrieved some sunblock, a towel and his new copy of *Undercurrent*, the most recent novel by David Kingston. Marc had been a fan of Kingston's since early middle school when he first developed an affinity for reading. He celebrated the author's entire catalog, collecting everything of his including the weird stuff he put out under a different pen name.

"Ewwww! David Kingston? Bleeeehh! That guy was such a fuckin' hack," Kelly interrupted while making fake gagging motions as she set her things on the other side of Marc.

"Some of his stuff was a little weird, but he was not a *hack*," Marc replied as he shook his head.

"Sweetie…he was a hack. I would rather be trapped in an elevator with Gilbert Gottfried as he narrates the entire *Fifty Shades of Grey* trilogy to me, all while he has a big glob of peanut butter stuck to the roof of his mouth, than read another David Kingston book cover to cover," Kelly replied with a chuckle.

She continued laughing at her joke as she gazed out at the waves crashing along the shore. Marc ignored the jabs and instead settled into his spot for the day nestled in his lawn chair.

"Hey, we're gonna go check out the rest of the beach. Ya know, see if there is anything else worthwhile out here. Maybe walk down to those rocks. You wanna tag along?" Kelly asked.

"No, that's cool. I'm just gonna hang out here and relax," Marc responded.

"And read that snooze fest?"

Marc just shook his head at her without responding.

"Ok, suit yourself, bubby. We'll be back in a little while," she added.

After a few minutes of mischievous giggles and inaudible inside jokes, Kyle and Kelly were off to check out the rest of the beach. Marc was left the way he truly desired: at a quiet dune with a chair and a hardback.

"Come on!" Kelly blurted at Kyle.

The two chased each other in a perpetual game of grab ass down the unoccupied shoreline. There was nothing around for miles; not a soul or any sign of civilization as far as the eye could see.

"Do you think Emma will freak when she finds out Hashi got accepted to NYU?" Kelly asked as they slowed down to a brisk walk.

"I don't think she's going to take it well. She doesn't do well with change."

"I mean the long-distance thing works for some people. My parents dated in college, and they toughed it out," Kelly replied.

"It's not impossible. I just don't know if Emma can handle that."

"I wonder if Hashi's dad pressured her into applying there instead of State?" Kelly asked.

"It wouldn't surprise me."

"Well, I mean, he's just kind of a hardass. You remember that time when she brought home a B+ and he grounded her for like a month?"

"Pfft, yeah I remember that," Kyle said with a chuckle. "My mom and dad would think I paid someone to do my work for me if I started bringing home Bs."

With almost a mile behind them, the smooth stone peninsula grew in scale as it came into view again. Seagulls cavorted about the wet rocks like a midday mass. Churning waves broke against them sending ocean spray soaring up to the heavens.

"Has Marc said anything to you about college?" Kelly inquired.

"No, and he's been acting kinda weird lately. Like something's bothering him, but he won't talk about it."

"Yeah, he seemed really out of it last night. Like I know that stuff isn't really his scene, but I still thought he wanted to be there."

Her query hung in the air for a few minutes as they continued to separate themselves from the others. The beach tapered inwards as the grassy slopes bordering the shoreline transitioned into rock formations and then a steep cliff stretching a couple hundred yards to the sky. The crashing of ocean waves began mixing with other white noise that crept in increments at first but revealed its presence as the two got closer.

"Do you hear that? It sounds like a rapid," Kelly inquired while holding her head higher to see ahead.

"Yeah, I hear it too. It's coming from behind that cliff."

Curiosity pushed them both further and faster as the sound of running water became more apparent. They rounded the corner of the cliff to find a stream of fresh water feeding into the ocean. Its source was unknown, and for that reason Kelly and Kyle ventured forward in pursuit after a brief glance at one another. They hiked upstream for another five minutes through thick tall grass and woods until they approached the genesis of what they sought out.

"Man. That is…that is dope," Kyle said without removing his eyes from it.

"It's gorgeous!" Kelly added.

Marc reclined back as far as the beach chair would allow him. His new hardback copy of *Undercurrent* rested open and upright on his chest so he could breeze through it while being completely horizontal. The warm summer rays lulled him on the cusp of a mid-day nap. He scanned over a page or two and then his eyes grew heavy as he succumbed to the melody of Atlantic Ocean waves crashing on the shore paired with the occasional griping of seagulls fighting over lunch. Ten maybe twelve minutes passed at a time, and a gentle breeze or a cough would snap him back to the real world. After he was unable to finish more than the first two chapters of David Kingston's latest novel, Marc put it down on the towel and committed to laying back in the foldable chair to see where the afternoon took him. Within a few minutes he had no desire to hold his eyes open. Rolling his head over to the side, he took in a deep inhalation and prepared to drift off into the black.

"...hey!"

Marc opened his eyes to see Kelly and Kyle coming back earlier than expected. Both had a strange look of excitement on their faces, like two children that had just discovered where "Santa" had been hiding their Christmas presents. As they got closer to being within earshot, Kelly tried to get his attention once more.

"Hey! You guys need to come check out what we found!"

The two of them stopped by the cluster of beach chairs and towels trying to catch their breath as if they had run part of the way back. Kelly motioned over to Hashi and Emma in a wild frenzy, trying to wave them back over to their congregation.

"What is it? It must be something good to get you all wound up," Marc said looking at Kyle.

"It's really fuckin' cool," Kyle blurted out in a fit of excitement. "You guys are gonna want to see this," Kyle replied.

Emma and Hashi emerged from the ocean waves behind Kelly. They draped themselves in towels and huddled together by everyone else.

"What is it?" Emma asked.

"Just trust us. You're gonna love it," Kelly replied.

"How much further is this thing?" Emma inquired, pushing her glasses back to her face.

"Not much further," Kyle replied. "Should be just up ahead."

The uproar of the stream baited their curiosity, dangling its carrot for even the most skeptical among them. The forest canopy flooded their path with cool shadows as it stood at the ready against the mid-day sun.

"There it is!" Kelly exclaimed as she pointed to a raging waterfall.

The teenagers stood in front of a series of cascades all feeding into a deep blue pond. The crashing of fresh water against the rocks drowned out the ocean waves behind them. Kyle and Kelly both stood back as their friends approached it first. A contagious shock and reverence swept through the teenagers. What they took in now must have been the grand secret bestowed on them by the locals, not the vacant shoreline. Maybe they took a wrong turn somewhere and should have wound up this far up the coast instead. A rich green tapestry of vines surrounded their paradise, hanging from trees serving as home to several choirs of local birds. The avian wildlife welcomed their new guests with a soft, hypnotic melody.

"Well, I don't know what you guys are waiting for," Kyle said as he pushed past his friends, and catapulted himself into the water.

either jumped in after Kyle or teased the water with their toe tips before committing to the cool spring water. The five spring breakers lost several hours in the freshwater pool. Their new utopia revealed its secrets to them as the world around them stopped turning. The late afternoon sunset crept down until it hovered just over a hillcrest, now blanketing them in shadow.

"I believe…someone…owes me an apology," Kyle said with a smirk while wiping wet hair off to the side and out of his eyes.

A humbled silence lay over paradise as Kyle waited for smartass counterpoints.

"Well?" He added.

"Yeah, yeah, yeah, you were right for once, Kyle. This is pretty fuckin' cool," Hashi replied.

"I'll admit, I didn't know what to expect, but this was worth it," Emma added as she began drying herself off.

The back and forth between his friends came out as ambient noise in Marc's soundtrack. The apologies to Kyle for his discovery might as well have been tinnitus ringing incoherently in his ear. Even here with what he considered to be his real family the melancholy bubbled up inside his cerebral cortex. He remembered a passing soundbite or online article he had read once said something about drowning being one of the most peaceful ways to go. The idea kept repeating in his head like vinyl: *How long would it take? Is it really peaceful? I wonder how deep this is?*

"I wonder how deep this is?" Marc asked himself out loud, even though he meant to say it in his head. Marc looked up from the spring water to see Kyle staring back at him with a face that said *challenge accepted.*

"I don't know, but there's one way of finding out," Kyle replied as he gazed up at the rushing waterfall feeding the pool they now occupied.

Pulling himself up and out of the spring by an ensemble of smooth flat rocks, he exited with his eyes locked on the tallest fall feeding into the spring. Picking up a little speed he jogged up a dirt path climbing up to the waterfall.

"You can't be serious," Emma shouted at him from the comfort of her beach towel, which was now wrapped around her torso.

"Oh, I am. You just watch me," he replied as he vanished behind a rock wall.

Everyone exited the pool one by one as an unspoken nervousness fell over them all. Marc, Kelly, Hashi and Emma all stood among the pile of towels and beach chairs as the pitter patter of his footfalls stopped somewhere behind the cliff. The four stared in anticipation while nothing happened for several minutes. Only the rushing of freshwater over and under smooth worn rock and the crashing of that same water into the pool below could be heard.

"Kyle?!" Kelly blurted out as she returned her towel back to the gym bag, she retrieved it from. She waited once more, hearing nothing as way of reply. "Fuck this," she said under her breath as Kelly marched up the same path behind Kyle.

The rest followed in line behind her. They called out to Kyle as they got closer to the top. The half-beaten path restrained them at first with tree limbs, ancient bulging roots protruding from the ground, and steep inclines. Once they broke through to the top plateau, they met a calm stream flowing across their path and into the cascade.

"Kyle?" Emma blurted out as she looked around in desperation to find her friend.

"Hey, over there," Marc said, pointing across the hilltop to a little thicket of trees.

Kyle stood motionless with his back to them. Even as his name was called out several times in a mantra, and as his friends approached where he stood, he didn't flinch and remained frozen in place. Crossing a rock path across the stream, they soon found a place by his side, and like their friend, the speech had been all but dissected from them.

They stood in the maw of a gigantic cave buried in a wooded thicket. No words could describe it with any accuracy. Bright iridescent climbing plants with thick vines ran up the rock and into the dark entrance of the cave. They pulsed with intense violet and blue radiance like a gargantuan intersection of arteries feeding an unseen heart. Faint flickers of light sparkled like sprites along the walls inside just past the last remnants of daylight, hypnotizing all who peered into the void. A sweet, unidentifiable aroma crept from the cave entrance, tempting all who dared look in. It smelled like fresh picked lavender and warm honey to some, or ripe citrus fruits to others.

"It's...I mean I've never seen plants like that. It's so..." Hashi said with awe as she shook her head.

"I mean it's so soothing. It's like staring at a snow globe or a lava lamp. I just can't look away," Kelly added.

"And that smell," Emma said as she took a deep breath into the bottom of her lungs. "It smells like my Nanna's house in the summer."

"You guys wanna check it out? Like to see how far it goes?" Kyle added.

"Hell yeah!" Kelly replied.

"Oh, no!" Marc added, shaking his head.

"What? You know what they say about *the road not taken*?"

"No! No, no, no, Kelly," Marc rebutted in protest. "You know what kind of people quote Robert Frost?"

She just shook her head at him and frowned at the oncoming sarcasm.

"People who die from hypothermia or like…sharks," he added with a nervous chuckle, halfway between deep sarcasm and real concern masked with dark humor.

"Sharks?"

"It happens…ok."

"Ugh, whatever Marc."

Marc stood back as the rest of his friends inched closer to the entrance. With every step, more of its features opened up and made itself known to them almost like a new acquaintance. The vines pulsed faster and brighter as they closed in proximity. Unseen flower buds clumped on the greenery began opening up wide exposing vivid red and orange petals. As they blossomed, the sweet aroma flooded the area, welcoming its guests inside with unspoken promises of baked goods and sweets.

"Look, I'm just gonna stay out here, ok? I don't really do confined spaces. You guys just go on and I'll wait outside," Marc said as the color left his face.

"Oh, come on, Marc! Don't be such a pussy," Kyle said as he patted him on the back. "It'll be fine. We'll just take a quick look and-"

A faint cry fell in the distance, cutting Kyle off mid-sentence. Everyone remained still as the same thought passed through their heads. Until they heard it again. Low in volume at first but echoing through the cave and out onto the hilltop. A whimper, like an injured dog crying out for help.

"You guys hear that too, right?" Kelly inquired.

The mysterious yelping sound answered her question as it reverberated louder this time from the cave walls.

"Sounds like an animal stuck in there," Emma replied.

"What if someone's dog got loose and trapped itself under a rock?" Said Kelly with a look of deep concern. "If it is, we need to get it out."

Almost on cue with the conversation, the whimper intensified into a sharp, painful yelp followed by several barks.

Kelly didn't wait for anyone's permission before darting off into the cave with her cell phone flashlight leading the way, followed by Kyle. Emma, Hashi, and Marc all exchanged looks back and forth with one another before chasing after their friends.

"Kelly! Wait! Slow down. We don't know what's down there!" Marc screamed as he fumbled to open up the torch on his phone.

Bright vines raced along the walls and ceiling of the cave, pulsing faster as the teens darted after their tenderhearted friend. The sweet aroma that had once breezed out onto the cliffside, had now become intoxicating, almost choking the air from their lungs so the odor could take up residence there instead. A few hundred yards ahead of them the neon pulse glowing from the strange plants stopped, tapering off into the darkness of the cave. Kelly slowed her approach to a brisk walk, setting the pace for everyone else, and giving Marc the chance to catch up with the pack. They pushed so far inwards that the daylight from the hilltop left just a small glimmer on the rocks behind them. Only their individual cell phone lights guided them.

The teens paused for a moment to orient themselves, when suddenly the painful howling picked up again, this time much louder and direct. The faint call that could have been confused earlier with anything else, now sounded pitiful and desperate.

With the potential death throes of a family pet resonating in the dark cavern, Kelly and Kyle led their friends through the dim passage. The phantom cries grew with every cadence until a break in the cavern path stopped the group. The left side continued further down into the black, while the right forked off to a small cliff overlooking a steep drop off. The last whimper came from the murky black hole in the ground. The smart phone torches did little in cutting into the void.

"I can't see anything down there," Emma said as she slung her phone back and forth.

"What are we even supposed to do? All we have are some beach towels and a cooler! We need to go back and get help," Hashi exclaimed.

A look of desperation hung low on Kelly's face as she turned back around to face her friends.

"What if we don't get back in time to help it? We need to-"

Kelly's words were cut short as she slid backwards into the void. One brief scream was silenced as she disappeared into the abyss. Her body never made a sound to confirm its collision with what lay beneath. She merely ceased to exist.

"Fuck!"

The morbid terror shook Marc awake from his cat nap. He shot up out of the beach chair, catapulting the book from his body and out onto the sand in front of him. His chest heaved with exhaustion as his heart beat out of time. Only after seeing Hashi, Emma, and Kelly standing around in the waves chatting amongst themselves did his composure return to him.

"You ok?" Kyle inquired as he looked down at Marc.

Marc dwelled on the dream for a moment as the vivid flashbacks melted away until he could not recall the main points. Only the shiver it left in his spine and the cold clammy sweat remained as a souvenir.

"Yeah, I'm fine. Just a fucked up dream."

Marc leaned over to retrieve the novel and knock the sand out of its creases. Kyle didn't wait around to let him elaborate, just obeyed Kelly as she beckoned him to come join her in the water.

The day carried on and soon Marc passed out again in the summer sun with another failed attempt to finish more of his book. Soon nightfall brought the five teens on their way back to the hotel rooms. The last few days of their trip brought them to pool parties, live bands on the beach, one late night rave in a penthouse suite that didn't stop until later the next morning, but never back to that secluded beach. The following Sunday morning the two cars set out for home. Time lost its meaning once the seniors got back into their normal routine. For Marc, hours slipped away in seconds, days flew by with such haste that they began and ended out of order. Sunday evening cross faded into a Thursday mid-morning. An early Friday with a hazy vignette morphed into Tuesday of the next week.

One afternoon Marc blinked, and the day had arrived to walk across that stage, bringing him one step closer to his independence. The moment he had fantasized about for so long was now within his grasp. His dad sat in attendance that afternoon along with his only living grandparent and a few other people that he vaguely remembered from his childhood. The indoor basketball stadium that on occasion doubled as an auditorium for one of their local colleges had been rented out again like every other year for their graduation ceremony. Seats were jam-packed all around the arena with more attendants standing along the second floor that ran the perimeter. Parents and grandparents all held up colorful homemade banners with their child's name scribed across in various shades of permanent marker or glitter ink. Beach balls vaulted back and forth over the crowd despite the strict warning from administration not to bring those inside. On occasion someone would test out their air horns or cowbells to make sure they were as audible and obnoxious as intended.

Seniors were lined up in alphabetical order, staggering males and females so that it could show both royal blue and tangerine orange school colors off in perfect symmetry. Marc stood between Teressa Bellaroux and Jackie Bellman. Neither of the two girls ever associated with Marc while in school. The only friends he had there stood in the opposite end of the line with a few hundred teenagers between them. Stuck inside his own head as usual, Marc ran the mental gambit of anxiety before he would have to walk across the stage. Despite how he longed for this day to come, his uneasiness still plagued him as it would any other day. His spine tightened up like a steel cord. Every half step forward left his body shaking him like a bobble head. His panic made it clear to him that everyone in the auditorium was indeed staring at him (even if they weren't), which became the catalyst for his muscles tensing up even further, which caused his gait to look and feel more awkward, which then led him further into the paranoia that everyone was staring at him. By the time he approached the stair set leading to the stage, he hopped and bobbed across the floor, leaving him to overcorrect by easing his shoes from the ground with each step. Marc took in a deep breath and held it as he waited for someone to say his name.

"Marc..."

"Have you talked to her?" Kelly asked.

"No. Not since yesterday," Emma replied, shaking her head.

A heavy silence lay over the booth as Emma held her face in her hands. Kelly swapped worried looks back and forth with Marc as Kyle pawed at a half-eaten basket of loaded cheese fries. The crowd inside Frank's Wings N Things packed the bar area and left a thirty-minute wait time for a table in the restaurant. Over a dozen different games played on the big screens and projectors hanging throughout. Most covered current baseball games, while some just showcased basketball highlights and replays from last night's MMA title fight. One game in particular had a large party of eighteen people in an uproar every few minutes not being taken up by commercials. Four normal size tables had to be merged to accommodate their group.

"I mean, I thought we agreed we were both gonna go to State," Emma added. The levy holding Emma's tears back gave way, leading to an uncontrollable outburst. She closed her eyes tight holding the tips of her fingers into the corners of her eyelids to calm herself. "I just…"

"Look, I know it's not what you want to hear, but the long-distance thing works for some people," Kelly interjected.

Emma took a pause to compose herself after the statement.

"I don't think she wants to try that. I…think she just wants to see other people," Emma said in between sniffles.

"Aww, sweetie," Kelly said as she leaned over putting her arms around Emma.

The hustle and commotion enveloped the booth as the four teens sat in silence.

"AAHH FUCK!" Kelly screamed as she sat back up and pulled her left arm into her chest, cradling it as she winced in pain.

"What's wrong?" Kyle asked as he contributed to the conversation.

"I don't know. My arm just...it fuckin' hurts! It feels like it's dislocated."

"Dislocated?" Kyle responded with a tone of condescension.

Kelly only responded by pulling it tighter into her chest. She reached up with the same hand and latched onto the opposite shoulder making a V across her chest with the limb in question. Grasping at the triceps with her good hand, Kelly doubled over across the table wincing in pain as she clenched her arm.

The scene unfolded in slow motion for Marc. He watched in horror as Kelly held her arm in pain while Kyle shot over to the other side to help her. People sitting all around them eased their attention away from the TVs and onto the booth. The audio muted itself in Marc's head as if someone yanked the aux cord on the world. A low garbled buzz had replaced every sound from the world around him. He watched as Kelly screamed at the top of her lungs, clenching her arm as she teetered on the verge of tears, and yet no sound left her lips. Only the steady hum remained.

Marc blinked as the world darkened before his eyes. Like a blackout from mild alcohol poisoning, the time, place, atmosphere, and source of light all changed in a fraction of a second without transition. The restaurant walls transformed into barriers unknown to his eyes as they adjusted to the darkness. A musky, damp odor replaced the enticing smell of hot wings and cheese fries. Instead of the soft booth cushions, Marc sat on what

115

felt like a wet stone. Confusion set in as his initial reaction to sit up had been met with unseen restraint. His muscle memory couldn't comprehend why Marc could not move his arms to prop himself to his feet, or even bend his knees to put his legs under himself. He remained where he was against his will. An oily residue caressed his cheek more when he labored to wrench his neck to the sides. Whatever restrained him gave Marc little to no mobility. After adjusting to the darkness, vague outlines began to take shape.

The silence of his new surroundings was broken by a whimper from his left side that escalated into a blood-curdling scream before tapering off into violent coughs of exhaustion. The sound rose and fell in a haunting cadence. A silence would settle for a few seconds just to be shattered by the shrill cries. His neck was still restrained, which only allowed him to search the edge of his peripheral vision to find the source of the violent bellowing.

Marc started making out an ambiguous silhouette in the murky darkness about ten yards ahead of him. What appeared to be shoulders and a head, or maybe a rock formation of comparable size. The shape shuffled along sideways in the darkness followed by a few more of similar shape and stature behind it. A scraping noise followed the movement, like a rake being scratched across sand or loose dirt in small intervals. Every few seconds the scratching sound came closer until the dark silhouettes eclipsed what little vision he had in the darkness. Heart pounding in his chest, Marc fought against whatever restrained him to the ground. He tried twisting and contorting to free himself but to no avail. The screams still echoing beside him were cut short as a blunt object struck him in the forehead and forced his eyes closed.

"Hey! Hey! You still with us?" Kelly said as she reached across the table to put her hand on Marc's arm.

Marc looked back over the booth with confusion. Kelly was no longer holding her arm or wincing in pain, and she looked more concerned for him than anyone else at the moment.

"You really had us worried. You turned pale as a ghost and then you fainted headfirst into the table," she added.

Marc held his now shaking palms in front of his face. A fierce tremor rose up through his forearms and into his fingertips. If the skin on his hand was any indicator of what they were saying, then he must have looked flushed.

"Man, I thought for sure you had broken your nose on the table. One minute you were here, the next you dozed off," Kyle added. "Smashed your face pretty good, too."

Marc laid his hands on his forehead and sinus region confirming what Kyle said as he ran his fingertips across a knot swelling up above his brow. The soreness of it was sharp to the touch.

"Is your arm ok?" Marc asked as he did the best to ignore the bruise growing on his face.

"What do you mean?" Kelly said shaking her head. "My arm's fine. You should be concerned about why you just passed out for no reason in the middle of dinner."

Emma composed herself once more and with bloodshot eyes and blushed cheeks she looked up from her hands toward Marc.

"We should take you to the hospital. Seriously, you look like shit."

"I'm fine."

"You don't *look* fine," Emma added.

He ignored their concerns as Marc put the notion out of his mind.

"I need to use the bathroom," Marc said.

Marc scooted across the booth and stood out beside it as a pair of servers maneuvered by him on the way to another table. As soon as the coast was clear Marc took a few steps across the restaurant toward the men's room. As he did, a faint ringing started up in his ears. His peripheral vision turned fuzzy like an old TV left on the wrong channel. Grey scale static flashed by his eyes, creeping inwards until the vignette made a tiny line of sight just outside of arms reach. Only four or five steps connected with the carpet before Marc stumbled sideways into another booth and then hit the floor. Prior to his vision blackening out, he glimpsed the underside of a table and its assortment of chewing gum glued underneath.

"...someone call 911," Emma blurted out through the ambient noise.

With eyes too heavy to open, Marc remained still as fragments of audio flirted with his conscious self. Lulled into a peaceful rested state, the strength to open his eyes for any prolonged amount of time eluded him. But the sounds, the sounds crept into his placated state, feeding his curiosity. He heard skittering noises like the clicking and clacking of small animals waddling across a hardwood floor, the shifting of earth as unseen objects dragged across rock and through dirt. One at a time he cracked a lid open for a few seconds before the labor became too much and he drifted off again. Back and forth he took in small fragments of his surroundings. Shadows walked by leaving dark shapes against the inside of his eyelids. After what could have been a few minutes or a few hours in the shadows, Marc forced his eyelids open. The cave.

He remained alone trapped deep in the gullet of the cave. The same iridescent vines tangling around the entrance continued their creeping influence all around him far away from the light of day. They glowed with a steady pulse as they fed into parts unknown. Marc stood upright with his back cemented to a rough stone pillar. An oily gel adhered him in place like a pest in a glue trap. The ceiling went as far as Marc could see, eventually being swallowed by the darkness above. As Marc's auditory powers returned to him, the roaring of an unseen body of water made its presence known to him from the caverns below. The walls moved as if the chamber owned a set of lungs and had been taking in oxygen and releasing carbon dioxide. His eyes strained in the low iridescent light emanating from the abnormal plant life, but after a few minutes he recognized the walls were not breathing; they were crawling with insects. Hundreds of ten-legged monstrosities the size of greyhounds squirmed over one another in a chaotic network. Long oily black appendages skittered across the walls of the cave in unison.

"Help!" he cried.

But no one answered him. He watched as shadows shuffled around in the sections of the cave beneath.

"Help!" he screamed once more.

Off to the left of him, a figure moved back and forth while the radiation seeping from the plant life revealed small clues at a time. The upper torso glimmered with dark wet stains running from the base of its neck down to its hips. Arms hung low at the figure's sides, swaying as if they had lost all muscle retention. The person stared at the ground as its gait threw it into random configurations. Like a knight on a chess board, the dark figure moved a few steps toward Marc and then one to the left or right, then again in reverse. Every movement appeared random and with no initiative directing it.

"Hey! Help me, I'm stuck in something!"

The last sentence stirred something in it. The shadowy figure reared its head up and began galloping in wide unpredictable strides toward Marc. In a few seconds, the anonymous figure stepped out of the dim light and in front of Marc where a bright vine over his head shed a teal light on its features.

"No...No."

Kyle stood before Marc as the bluish green light washed across his face. His mouth contracted and released with his jaw hanging down as if he were struggling to complete a sentence while choking to death. A series of gurgles and moans left his throat, but nothing else. His swim trunks now hung from his waist, torn to shreds and only covering his thighs in scant pieces. Blood soaked through what remained of the nylon and left slick wet streaks down his legs where his wardrobe hadn't absorbed it. But it was the eyes that made Marc hold his breath in shock. Kyle's eyes had rolled back until only the whites stood out between his heavy lids.

Kyle reached out and put his left palm over Marc's face, silencing him from any more protests. His blood-stained dirty fingers ran up Marc's forehead, covering part of his vision. Marc continued protesting against the grimy skin pushed to his lips, but nothing audible made it to the surface. Kyle reared his head toward the ceiling of the cave once more letting out a chattering din from his throat. Upon returning his gaze, Kyle reached behind Marc and tugged at something stuck to his back. With every pull Marc felt the beginnings of a sharp pain around his kidneys pricking away under his skin. Something was holding him back in the darkness, something in his skin that he hadn't noticed until the moment it was being removed.

"AAAAAHHH!" Marc screamed into the hand muffling his cries.

What felt like a long tube had been unsheathed from his lower back, leaving Marc to acquaint himself with a new stinging sensation as an unseen wound opened up. A warm wet feeling ran down his hips, soaking into his shorts. Kyle removed his hand from Marc's mouth and used both to reach behind him again, removing another foreign object Marc had been unaware of until now. This one was lodged deeper into the flesh and needed both hands at once to uninstall. Marc teetered on the brink of tears as this chattering silhouette of his friend dissected him. Upon removing the second Marc fell to his knees in agony. His sweat-drenched cheek hit the cave floor and at once absorbed the earth beneath him, coating his face in coarse sand and small rocks.

The physical pain and exhaustion forced his mind in and out of this space in time like someone flipping through channels without care. Most of the time when his eyes were open, he remained in partial light only knowing he was awake by the coarse sensation of sand near his eyelid.

After an unknown number of disorienting episodes, Marc awoke to lights passing as he slid along his back down a beaten path of sand so condensed it felt like stone rubbing against his clothes. He came to as Kyle stopped at the epicenter of the cavern. Deep in the core lay the beating heart of its plant life. The glowing vines all met here, intersecting, and feeding into a gargantuan bulb. Towering over three stories, the body of this mysterious plant throbbed with light dwarfing the dull pulses from its appendages that stretched to the surface world. It glowed with such radiance that if not for its light, Marc would be ignorant to the horrors surrounding him. He rolled to his side and looked up to see dozens of people in various stages of rot shuffling through the underworld like mindless worker ants. Some carried varying loads of raw materials back and forth to other platforms while others tended to the plant like obedient children to their matriarchal figure. He stared in awe at the army of half dead marionette puppets marching along on invisible strings. A few side stepped near Marc, giving him a better glance at their decomposition. One carrying what looked like an arm load of fruit the size of pineapples but shaped like bird eggs stopped for a moment in front of him. Its face had been halfway torn away leaving one eye and most of its nose intact. Its jaw was missing which left a guttural wheezing sound as it toiled through its task.

A low whimpering from across the chamber caught Marc's attention. It originated from the center of a small cluster of the workers. As the sound intensified, the drones began shuffling away to other tasks, leaving the line of sight open to Marc. Kelly lay attached to a dirty slab of rock a few feet off the ground. Someone had glued her torso and legs to the surface with an oily gel. Somehow her left arm had been removed from the shoulder all together and the empty socket covered in more of the same gelatinous substance. She rolled her head over to the side and caught sight of him. Her face had been drained of all color and her eyes looked straight through him like someone who knew the end was moments away. Her mouth opened in an exhausted motion and then closed in agony before she could form a word. Her head rolled back and forth as a shrieking cry came bellowing from her very core. Kelly screamed as an arterial spray shot from her chest, washing her neck and chin in crimson. A series of seismic jolts ran through her body forcing the unrestrained parts to arch up from the slab. The last left her sinking back to the stone in silence as tiny insects began crawling from her body one by one. Like a visceral clown car, a dozen or more bugs exited from Kelly's lifeless form to join the rest of their hive.

Covering his mouth with his hands, Marc sobbed without pause as he lay with eyes locked on the corpse of his childhood friend. His mourning had been short lived as the parasite controlling Kyle snatched him by the legs again and began dragging Marc across the chamber. Not knowing what else to do, he struggled against it. He struck against his friend's grasp until a foot came loose enough to free itself. He reared back and kicked his free foot as hard as he could into the back of Kyle's knee causing the teen to stumble forward and release his other leg. Losing no motivation, Kyle turned around and advanced toward his prey. Marc pushed himself backwards but could not keep Kyle from closing the gap. In a hurried desperate motion, Marc grabbed a handful of dirt and flung it into Kyle's face. It forced him to halt his advance for a moment. Kyle's arms hung low at his sides as he stood hunched over from shoulders to head. His torso throbbed with every breath. In one motion he clenched his fists before swinging both arms up and out from his shoulders. As he did, six oil-slick, black legs burst from his back and stretched out twice the wingspan of his human limbs. Three appeared on each side with four knuckled sections on each leg. A clear viscous gel dripped from the newborn appendages as they vibrated in unison with the frustrated howls coming from Kyle's throat. A violent chattering like that of a cicada bellowed from his mouth while his head reared back with violent intent. Without warning, Kyle shot forward toward Marc. His new appendages clawed and scratched in unison with his arms. The terror pinned Marc where he was. Unable to avert his eyes from the nightmare unraveling before him, the best he could accomplish would be to halfway slide, halfway crab walk backwards until his body found the unflinching side of a stalagmite.

Kyle lashed out again. Securing both legs, he dragged Marc across the chamber floor once more. This time his hands locked down with such force that if he had tried any harder, Marc's ankles might have fractured. They stopped in front of a cluster of stone slabs surrounded by large honeycomb cells embedded into the wall and climbing as far as Marc's vision would allow him to see. Being closer to the walls than he wanted to, Marc witnessed the true scale of the creatures slinking about the walls. Ranging in assorted sizes, most were as long as Marc was tall, and stood as erect as large dogs when their multiple oily black legs extended them to attention. The din of clicking and scratching appendages paired with a choir of chattering noise set his stomach on edge. The bugs worked without rest milling about their home.

Grabbing Marc by the upper arms, Kyle flipped him over on his stomach and brought him face to face with a cluster of red bulbs nestled in a dirty patch of earth. Thick black veins branched across the eggs from the top down to the roots buried in a row of vines. Marc struggled against it, but the thing controlling Kyle's mangled corporeal form pinned him down into the dirt. Soil caked against his cheek as his futile efforts dug a pit in the earth for the right side of his face.

Inches away from his forehead a bulb began to throb from the base, halfway up. It pulsed with its own heartbeat. Marc stared in horror as the outer shell fell away like flower petals, leaving a soft pink membrane exposed to the damp cave air. The core rippled and shook as a pale worm larva slithered through the side of it.

"No. NOOOOO!" Marc shouted as it crawled an inch at a time toward his face.

The puppet wearing Kyle's skin held his grime ridden palm across Marc's cheek, pressing him into the dirt without any slack. The bug worked its way over a little at a time until it climbed his face. Tears began welling up in his eyes as the parasite slinked across the side of his head, resting just outside of his left ear. Thin wire tendrils Marc could only imagine were eye stalks or whiskers of some kind kissed the outside of his earlobe.

"Kyle. Kyle, I know you're still in there. You have to stop this."

If there were any inkling of his friend's consciousness left in him, it didn't have a chance to surface as a deep thud crashed into Marc's captor. Whatever happened in that instant, it freed Kyle's hold on him. Marc shot up, bringing both his hands to the worm working its way into his ear and tore at it without mercy. The bug dug in deep, and with one final pull Marc yanked out an eight-inch creature akin to some tapeworm, along with a piece of his cartilage still clenched in its mouth.

"Goddamnit!" He shouted as he flung the monster from him and across the cave floor. Looking over beside him he found Hashi delivering a fourth and fifth blow to the back of Kyle's skull with a rock the size of a volleyball. She reared back over her head for the last time and brought it down with a guttural scream as it found its new home in the slathered grey paste of their friend's brains. She looked over to Marc with gritted teeth and a heaving chest.

"Come on, we have to get the fuck out of here now!"

"Kelly..."

"Kelly's *FUCKING* dead. We *have* to go!"

Lacerations and gashes split Hashi's face open from her forehead to her chin. Clumps of her black hair had adhered to a clotted bloodstain originating from her temple. Her hands were dripping with blood (both hers and someone else's). A groggy and bloodied Emma lay on the ground behind Hashi.

"Come on and help me carry her out of here," Hashi said as she looked around at the rotting drones still unaware of her presence.

Marc and Hashi dragged a half-conscious Emma up steep winding paths through the cave with nothing to guide them but the camera light on Emma's phone. Arm in arm they pushed through the dark with the skittering din of insects closing behind them while the phone's battery hovered in the single digit percentile. The further they went, the more the weight of Emma's body taxed the both of them. They neared a sharp bend where the cave began to level out when the aroma of freshwater hit them.

"We...have to be getting...close to the entrance," Marc said between fits of exhaustion.

With every step the smell grew as well as the faint echo of rushing water crashing over the falls. But as the soundtrack of their exodus began to play, the hungry cries of the cavern screeched behind the teens in unison. The clawing and scratching along the walls and ceiling paired with the crunching displacement of rock and sand as feet pounded the earth in pursuit. Fatigue set into Marc's arm that was holding up the phone making it impossible to hold it steady. The sporadic use of light left them stumbling into walls and stalagmites.

"GIVE ME THE GODDAMN THING!" Hashi screamed at Marc as she reached across Emma to take it from him.

"They're getting closer!" He yelled.

"I know! Just keep moving."

A series of low whispers materialized just behind them. They were inaudible at first until they were right outside of Marc and Hashi's ears.

"Guuuuuuuuuys...don't leave me," came a voice from behind them.

"That can't be-"

"It's not!" Hashi exclaimed. "It's a fuckin' trick, just like that dog!"

A lone series of beeps interrupted the dispute as the phone alerted them it had now consumed all of its power and would shut down. The dying light was now accompanied by a black screen with a hollowed out red battery symbol.

"FUCK!" Hashi screamed.

Fumbling through the dark, Marc waved his free hand in front of him and to his side feeling for walls or obstructions on their way out. The taunts made to mimic their dead friend Kelly continued to haunt them at every turn.

"Wait, do you see that?" Marc asked.

"Is that?"

Thin rays of sunlight splashed along the walls of the cave, unveiling another bend up ahead.

"Daylight!" Marc replied. "I bet it's coming from the entrance."

They rounded the corner and with a quickening rush of relief a brilliant flash of sunlight flooded the other end. With the light at the end of the tunnel guiding them, they picked up the pace as much as possible while still dragging Emma along. Freedom lay just a couple hundred yards ahead of them.

A new frenzy of scratching noises came down the final stretch of cavern with them. This time the noises came from all along the walls and ceiling. Jagged shadows danced all around them as piercing rays of light hit thin pointy legs and dark bodies. Shapes scurried about ahead of them, narrowing the opening to the cave.

"EMMA! EMMA! You have to wake up and run! We have to run, NOW!" Hashi screamed until Emma stirred again. "Come on, baby, I need you to run!"

Emma turned her head to meet Hashi's gaze.

"Ok. Ok, I…"

Her reply was cut short as an unseen force jerked her out of their arms and to the ground. Before either of them could react, something grabbed Emma by the ankles and pulled her back into the shadows in a second.

"NOOOOOO!" Hashi screamed while Marc put all of his weight back on her to keep Hashi's momentum forward.

"We can't stop running!"

The two of them darted through the darkness as the din of freshwater streams competed with the chattering things in pursuit. Ten yards and closing, the grassy path lay in plain view as it had been earlier.

"Almost there," Marc said.

Flinging themselves from the darkness of the cave and onto the warm grassy plateau, they both chanced a look back behind them to find that the creatures halted their pursuit within the shadows. Where the sunlight touched, they dared not trespass. Instead, they skulked around and taunted the two escapees before receding into the murky black.

Hashi dropped to her knees sobbing. She gasped as hyperventilated spasms sent her spiraling into the prelude of a breakdown. Falling forward to her palms and knees, her long black hair veiled her head and dipped down to the surrounding earth, hiding her reaction from Marc.

"AAAAAAAAAAAAAAAAAHHHHH!" She screamed into the dirt from the bottom of her lungs until the last molecule of oxygen had evacuated, leaving her in a coughing seizure.

Marc darted to her side and held Hashi to his chest as she belted out another protest before sobbing in his embrace.

Marc pulled up to the house around 7:00 that evening with several cardboard boxes busting at the seams with the last forty-two years of his life in tow. Retirement. That is a word he never understood the definition of until it stared him in the face. The rest of his life to do as he pleased, go as he pleased, just live. But even at 64 the idea of taking liberty for all it is worth felt foreign to him. What would he do with his time now? As he put the hatchback in park and grabbed a stack of junk, he put together a bulleted list in his head of different hobbies he could pick up in his spare time. Sculpting, painting, take on a project car, maybe? Atop the box of knickknacks lay a small gold colored picture frame. Enclosed underneath glass and several decades of dust lay an eight by ten photograph of Marc, Kelly, Kyle, Emma, and Hashi standing on the boardwalk behind the hotel they stayed in all those years ago. *We all looked so happy* Marc thought to himself as he ran his fingers across the photo.

"Fuck," he muttered as he dropped his keys on the front stoop fumbling to find the one to the house.

Scooping them back into his palm, he made a mental note to change the burnt-out bulb over the front door as he held his keys out of his shadow using the ambient light from neighboring streetlamps to pick out the one for his front door from the rest. Finding it, he tried once more with caution to unlock the door.

Shuffling through the darkness of his living room, Marc dropped the boxes of picture frames and knickknacks over by the couch where they would be out of the way while he acquainted himself with the light switch.

"SURPRISE!" A choir of voices rang out as the overhead fixture burst to life revealing a room packed with his family, close friends, and former coworkers all adorned in festive party hats. A large electric blue banner stretched across the wall opposite him that read *HAPPY RETIREMENT!* Streamers ran the perimeter of the room and lay draped across lamp shades.

"Did you have a good last day, honey?" Linda said as she planted a soft kiss on Marc's cheek.

"I did," He replied with a smile.

"Did we surprise you?"

"Haha. Yes. Yes, you did!" He replied while scanning the room.

Marc removed his coat and made his rounds through the room saying hello and thank you to people one by one for being here for him today. The sentiment brought a tear to the corner of his eye that he played off as an unwanted eyelash sticking under his lid. Never one for spontaneity, he stepped away from the crowd after almost an hour of handshakes and warm gestures. Marc took a plateful of cake downstairs to the den where several grandchildren had set up a few tabletop games.

In the back of the room, a familiar face stood out among his old friends and colleagues. Hashi Iwai sat alone on the faded navy-blue suede couch staring off into space as the party continued without her. Solemn and reserved, she only glanced his way once before gazing back into her own daydream. They never spoke much of that day. They talked often about every other controversial topic from politics to theology, but they let that one memory lay where it was.

He sidestepped guests and made his way over to that same navy couch looking for a little relief from forced social interactions.

"Hey there, stranger! I haven't seen you since the last school reunion," Marc said as he took a seat next to her.

Hashi said nothing in return, only shot a forced smile in his direction.

"So, are you going to be back in town for long or...?"

"We're ssss," Hashi said just above a whisper.

"I didn't hear you. What did you say?"

"We're ssss..."

A sharp ache ran through the left side of Marc's back, throbbing until it took fire in his chest and his left arm. The spasm shook him so hard he dropped his plate to the floor as he doubled over in a knot and fell to the carpet. He rolled to his back gripping his chest with his right hand while he labored to breathe.

"LINDA!" a voice called out from somewhere in the basement. "Someone call 911!"

"Oh, God! I think he's having a heart attack!" Another voice muttered as a group of guests stopped what they were doing and rushed to his side.

A dark haze began to settle around his vision as his breathing thinned into shallow rasps. A series of loud, thundering explosions went off as a dozen or more people ran down the basement steps headed by Marc's wife, Linda. She pushed her way to his side holding his hand in hers.

"Sweetie, what's wrong? SOMEONE CALL 911!"

Hashi got off the couch and stood over Marc looking unphased by the events unfolding. She mouthed some words over and over that came out inaudible under the commotion racing through the den. Marc locked eyes with Hashi through his darkened tunnel vision and tried to read her lips, but to no avail. Hashi knelt down by his side and put her face beside his so to bring her lips just outside of his ear. She spoke again. This time her modest whisper drowned out every piece of ambient noise around him.

"We're...still...here. We're...still...here."

THE SWANSONG OF WILLIAM DELACROIX

The Sandman cometh, and Hell followed him. William Jean Delacroix; murderer, only child, sociopath, loner, apex predator, Columbia House Record Club member, extinguisher of light. For several years William Delacroix took his one man show all over the state of Texas before settling back in the fine city of San Dismas. His act swallowed up over four dozen men, women, children, and household pets inside the gaping maw of his shadow. Like the fabled Azrael swooping in low to collect the firstborn of Egypt, the Sandman delivered his violence with haste and indifference. Whole families went to bed dreaming of book reports and board meetings just to find themselves gobbled up by the earth, never to be seen again. With blades, steel wire, and even his fists, he culled the herd with a precise lethality. Like many famous epics, it was pride and arrogance that ended his reign of terror. Ultimately, his ego would smelt away to form the final nails in his coffin. But every legend must reach its climax and finale in proper time. Such is the ballad of his final act.

On a cold January night under a dark starless sky, the Sandman made the fatal error of mistaking a predator for prey. Soon after his capture, every news outlet across the country fought for the opportunity to catch him on film. Like other executioners before him, the macabre eroticism around documenting his life dwarfed anything and everything noteworthy that year. Everyone's inner voyeur came out to the spectacle of media outlets putting his biography under the microscope for the world to bear witness. Once his death sentence came down, Channel 14 outbid all competitors to interview the Sandman for the first and last time before his transfer to another facility and later, death row.

In less than an hour Sarah Kim's crew had turned an administrative office at the Breckenridge Penitentiary into a studio set tailored for William Delacroix's last confession. With feet and wrists bound by chains, William Jean Delacroix entered the room accompanied by two armed guards. For someone awaiting state sanctioned extermination, he grinned like he held a winning lottery ticket. A cameraman motioned for him to take a seat in a chair already set up for him underneath two soft box lights. Sarah Kim straightened some loose papers into a uniform pile in her lap as she took a seat across from William.

"Hello, Mr. Delacroix. I'm Sarah Kim."

Delacroix took his seat in front of the reporter and postured himself accordingly. His brow remained firm, his eyes were unblinking and wide, and he stretched his mouth muscles from corner to corner in a faux clown-like grin. His cheeks twitched as he held his pose before returning it to his normal cold expression.

"Well, hello, Ms. Kim."

"You can call me Sarah."

"Well, you are looking lovely this evening, chér. The cameras don't do you justice."

"Thank you," she replied with an uneasy and cautious tone. "So, if you're ready, then we'll get started."

Delacroix said nothing in return, just nodded and gave another smirk.

"Let's talk about your earlier years. You were born in Louisiana?"

"Mandeville."

"Right, but your family didn't stay there, did they?"

"No, we started moving when I was three. My father always had a tough time finding work, so we traveled from town to town."

"What kind of work did your father do?"

"He was a brick mason by trade. Did construction work wherever he could find it. Sometimes he would luck out and find jobs in the surrounding counties. Whenever that happened, we usually stayed in an area for a few years at a time."

"Where did your family stay?"

"Sometimes we would stay with relatives, but mostly we lived in these tiny apartments wherever Dad could afford them."

"How would you describe the relationship with your father?"

Delacroix sat in silence staring into her eyes unblinking, as if the question unchained something in him once restrained. He moved his tongue back and forth around the front of his teeth, biting into his gums and lips as he looked for a word or a phrase to respond with. Knowing that some inquiries tread on paper-thin sheets of ice, she withdrew her question and redirected the conversation.

"So, I guess it must have been hard making friends, let alone keeping friendships, as you moved around the country. Did you feel lonely growing up?"

"It was mighty rough. I think I found my place when we moved west to El Paso. I was there 'til I finished high school."

"Did you have any hobbies or special interests?"

"Reading. I read a lot, whatever I could get my hands on from the library. I didn't have siblings and my mother was terribly withdrawn and quiet, so I learned at an early age to live in my own head. I relied on my imagination to entertain me."

"Who's your favorite author?"

"Oh, I read a lot of Henry James, Shirley Jackson, Tom Clancy, and a 'lil bit of John Grisham's stuff. But I always enjoyed the classics more: Cervantes, Dostoevsky, Milton," he said while reclining as far as the static office chair would allow him. "My eighth grade English teacher, Madam Dubus, now she put a fire under me. She pushed me harder than any other. Got me to read well above my level and inspired me to learn everything I could 'bout the world."

"I want to shift the questions to your adulthood if that's ok with you."

Delacroix nodded in agreement giving the journalist free rein to continue.

"When did you first have thoughts about harming others?"

Delacroix paused for a moment before responding. He looked down at his hands, and then around the room as he scoured the recesses of his mind for the right answer (or at least the right answer he debated giving up).

"You know, chér, I think I've always had that in me, the desire, the drive. I used to fantasize 'bout making some of my classmates disappear. The ones that fucked with me the most."

"William, I need to remind you that you can't use that kind of language during the interview."

He met her criticism with a faux smile that his eyes and brow could not meet halfway with the same sincerity.

"My apologies, chér, I mean to say the ones that *messed* with me the most. I would daydream about making them hurt. As the years went by and my understanding of the world matured, I came up with new and inventive ways of dealing with them in my head. Sometimes I would ponder on what sounds would come out of Colin McElroy's mouth if he went feet first into a woodchipper."

"What about as an adult? When did those urges strengthen enough to drive you toward murder?"

"I think the first time I gave myself over to it was when I started working downtown."

"At the machine shop?"

"Fentco, yeah. So, I worked there right out of high school trying to get my Journeyman's card. I was slaving away twelve hours a day not leaving 'til two in the morning. I didn't have a car back then, so I just took the bus to work and walked back home to my apartment over on McCormick Street. That's when I started carrying a buck knife on me. I told people it was for protection, but I carried it because it made me feel powerful. Those late nights made me restless. Sleeping during the day, coming alive at night. It woke something fierce in me chér. Something ornery and…hungry. One week during the summer of '98 the plant got caught up on orders, so they let some of us go home a bit early. That Friday I left just after midnight and made it down to the local cineplex hoping maybe I could catch a late showing of something. I think *Blade* had just come out that week.

When I got outside the theater, a group of these college-age kids were just leaving the building. I stood in front of the ticket kiosk and looked at the showtimes, but my mind couldn't focus on that. This hunger, this need to have something that belonged to them started rising in me. At first it was like a stomach ulcer, or at least what I think a stomach ulcer would feel like. It was this burning in my guts, and it just got worse the longer I stood there staring at a list of movies I knew then I probably wouldn't see. I turned and started following these people. I followed behind them for about a block until they started to disperse to their own cars. Moments passed by where I was scared for what I was about to do, and those led into moments that I couldn't control, moments where something else, something in me took the steering wheel and wouldn't let me turn back. After another half block, a young girl about twenty or twenty-one veered off into an alleyway leading into this double decker parking lot. I didn't blink, I didn't breathe, I just turned with her into the parking garage."

"They didn't notice you following them?"

"No, chér. They never looked back. It was like I wasn't even there. I can't remember how I got there. I think I blacked out for part of it. I just remember turning in and ducking behind a row of cars, and the next memory after that is me pinning her against a car with my left hand over her mouth and my right hand driving the buck knife into her ribcage just under her heart. I pulled the knife out and returned it several times until only a low whimper came from behind my hand."

There was a long silence between them where only the hum of studio lights filled the office. Mild tempered journalist Sarah Kim went into this interview excited for the opportunity of her career, but unaware of the Pandora's box she would be opening. She cleared her throat and prepared herself for the next series of questions.

"How do you feel about killing? What comes over you in the moment after you've ended someone's life?"

"I don't..." he responded with his eyes fixed on the corner of the ceiling.

"What I'm saying is how..."

"I don't. It's like turning off a light."

"I don't understand. What do you mean it's like turning off a light?"

"When it's over, when they've finished breathing, finished blinking, finished pissing themselves...when the light behind their eyes dwindles and dies away, there is this...nothing. The nothing you feel from unloading your groceries, checking the lint trap for debris, or turning off a light switch. When it's over..."

"Here, let me reword that," Sarah interjected as tension in her subject began bubbling to the surface. "Tell me what it was like living a normal life while keeping your secrets."

William put on the brakes from his last question and took another quiet moment to work on his response in a composed manner.

"At first it was like taking a step outside of my body. Like being on autopilot while the world moved on around me. I found myself giving into my compulsions out in the open, sometimes in broad daylight, almost daring someone to catch me. I remember this one night in the spring of 2014, I went back to my apartment with a backpack that belonged to a young woman I'd met earlier that evening. I had her head in the backpack. On my way up the stairs I passed this couple. They said *Hi*, and I said *Hi* back and told them to have a good evening or something and the whole time I've got this woman's head in the backpack. As they passed me, I couldn't help but wonder where they were heading off to that night, and if I should join them. That was my reality, my truth. I walked like other people, talked like other people, held down a job, subscribed to a fitness magazine, I even had a video rental membership. After a while, the line blurred, and it became more difficult to fly under the radar."

"Is that why you moved outside of the city toward Fairbank? Were you looking for seclusion?"

"That was part of it."

William Delacroix, with the shimmer of soft diffused studio lights dancing around his pupils amid the line of questions, sat in silence as he composed himself in his chains. He lowered his head until his brow began casting a slight shadow over his eyes. William Delacroix, Mr. Suave himself, pulled the corners of his mouth up into a wicked smirk like an unsupervised child elbow deep in the cookie jar.

"Now, I want to ask you about Fairbank. Let's talk about the night they caught you," Sarah Kim asked as the last syllable of her statement transformed William's grin into a cold stare.

"You're gonna fry, Delacroix!" an inmate shouted from the top of C-Block.

"Wooooooo!" another screamed along with a choir of grizzled men in cages.

A week to the day after Sarah Kim gave him his last rites, William Delacroix marched through C-Block with ankles and wrists chained together. Like so many at his own hand, death awaited The Sandman. The late summer thunderstorm pounded against the skylights of Breckenridge Penitentiary leaving deep shadows throughout. Four guards escorted Delacroix through the facility armed with Mossberg 500s, two behind and two in front of him, leading the way to the south exit.

"Well, this is it, Delacroix. Soon, you're gonna be someone else's problem," one of the rear guards said taunting him.

William turned his head sideways to the right so he could catch a view of the guard in his peripheral. A small smirk formed over his face as he stared at him through the corner of his eye.

"EYES UP FRONT, DELACROIX!" the second rear guard barked at him.

William turned his head back around to face the direction they were marching.

"Yeah, and soon after that you won't be anyone's problem anymore," one of the point guards spoke up.

Together they escorted him through processing before exiting to the south side where a black Yukon awaited them. Three men in plain clothes stood by the vehicle waiting for their new prisoner. Despite their outfits which varied from blue jeans to khakis, with polos to blue and grey plaid long sleeves, they all wore the same matching black plate carriers over their shirts with bright yellow U.S. Marshals tabs Velcroed across the fronts.

"How you boys doing today?" One marshal said as he pulled a handful of papers from the front seat of the SUV.

"Not too bad. Be a lot better once we unload this piece of shit," one of the forward guards said while keeping his eyes on Delacroix.

"Yeah. Well, we're here to take him off your hands," a marshal replied while handing the transfer papers over to a guard.

A marshal in blue jeans and a blue polo shirt opened the door to the back seat and motioned for the prisoner to take the row behind the driver and passenger seats in front of the back row. Delacroix looked back at the guards behind him and smiled before stepping forward to the vehicle. Tearing off the carbon copy for himself, the guard handed the remaining paperwork back to the marshal with a smirk.

"You watch this one now. Don't take your eyes off of him," the guard reminded the three marshals.

"We won't," a marshal in a grey plaid shirt and black denim jeans replied. "C'mon now, Frenchie. Get your broke dick Cajun ass in the seat."

The heavens opened wide releasing the full brunt of the afternoon storm as soon as the marshals exited the highway for Route Six. With wiper blades slashing away at full speed, the golf ball sized rivulets of water narrowed the driver's line of sight down to thirty feet, forcing him to slow down to around twenty miles an hour. Every mile down the road brought the crashing of thunder closer to them. William sat in the middle of the seat behind Tom Heller as he drove them through the storm and onwards to William's final stop. Agent Randy Willis sat to Delacroix's left with André Martinez to his right, sandwiching the murderer inside the SUV.

"You know what, fellas? We should play a game to pass the time. You know like, license plate bingo or something," Delacroix said over the deafening silence in the SUV. All the marshals ignored him, staring off ahead of them while the summer storm beat the frame of the vehicle without mercy. "Or how 'bout 'tis, what 'bout a game of I spy with my little eye? I'll go first. I spy with my little eye..."

"Can it, jackass!" Heller barked at Delacroix as he struggled to see the road.

"What? 'Tis all in good fun. How 'bout this? We all go 'round the car and tell stories about our first times? You boys know all my dirty secrets, maybe you three should share some. Tell the class all 'bout the first time you ever stood over a man and watched the light die behind his eyes."

Randy answered his question by driving his elbow straight into the prisoner's teeth, thus silencing him.

"I don't know much about the light in a man's eyes, but if you don't shut your cock holster, then we'll be stopping on the side of the road instead of taking you to Mayfield, and I'll personally save the taxpayers some money."

Delacroix sneered at him, then cocked his head back and spit a gob of blood and phlegm on his vest.

"You're no fun," William added.

The whirring of wiper motors and the shrill patter of rain against the car body and road created a hypnotic tone lulling the occupants. This comforting silence ended in a flash of fire and smoke as an explosion near the passenger side tire knocked the right side of the Yukon off the road for a moment. Rocks and debris collided with the side of the car shattering the front passenger side window inwards. Snapped out of his concentration on the road ahead of him, the driver over-corrected the now fishtailing car, sending it off the road and down an embankment. The Yukon slid down the hill for what felt like an eternity. Branches slapped and scratched the windshield making it impossible to see what lay ahead. It wasn't until the engine block wrapped around a tree near the bottom of the hill that the illusion cracked.

Martinez lulled himself back from unconsciousness to find no William Delacroix beside him. Aside from where he sat, the backseat remained empty. No agent Willis, but more troubling, no William Delacroix. He shot up, sending throbbing pain through his skull and upper torso. After clearing his weapon from its holster, the marshal freed himself from the seatbelt and checked all around the car. A sheet of perpetual rain plummeted in front of the open passenger door opposite him. Keeping his Glock trained on the door left ajar in the middle of the storm, he glanced around the Yukon to find the driver still enveloped by the airbag.

"Tom? Tom?" he said just above a whisper hoping the marshal behind the wheel would give him a sign he was conscious.

Without a response, the marshal exited through the open door with care and tactfulness. The storm pounded him outside of the Yukon. Concentrations of rain fell so thick it left his sightline down to just the immediate area around the crash. Not only did the engine wrap around a tree, but it had become imbedded in a cluster of smaller ones, making it difficult to pry open the driver's door.

"Tom!" the marshal cried as he pulled the door open enough to slide himself in. "Tom?"

He stopped himself before calling out to his friend again once he laid eyes on the scene in front of him. Shards of glass from the exploded window had embedded themselves in the right side of his face and neck. One large piece entered through his jugular, killing him before the airbag even deployed. Hot sticky rivulets of blood covered the dashboard and windshield.

"Fuck!" the marshal muttered to himself.

The frigid realization that Tom had bled to death inside his airbag, and his other companion and their lethal cargo remained unaccounted for, crawled up his spine where it settled at the base of his skull. The marshal turned around a hundred and eighty degrees and scanned around him with his sidearm at the ready. Starting with the crashed SUV to his left, he pushed up ahead with care until he rounded the back of the car and then went to the other side. Without a sign of life or death near the crash, Martinez picked a direction and swept through the woods. Crashing thunder detonated closer to him with every step, throwing off his focus with each strike. Flashes of light tore against the forest canopy leaving ragged shadows dancing amongst the greenery, which led him to draw down on figments of his imagination. The torrential downpour against the leaves masked his footsteps as he chose every movement with care.

"Goddamnit," he whispered to himself as he stopped in the deep shadow of a tree cluster.

Rainwater cascaded down his brow and into his eyes making his scan of the woods that much more daunting. After a minute of calm, another deafening crack of thunder preceded a prolonged flash of white through the trees. The spark glimmered against something on the ground about a hundred yards ahead. He set himself into motion with haste. Still minding his footfalls against the forest floor, he pushed up with his service weapon at the ready. As he closed in, another series of quick flashes left him with a bigger picture of what lay in front of him. He stopped just above the broken shell of the missing agent.

"Randy?!" He muttered at a low volume, still keeping a watchful eye for his prey.

He crouched down beside him and ran his fingers down to the side of Randy's neck searching for a pulse while keeping his head up in vigilance.

"Jesus. Fuck," he whispered as his quest for any sign of life came back fruitless.

He looked down at the slain agent for the first real time since he found him. A cherry red stripe ran the span of his throat, and in a pile of dirt-caked leaves next to him lay his prisoner's chains. Eyes flooded with the blood of burst capillaries gazed off without emotion into the abyss.

An abrupt hard blow to the back of his skull interrupted his brief mourning. The pain dropped him to his knees with his left-hand clinging to a sapling and his right still gripping the pistol. Before he could orient himself to turn and aim at his attacker, another strike found the base of his neck, releasing his hold on the weapon and dropping him to the ground beside Randy's corpse. From where he lay, he could make out the scraping noise of his pistol being retrieved from the leaves. In one excruciating motion, the marshal rolled himself over to find an unchained William Delacroix standing over him with a bloody rock in his left hand and André Martinez's Glock in his right.

"Now that's a nice shirt you're wearing there, friend. Is that a large or an extra-large?" Delacroix said with a sneer.

Between the tall and slim one missing the back of his skull, and the shorter and more toned one with purple and crimson witness marks across his throat from William's chains, Delacroix assembled a suitable outfit for his voyage back home. Rain continued crashing all around him while he made his escape through the woods. Aside from some sag in the waist and a stretched-out collar, the clothes almost fit him. The extra slack allowed William to stash the agent's service pistol in the waistband of his lower back. Deep shadows bred from the forest canopy distorted Delacroix's vision, making it hard enough to navigate without the torrential downpour.

A few hours later he had found his way out of the woods and back onto the main road. He had put enough distance between himself and the crash that he began to relax his gait and travel as someone who didn't just escape from prison. No, that wasn't him. Not at all. Just a poor hitchhiker with car trouble. Though it may have appeared to the powers that be this would be the final act of William Jean Delacroix, it was all a ruse. Soon he would find his way out of this, and the show would go on. The Sandman cometh.

A set of headlights emerged around a bend in the road a quarter of a mile ahead of William. The ice blue halogens pierced the downpour, dispelling darkness the closer it got to him. Delacroix kept his head down as he marched along the highway hoping no one would recognize him. Soon the car barreling his way passed by flooding William in a sobering blue light and then leaving him again in the darkness he preferred. Where the stolen outfit had once been too loose, now it adhered to his body from the rain. The cold steel of the Glock's slide left a constant reminder that it rested in his lower back, waiting.

The storm ceased after dark. Without a watch, William had no idea how far into the night he had traveled. Overhead the clouds had parted leaving an unrestrained full moon to light his path. Off in the distance behind him, a motor became audible, followed by the sound of tires slicing through puddles, treading across soaking wet pavement. Beams began peeking over the crest of the hill he had climbed fifteen minutes ago until they poured past his body and shed light on the road ahead. William turned around to face the car approaching and prepared himself for whatever came next. He extended his left arm in front of him with his

Michael Tyree

thumb out in the direction he was heading in hopes of someone
trusting enough to give him a ride away from here. His other
hand remained behind him, pulling up the shirt just above the
pistol. He wrapped his middle, ring, and pinky fingers around
the grip while pushing his index finger down along the side of
the trigger guard, readying himself with Plan B. The car closed in
enough that Delacroix could see it was not an obviously marked
cop car or EMT. A cobalt blue hatchback drove past him kicking
up puddles of water on him as it did. To his surprise, the car
slowed down to a stop on the shoulder of the road just a few
hundred feet ahead of him. Leaving the gun uncovered by his
clothes he removed his hand but kept it close to his waist just in
case. His good Samaritan had rolled down the passenger side
window by the time he had jogged over to it. Inside sat a woman
in her early thirties. Her long black hair was pulled into a
ponytail behind her head and restrained by a black ball cap. She
looked over the seat at Delacroix with concern.

"You need some help?" the woman asked.

"Oh, merci, chér!" William responded as he channeled the
demeanor of a wounded animal hoping this person would let
him in close for his next performance. "You see, my car broke
down, and my phone is dead," he said with a sigh.

"Well, you've got a hell of a walk ahead of you. There isn't a
service station for at least another ten or twenty miles. Hell, there
isn't really much going this way," she responded.

Delacroix looked defeated as he pretended he didn't already
know there was nothing down this road. The idea set his teeth on
edge at the endless possibilities racing through his mind; this
lone person, the desolate roadway, and the sharp end of
something.

"You want a ride somewhere?"

"Oh yes! I would be forever in your debt!" Delacroix responded.

He reached behind himself and acted as though he needed to adjust his clothes before entering so he could conceal the Glock once more. With a spring in his heel, he opened the door and slid into the passenger seat of the Subaru.

"Yeah, you're lucky I found you when I did."

Yes, yes, I am, he thought to himself. "My apologies, but I am soaking wet. If I had thought for one second that I would walk through that storm all night, I would have just slept in my car," he said with a chuckle.

"That's ok," she put the car back in drive and started off down the road once more. "Now I can't take you all the way to the city. The storm caused some flash flooding earlier and a lot of the roads are still washed out. I can take you as far as I was going, and I can call you an Uber or something."

"Are there any hotels near where you're going?"

"Not really. Not until you get closer to San Dismas."

"Well, I guess I can just..." he replied.

"Or, if you can wait it out, I have an old couch in the basement you can crash on, and I'll just take you into the city in the morning," she replied cutting him off.

The fantasies running rampant within William peaked at the notion of this good Samaritan.

"Well, that's kind of you, but I couldn't impose. If you can just get me as far as you were going and if you don't mind me using your phone, I'll just call a taxi."

"Well, it's up to you. No one is renting out the basement apartment anymore so you can just stay there tonight if you need a place to sleep."

"I mean..." always the chess player, William Delacroix planned his next five moves needed to calm the maelstrom raging in his veins, and then disappear before sunrise. "I can give you money for your trouble if you don't mind me crashing on the couch. I'm just exhausted," he said as he took in a deep breath and rolled through the possibilities waiting for him wherever his good Samaritan was now chauffeuring him off to.

"That's no problem."

"I'm John," William said with a wide smile and a nod of his head.

"Lilith."

After a few minutes on the road, William could hear what sounded like sirens in the distance. His confidence dialed itself down when the sound grew louder and then paired up with a caravan of cop cars and firetrucks heading toward them in the wreck's direction. As the authorities came close to passing them, William acted as though he had to bend over to adjust his pant leg, shielding his face from anyone looking inside.

"So, are you from around here?" Lilith asked.

"Not originally, no. I moved here from El Paso when I got out of high school," he responded while maintaining his cover.

After they had all passed, William sat back up and readjusted himself.

"How 'bout you?"

"I bounced around some as a kid. We lived out East when I was young and then moved out here just before I started high school."

"You know, I'm not used to people being so kind. It's refreshing. With so much awful shit in the world it's hard to trust people anymore. Know what I mean, chér? Most folks would have just passed me by without a glance. But you, you're going out on a limb for me, and I sincerely appreciate it."

"Well, that's no problem. You know what they say. *Do unto others.*"

After most of an hour on the road, Lilith veered off the main stretch onto a private gravel path just as the storm returned for its encore of the evening. As seclusion set in around them, a deep excitement rose in William, starting with a fluttering of his heart and a quickness in his breathing. Soon his guts stirred with every cluster of trees entombing he and his prey. They turned from the gravel road onto a narrow, hidden driveway through the woods. They traveled down beside a shallow creek and then up a few steep hills before emerging in front of a quaint two-story house. The hatchback's headlights lit up a pale blue sanctuary littered with quaint lawn ornaments. A battalion of gnomes and flamingos guarded the modest home and greeted the Sandman as the hatchback eased into the drive.

"So, you live here all by yourself?"

"I wouldn't have it any other way," she said while putting the Subaru in park and turning off the engine.

Delacroix sat in the passenger seat minding the pistol still tucked into his waistband, while he watched Lilith get out of the car first and head to the front porch. A visceral slideshow flipped through his mind as he studied her every move. He envisioned her entrails unwinding like a hot sticky ball of yarn, fingers gnawed to the bone, face crushed inward with a cinder block. The endless macabre possibilities flirted with him while real life continued moving forward around his body.

"You comin'?" Lilith said from the porch as her new friend had yet to move from the passenger seat.

The statement shook him awake from his daydream. Still maintaining his timid rabbit composure, he feigned modesty and leaped from the seat like someone embarrassed to be caught off guard that way.

The climate-controlled air sent a fresh chill up William's spine as he became reacquainted with the soaking clothes glued to his body. The reaction gave him a real shudder outside of the character he played.

"First things first. You need to get some dry clothes. I think some of my dad's old stuff might fit you," Lilith said as she set her keys down in a ceramic tray by the door. "I'm gonna go look through some of his things real quick. Just make yourself at home," she added while disappearing down a darkened hallway off the kitchen.

Oh, I will, Delacroix thought to himself as he covertly slid his hand over the Samaritan's keys and smuggled them into his pocket. He walked around the first floor, scoping out the layout of the house, making mental notes: *front door, side door from the kitchen leading to an enclosed porch outside, from that side a downhill slope to the back where another side entrance led into what must be the basement.*

If William Delacroix were capable of intimidation or fear, he might have felt something similar while basking in the den's décor. All varieties of big game stood, lay, or hung from the walls in exaggerated poses of aggression. A black bearskin rug stretched out before the fireplace, surrounded by two other massive predators posed on their hind legs with front paws to the sky, their mouths wide open in bloodlust. A collection of smaller beasts decorated the mantel as well as occupying random shelf space on built-in bookcases: foxes, hares, badgers, even a few dozen serpents. In a way, he admired the art of taxidermy. He took trophies over the years, but never had the artisan touch of others with the dead. Uncanny attention to detail in each beast left a sense of covetousness in the pit of his stomach. Maybe he should take up a trade like this, he thought to himself while standing in the cold gaze of a hundred or more stuffed predators.

Lilith returned after a few minutes with an assortment of clothes for him to try on.

"Here, some of this is from when dad lost all that weight after his surgery. So, it might fit you, but if not then at least it's better than that soaking wet mess you're wearing now."

"Merci," William said while taking the two shirts, two pairs of pants and socks. "So, I take it your dad is or was the big game hunter?" William asked while looking into the den from the kitchen.

"He liked to hunt, but those weren't all his. Dad was a taxidermist by trade. He acquired some of these from other hunters through bartering."

"So, pardon me if this is out of line, but is he still alive?" William asked.

"No. He passed away a few years back," Lilith added as she walked to the kitchen window to observe the death throes of tonight's second storm. "Cancer. After he died, I inherited the house," she said with a sigh. "I was tired of renting an apartment, and I wanted to live somewhere I could have some peace and quiet. That's why he liked it out here, too. No one around for miles."

That last sentence reverberated in William's skull like an early morning church bell. *No one around for miles.* Details like that gave him the inspiration for taking his time here, even though he had

153

a weapon within arm's reach with at least fifteen or sixteen rounds left. For his next performance, he chose a slow buildup to the final act.

"Bathroom's just through there, down the hall on the left," Lilith said as she pointed him toward the hallway.

To William's surprise the old man's clothes fit him better than his captor's ensemble. The faded blue denim pants left just enough wiggle room to continue securing the handgun out of sight. He returned to find his good Samaritan lost in a collection of framed photographs arranged on a cherry wood end table. With a casual stride he walked over to the front door just outside her line of sight.

"Sounds like it's finally slowing down again," Delacroix mentioned as he returned the keys (minus the one to the front door) to their dish with care.

"So, I guess they fit you ok?"

"Yeah, a little loose, but not bad."

"Good, there's a dryer in the apartment downstairs. You can throw your wet clothes in that later," Lilith turned away from the family photos and walked over to where he stood by the front door. "Come on, I'll show you the apartment downstairs."

Following her lead with modesty, William took the door to the front lawn again with her just behind him. Together they rounded the side of the house and sidestepped puddles on the way to the back corner of the home. She stopped and with a little work, opened the door motioning for him to walk inside with her following behind him.

"It's not much, but it's better than sleeping in your car. There are some blankets in the top of the closet, and the washer and dryer are just on the other side of the bathroom. I'll take you to town in the morning after the roads clear up."

"I really do appreciate your kindness."

"No problem. Try to get some sleep," she said while closing the door behind her on the way out.

Taking exceptional care to not disturb any of the decorations, Delacroix slid across the porch just outside of the front door. He retrieved the stolen key from his pocket and fed it into the handle with a slight turn to the left, releasing the lock. Darkness blanketed the house from top to bottom. Only pale shimmers of moonlight penetrated the windows leading into the kitchen. The aroma of vanilla candles lingered from the countertops near the stove, inviting William to where some of his favorite instruments lay in drawers or inserted into blocks with careful organization. A stainless-steel magnetic strip mounted above Lilith's cutting board held a few choice tools for his disposal. Of the variety for the picking, a six-inch blade, burning with the reflection of lunar radiance called his name through the pitch. The stillness in the atmosphere stoked his madness until it tugged his marionette strings into action.

His moment of introspection was interrupted by a commotion above him on the second floor. Clenching his teeth at the sound of footfalls, William wrapped his fingers around the kitchen knife handle until the color left his knuckles. After a few laps back across the hallway, the sound stopped for a moment only to be replaced by that of running water crashing against a porcelain tub. The fire roaring in Delacroix's bloodstream peaked with the pitter patter of the shower. This was it. With the stage set, the band began to play, and the curtain was only moments away from William Delacroix's next performance. With the knife pointed downward, he took the staircase one at a time, paying keen attention to the volume of any accidental creak along the hardwood in comparison to the din coming from the bathroom. Every few steps brought his blood pressure to new heights. His veins throbbed from his cock to his fist tightening around the blade. Stopping at the top of the staircase, William paused for a moment in part to listen with care at what was happening at the end of the hall, but mostly for breathing in the air of the calm before the storm. The moment prior to him standing before drawn curtains and fanfare. Deep breath in, deep breath out, and off to it. Taking a crouching stance, he slithered down the hallway under the radar, bringing himself face to face with the bathroom door.

Without any more pause for reflection, he pushed the door open enough to slide in. Never seeing the layout of the room, he oriented himself with care to position himself just outside the curtain from his good Samaritan. Without an exhaust fan running, the bathroom filled to the brim with steam leaving only a vague shadow of Delacroix on the mirror. Narrowing his eyes on the form outlined in the shower curtain, he raised the kitchen knife over his head, threw the curtain back with his left hand, and drove his blade into what lay ahead of him. To his shock, the knife didn't find its way into anything soft as he had planned. No muscle tissue or vital organs, no arterial spray, or guttural screams. Instead, his knife stuck into plastic, specifically the plastic of an adult mannequin. There standing in front of him underneath the downpour of a pulsing showerhead stood a female doll with its arms stretched upwards around its head as if it were lathering conditioner into phantom locks of hair.

"What…the…hell…"

His mumblings were cut short as a hard pinch gripped the side of his neck and then disappeared just as quick. William dropped the knife against the ceramic tile before bringing both hands up to his throat. His eyes swam in their sockets unable to focus on any one thing. Like the medicine cabinet covered in thick condensation, soon his vison blurred into a drunken blindness. Stumbling halfway through, he turned to see his good Samaritan, Lilith, standing behind him with a spent syringe in her hand. She cocked her head to the side and raised her free hand to wave at William as a parent waves to a child being put down for a nap. He opened his mouth to speak but lacked the cognition to form whole words. Somewhere between *how* or *who* he closed his eyes before collapsing to the floor.

William Delacroix, professional boogeyman, the Sandman himself, bested by his own prey. His vision returned in tiny increments. Somewhere out of his line of sight a few halogen bulbs lit up the area to his right. Lying on his back, William remained fixed in place. No matter how hard he willed it, he could not command his legs or arms to move for him, nor could he feel anything around them. Lifting his head upwards as far as his muscles allowed him, he noted the white sheet covering him from the neck down. With no context as to how, he remained motionless against his will, only able to move his head from side to side. With an agonizing wince he looked over to his right. Still sensitive to the light, his eyes blinked hard of their own accord.

Newspaper clippings and photographs littered the wall from ceiling to floor. Dozens and dozens of yellowing black and white articles dating as far back as five years ago, even some front-page eye grabbers, all showed the same common theme: each one focused on the Sandman, William Jean Delacroix. Mixed in with the newspapers were just as many photographs of him. Some originated from magazines and other papers, but the vast majority were pictures never captured by the lens of a professional photographer. His senses still flooded with drugs left him slow on the uptake. He blinked so hard it almost put him under once more. Letting out a deep exhalation, he rolled his head over to the left. Mismatched shadows from a fixture missing half of its bulbs lay across a sun-bleached wooden work bench. A chaotic pile of multicolored wire, circuit boards, electrical tape, and several pickle jars full of nails lay amid a cluster of other unidentifiable components and compounds. A large cork board hung from the wall behind the bench. Pinned across the left side was an aerial map of Wythe County. A series of scribbled out words near a road junction right of center drew his attention. Across the map scribbled in pen read, *1:00 P.M.*

The fog around his pupils cleared in small increments just to blur again.

"You have been a busy boy, William!" Lilith's disembodied voice emerged from the shadows behind him. "Or is it, John?"

Delacroix turned his head straight again and faced the uncovered insulation wedged between the rafters above him. Without the noise accompanied by shoes on concrete, Lilith appeared leaning over Delacroix, so she was upside down in his line of sight. Even from his strained posture he could still make out the beginnings of a content look on her face, like a child who had uncovered a lost plaything. She smiled before bringing her index finger down on his forehead with several taps to the beat of the humming rising in her throat. She placed both palms across his temples and rolled his head back over to the right facing him toward the pictures once more. The sharp movement rolled his eyes in a drunken stupor until settling on the collage in front of him.

"Do you remember that night?"

William remained silent giving her nothing in the way of a response.

"That was the night they caught you," Lilith said as she walked over and laid her fingers across a photograph of William walking into an old pipe factory near Fairbank. The picture appeared to have been taken from several stories up, looking down on him from an adjacent building. "To think, you might still be out in the wild if it hadn't been for that PI."

Lilith turned from the wall of photos to face him once more. She crouched down, folding her arms over one another on William's gurney, then plopping her chin on them like a child as she got eye level with him.

"Nothing? You don't have any witty remarks?"

"I'm gonna...fucki..." he whispered with a labored breath.

"I can't hear you?" she said while pinching his cheek. "Oh, well."

Lilith stood up, walking back behind William's head and almost out of his line of sight once more. Pressing her feet down on the locks holding the wheels in place, she set the gurney in motion across the basement.

"When I was younger, maybe fifteen or sixteen, I wanted this red leather jacket more than anything in the entire world. I saw one picture of Alicia Silverstone wearing it and that was all it took. I saved everything I had that summer; did chores 'til my fingers bled. I had never wanted something so badly in my entire life. Finally, by the second week of school I had enough to get it, and my mom being so proud of me for saving my own money, took me the first chance she could. And I loved that jacket. I'll never forget the first day I got to wear it to school. The way the other girls coveted it; the way Scott looked at me when I wore it. I felt like a model. Then, the next week Becky Connifer came into school with the exact same one. She didn't have to save anything, didn't have to sacrifice anything. She just asked her parents for it, and they bought it for her without question. Pretty soon people started to forget I had it first, and the ugly rumors went around that *I* was the one copying *her*. I was so angry. My mom tried to make me feel better in her own way. She told me that *imitation is the highest form of flattery*. But we both know that's bullshit. Take your story for example. It would have been bad enough if you were just a sloppy copycat getting caught with your own take on someone else's hobby. But you, you took credit for work that wasn't yours. Do you know what that makes you, William?"

He said nothing.

"A plagiarist."

She pushed the gurney around a corner into another room with more ample light than where he had stirred. Still unable to move his arms or legs, he remained docile, hoping she made enough of a mistake for him to get the upper hand.

"Fun fact, though: that's also the reason Becky Connifer needed reconstructive surgery in tenth grade to replace her missing nose and ear," Lilith said, punctuating her statement by booping William on the nose with her index finger.

The room Lilith brought him into was tidier than a surgical suite. Bright white halogen bulbs ran across the ceiling in rows throwing clean light over every corner. Along one wall laid a series of connected stainless steel tables with instruments laid out with care: saws, hammers, files, chisels, pneumatic pencil grinders, shelves loaded with various paints, and dies as well as anything else required to transcend art from the corporeal flesh.

"I have a surprise for you," Lilith said as they stopped moving once in the center of the room. "Are you ready?"

She laid her palms across the sides of his head once more and rolled it over to the left. Trophies decorated the wall from top to bottom, side to side. Instead of tools or equipment, this wall displayed her true art at its peak. Grotesqueries were arranged in shapes and forms unthinkable by anyone unaffiliated with he who rides the pale horse. A plaque hanging high on the wall within William's sightline had the jawless head of a young woman attached to it. Her original top row teeth were removed and replaced with the sharpened incisors of an apex predator. Polished antelope horns had been attached to the top of her skull, parting the chimera's auburn hair where they protruded. Glass lifeless orbs rested inside her eye sockets, staring through and beyond Delacroix. Below that on an oak pedestal lay two lovers interwoven like shrubbery. There were joints broken and rearranged until it was unclear where one hip started, and another ended. The couple's hands were clasped together with fingers from one jutting through the palm of another like bamboo shoots. The art of rigor mortis left the two heads contorted to the side where both pairs of lips connected them forever with wire and adhesives.

"I think your friends missed you," she said pointing to the largest display amongst the trophies.

She drew his attention to a special piece. There among Lilith's compendium of macabre stood her very own Cerberus postured to guard her treasures. The gargantuan body of a hundred and ninety-pound mastiff stood erect with black fur brushed and pampered until its coat glowed. The three severed heads of the marshals had been collected and stitched together in a row where the dog's own would be. All three still wore their death masks, locked in the last moments of their existence.

"You know what they say about well laid plans? Well, I had another idea I wasn't too crazy about just in case your friends were a little late to the party today, but I guess it all worked out in the end. I think the fireworks were a nice touch," she said while pointing at the nail and wood screw littered IED shrapnel embedded in Tom Heller's face. Lilith paused as she ran her hand across William's forehead. "All these years you've been taking credit for my work. Telling the world about your memoirs, admitting guilt to acts you only read about in the Sunday paper, putting on this show so they'll do a movie based on your escapades," Lilith paused for a moment to clear her throat and let the rage simmering under her tan skin taper off before continuing. "But, I think that's all behind us now. I think we'll be even Steven after tonight."

Lilith drew away the sheet from Delacroix's body draping it over a stool. She disappeared out of his line of sight for a few moments leaving him with the dead. His attention remained drawn back to what lay ahead of him as the gurney started tilting up in small gear driven increments until it peaked at a forty-five-degree angle.

If William Delacroix maintained the ability to feel anything close to fear, it bubbled to the surface in that moment. In front of him stood a full body mirror showing off in horrifying detail the exact condition of his torso. An ice-cold sobering wave crashed over William Jean Delacroix as he took in his new form in the mirror. It wasn't drugs or restraints that kept his sensations in check. She had amputated his arms at the shoulder and his legs just above the knee. A series of leather straps kept him bound to the gurney just under his armpits, while another strap wrapped around his waist with a large steel loop in the center.

"We are going to have so much fun together," Lilith said brushing his cheek with the back of her hand. She gazed at the same scene in the mirror, watching William Delacroix watch himself. "Yes, we are."

Michael Tyree

THE DEPARTMENT OF ACQUISITION

If he who rides on the pale horse felt so inclined as to take up residence in a vacation home, he would find it within the walls of 6023 Walnut Street. Inside, the modest Tudor hallways squared themselves against handcrafted crown molding. Stairs ascended with beautiful symmetric banisters and ornate hand carved balusters all stained as cherrywood. The heart of the home featured built-in bookshelves converging on a brick fireplace. Not one corner conveyed laziness or poor craftsmanship. No rough edges in a finished wall, no tile met its neighbors without perfect geometry, not a single drop of paint found its way to anything but what it was poured out for. The foundation held its home upright with the resolve of Atlas bearing our world. With no other to rival it, the Tudor sat as a crown jewel among the other houses on Walnut Street.

As the centuries came and passed, Death understood the importance of Feng Shui. The Reaper always believed the floor plan of the home needed some adjusting as it stood in the beginning, so over time pieces of furniture moved about as inhabitants vacated the premises for the last time. Sofas and love seats would go off to auction houses or be gifted away in wills. The mattresses that did not find themselves in a police evidence room would be tossed to the bottomless pit of a landfill. Atrocious beige shag carpet splashed with the touch of vermillion, then cleaned by professionals, would be dowsed crimson again a decade later. The last time that premature expiration changed the shade, it was stained so deeply the third to last owners resorted to ripping it from the floor, hoping to refinish the hardwood beneath. Paint touched up the walls of the master bedroom, children's bedrooms, and even kitchen multiple times over the decades, sometimes with more organic coats instead of lead or latex. Rich Kentucky Bluegrass bordered the Tudor, leaving it a sight of covetousness by its neighbors. The backyard remained especially green and manicured throughout the season due to the extra time put in by several previous owners who stayed behind to fertilize it. From its creation in 1922 through the rising of the sun this morning, 6023 Walnut Street knew death as intimately as the honeybee knows the sunflower. As life found comfort within its walls from time to time, soon they would all find the Reaper's embrace.

The original Da Vinci behind the erection of the Tudor was an architect by the name of Raphael Navarro. The self-made son of Spanish immigrants, he and his wife Elena finished building the home five weeks prior to their first wedding anniversary. Everything he did, he accomplished for her. The shade of tile, the wood that they had cut their doors and cabinets from, the scale and proportion of the dining room chandelier were all carefully selected. She milled over every facet, and he made each one breathe life. For five years the Navarros watched fireflies dance through their Sycamore tree, picked tomatoes in their garden, kept each other warm by the fireplace, made table space for family and friends as they gave thanks for their blessings, decorated Yule trees, celebrated the beginnings of new years, and found each other under the mistletoe. They lived and loved with eyes set on nothing but the present. Time showed kindness to Raphael and Elena, but time is merely finite, and the reaper is never tardy.

Michael Tyree

One late December night, just a few days before Christmas Eve 1927, a young man came calling at the front door screaming nonsense about his friend lying injured in the street. He rapped on the door with such violence it woke both Raphael and Elena from a deep coma of a night's rest. Raphael, being the honorable man that he was, opened the door for the gentleman only to find that his kind nature let three men with guns drawn into his home. Stealing more than just material possessions, the thieves left the bloodied and ravaged Navarros to empty their life into the cracks in the hardwood, and thus gave 6023 Walnut its first illustrated example of inhuman depravity. The viscera displayed that evening would put a certain taste in the Tudor's mouth, and a curiosity of things to come.

With no children or relatives to inherit it, the house stayed vacant until 1934 when a man named Martin Rawley purchased the home. A bachelor and successful lawyer, Mr. Rawley practiced for the offices of Wallace & Snead. Martin never married despite the incessant nagging from his mother whose restlessness for grandchildren wore him down at every social calling. Instead, he kept to himself and focused on his work with dreams that one day he would see his name on the office letterhead. Over the years he took on several high-profile cases for the firm which demanded long hours and little time to himself. His antisocial tendencies and the duress of his career path mixed into a seductive and fatal cocktail. The neighbors would see him from time to time talking to himself in his yard. Sometimes it would appear at first that he was reminding himself of some task on the way to check the mail or water the plants, but anyone who studied him long enough would see Martin Rawley debating with the surrounding air.

On an early October morning in 1947, just after the first day of fall, Martin came up with a plan to solve all of his troubles for the last time; a way to obtain the vacation he so desperately required.

He pulled out a ladder from his shed and climbed up the sprawling branches of his Sycamore tree. From a girthy section he sat up and looked out at the surrounding neighborhoods in awe for what felt like the first time. The virgin rays of sunlight sparkled against panes of glass and dew droplets scattered about lawns and bay windows. He took a deep breath at the splendor before cinching a slipknot around his neck and sliding off the branch. The noose reverberated as the weight of his body found the limit of rope and thus snapped his neck in one fluid reaction.

Over the years new life would walk into the Tudor's embrace with hope and promises of new beginnings. Some stayed longer than others. A few left in such an abrupt and impolite manner that 6023 Walnut stayed in a perpetual state of melancholy at its vacancy for almost a decade at a time. But like the moth to the candle, her corridors and rooms would find company again.

There exist some places where only thin stitches of hope and prayer hold the veil between us and the damned together. The malice and hatred manufactured by humanity forms little tears in that fabric that over time split and run until nothing separates the two. Places where what waits on the other side peek through from time to time. If one were unfortunate enough to find themselves in one of these locales, not only would they be able to look behind the sheet at the other side, but maybe, just maybe, they would find things on the other side that wished to do more than look back at them. In the deepest corners and darkest shadows of 6023 Walnut Street nothing remains as even a placeholder of a border. With every final breath, every drop of life spilled between hardwood beams, every cry of anguish left unanswered like a neglected newborn, the door separates itself from the threshold in increments. Evil in its most sacred form waits with unshakable patience for the brief moments when the curtain tears from its windowpanes and the nasty things get a day pass.

"Hey, do you want to go by the cineplex? The Howling is still playing, but I don't want to see it by myself," Megan inquired.

"I would, but I already made plans," Hellen replied with a shudder as an icy breeze caught her cheek, forcing the teen to take refuge deeper into her lavender wool scarf.

"I promised Mateo I'd help him with his school applications. He's hoping to get into NYU, but he's so overwhelmed right now he doesn't know what day of the week it is."

"Well...I can help with that. I've filled out a couple of those so far," Megan replied with a newfound upbeat chirp in her voice.

"No, that's ok. I don't want to bore you to death. I should be free tomorrow, so we can go see the movie then."

Megan paused for a moment before replying. After the teens passed the Anderson's weather tattered colonial that marked the last block before Megan's stop, she pushed once more with the same insistence. "I wouldn't be bored. I just..."

"It's just...he and I were gonna hang out...you know, just the two of us."

"Oh...Ok. Well, I don't wanna be a third wheel or anything. So, is he not seeing Katie anymore?" Megan replied as she gazed across the street while her home crept into view.

Hellen just looked back at Megan with a little smirk and shook her head. Megan returned the gesture with a half-smile before bringing her attention back to the house towering in front of them across the road: her stop. The Tudor demanded her full attention in that moment. It existed for it. She became so hypnotized that she did not notice the long strands of cinnamon brown hair blowing across her face by the violent winds. Megan's gait slowed as they got closer to her home. A heavy uneasiness washed over her when 6023 Walnut Street came into view. As they stood on the sidewalk in front of the house, Megan turned to granite. Her muscular system protested the command to move from where she stood. Deep down she prayed for a miracle capable of spiriting her far from here. She fantasized of the things she would sacrifice for the freedom to turn and keep walking past the house until she hit mountains or ocean, whichever came first. But no, 6023 Walnut Street fixed its eyes on her. Its gaze refused to allow Megan passage to anywhere but the halls within.

"Are you ok?" Hellen asked.

"Yeah...I'm fine," Megan replied, knowing it was a lie. Hellen would never understand, and Megan did not know the words to start the conversation, so she shut down and internalized her dread. "I'll see you tomorrow, Hellen."

"Yeah...see you tomorrow."

Megan crossed the road with her head down low, watching the asphalt with every step. So many days like this had slipped through the hourglass. She had memorized every crack and pit in the road in front of her home. The frigid March evening grew bitter as she closed in proximity to that house. The same house that had only been her home since last summer. Even now its front porch stood out like the gaping maw of a symmetrically carved monster, waiting to swallow her whole. Its windowpanes glared like eyes emulating the orange fire of the sunset. As she approached the stoop, a rotten onslaught reached into her nostrils, pulling at every receptor until her body commanded she throw her right palm over her mouth and nose before gagging. A dead cardinal lay spread apart on the front stoop, already in advanced stages of decay.

An icy chill ran through the corridor, meeting the bare skin on Megan's face as she walked through the door. The frigid bite made her shiver from toes to hair follicles. The odor of decomposed poultry followed her into the foyer. No one had turned any of the inside lights on, even though everyone had been home long before her. Only thin beams of low hanging light from the setting sun snuck past the heavy curtains that were wrapped tight against every window of the house. The dominant light source came from the black and white Zenith TV in the den. Her Mom's boyfriend, Tony, was washed in a bluish grey light as he stretched out on the ripped and stained floral pattern suede couch. His grimy wife beater pulled to its limits as it contained most of his gut. Rough stubble bred patchy inky shadows across the bottom half of his face, leaving his eyes and brow accented the most in the television light. His unkempt, black, thinning hair was slicked over to the side and held in place with three days of oil and sweat. The bargain barrel jailhouse tattoos on Tony's upper arms looked like they were once outlined using a six pack of crayons by someone's brother-cousin with Parkinson's. One might have been a crucifix and a crown of thorns in another life, but in this reality, it appeared more like a nonsensical pile of squiggles. Tony's narrow eyes moved onto Megan without the rest of his face. He squinted at her through the corners of his eyelids without saying a word before returning to the evening news.

... at 2:27 PM this afternoon, a failed assassination attempt on President Ronald Reagan took place outside the Washington Hilton Hotel...

A shuffling commotion arose from the kitchen as Megan set her backpack down in the hallway. Scant beams of dying light reflected from other houses broke through the dusk settling in the kitchen. Upon entering, she found her mother on her hands and knees brushing broken glass debris into a dustpan. Rivulets of blood rolled down her knuckles in streams, that were slowing to a clot across her dirt caked hands.

"Mom? Are you...ok?"

Her mother, Patricia, remained crouched down on all fours, sweeping up another mess from the beige linoleum. The first inquiry fell on deaf ears as she continued at her task while her dirty blonde bangs hung down low almost covering a fresh bruise on her face.

"Mom?"

"HEY! You leave her alone. She has some tidying up to do," Tony bellowed out from the den.

Megan didn't respond to him. She knew how these days went, and what she needed to do to ensure her survival. She just knelt down and embraced her mother. Megan wrapped her arms around Patricia tight. A little at a time, Patricia let go of the dustpan and broom in tiny increments until they sat on the floor. Without making a sound, she brought her arms around her daughters' waist. Resting her head on Megan's shoulder, she shuddered and seized as her face fortified itself against the tears pushing for release from the corners of her eyes. Patricia clenched her teeth so as not to moan or sob at an audible level. Both women knew what it meant if she did not restrain herself.

"It's gonna be ok, mom," Megan whispered into Patricia's ear.

Patricia pulled away and smiled before planting a soft kiss on Megan's forehead. Tony tread past the endearing moment on his way to the kitchen cabinets. Patricia kept her head down, pushing Megan back so she could continue sweeping the broken pint glass into the trash. With an exasperated sigh, Tony opened the fridge door. He stood there in silence for a moment and took a quick inventory.

"Patty? Did you go to the store today?" Tony asked after taking in a long deep breath.

"Yes...yes, I went this morning while you were asleep."

Patricia's distressed response hung in the air as only the evening news served as a soundtrack inside the Tudor. Static filled clips of today's events filled the gaps between the pounding of Patricia's heart crashing in her ears and the grinding creak of Tony's fist tightening around the door handle.

"Did you? Did you really?"

"I did. I swear."

Tony sifted through the crisper until exhuming another light beer. Without waiting for the fridge door to shut, he had the top open and bottom of the bottle to the sky. With eyes narrowed into slants, he focused all his attention on the two women. Keeping his eyes on them, he took slow strides until he stood just behind Megan as she still crouched down by her mother. As he walked by, Tony ran his index finger up Megan's left arm, across her shoulders, and down her right arm before letting out a belch on his way out of the kitchen and back to the evening news.

"I'm just saying that I thought it was a little weird. I mean sometimes she acts like she'd rather be anywhere but home, but today…she was just in outer space. She offered to come over here and help with your college applications," Hellen said, shaking her head.

Hellen laid her head back against Mateo Sandoval's chest as the two stretched out on the faded, grey, corduroy sofa occupying his parents' basement. Her golden blonde hair draped over his Van Halen shirt.

"I dunno. Megan is a little flaky."

Mateo sat up so he could reach over to the coffee table for a small brown cigar box resting on the top. Digging through it, he procured a joint and a discolored steel lighter before repositioning himself on the couch. Holding it between his lips, he struck the old Zippo until it delivered a flame.

"You're gonna share, right?" Hellen asked with a chuckle as she watched Mateo take a light drag.

He laughed and passed the joint over to her as she remained propped up on his chest.

"I've known Megan for a long time. Whatever's going on is new to me. She wasn't this secretive or flaky when she lived across town. Ever since her and her mom moved things have been weird," Mateo added as he exhaled a thin cloud of smoke.

"I remember last summer after they got settled into the new place, she was supposed to go to the lake with our family before school started back up, but she backed out at the last minute and just disappeared. I didn't see her again until the first week of school. Even then, when I saw her, she just looked so...distant. Like she was there, but not *there*."

Darkness came over 6023 Walnut Street with an unexplainable sense of dread in the late winter of '81. The bitter cold still held its steel grip on the month of March with no sight of spring. Megan lay in her bed under four layers of blankets in a desperate bid to fend off the frigid air seeping through every pore of the Tudor. Most nights allowed her anywhere from three to four hours of sleep if not less. Fists penetrating drywall, doors slamming against their frames, curses brought to inhumanly audible levels, and the silence between scored the soundtrack to her insomnia. That night started off with white noise generating from the TV in the den paired with sharp winds that built up to shrill war cries piercing through the Sycamore tree beside her window. The crescendo of the evening arrived with a blunt scream from the master bedroom down the hall.

Michael Tyree

"NOOOO! I want you out of this house! I already called the cops…You hear me? OUT!" Patricia bellowed out between sobs.

The resonating din of feet stomping down the hall and past her bedroom door left Megan terrified and curious at the same time. With the utmost caution, she peeled back the blankets and crept across the room to the door to listen more closely. Just as she did, a second set of footfalls came by the door faster and heavier. Megan peeked through the crack in her door to see Tony crashing down the hallway toward the stairs. Before he reached the banister, Tony stopped and cocked his head to the side so that his peripheral vision caught sight of Megan's bedroom door. He turned and walked back down the hall. In a panicked state, Megan ran back and jumped into bed, covering herself in the blankets as she pretended to be sound asleep. She lay there with her chest heaving from terror and exhaustion. The subtle footsteps ended at her door. She clenched her eyes shut tight as her door creaked open and Tony stepped inside. A deep chill followed her mother's boyfriend into the room as if he had just emerged from a freezer. The cold followed him over the floor along with a rancid odor akin to a dead animal. Through tiny slits she watched as Tony glided over to her bedside, triggering every creaky loose board along the floor. She tightened her eyelids like vice jaws, hoping if she willed it so, he would just go away like so many boogeymen living in her closet and under her bed. Tony squatted down, bringing his elbows to rest on his knees, as he hooked his index finger under her blanket and tugged at the cover until it rested just below her collarbone. Megan clenched her teeth as the odor of cigarettes and PBR wafted over her. She found herself at the point of tears when he brought his motor oil-stained palm across her cheek.

He halted when an eruption of noise downstairs drew his attention away. The sound of doors opening, and closing were followed by garbled voices from below. Tony stood up a little at

174

a time as he stared down at her. Mumbling incoherent profanity under his breath, he turned away and walked out of the room.

Megan shuddered in revulsion as his pungent stench still hung low in the air. Her muscles constricted and locked against her curiosity. She remained wrapped tight in the blankets as the commotion beneath her began escalating. One nerve shredding curse after another fired off while she hid under her covers. After a few minutes she worked up the courage to leave her room and venture out onto the landing overlooking the living room. The shouts and profanity still echoing through the house now emanated from the kitchen. She crept down the stairs one at a time as the frosty air tightened around her limbs.

"KEEP YOUR HANDS WHERE I CAN SEE THEM!" A commanding voice bellowed out from the kitchen.

"Have it your way," Tony responded with a condescending tone.

Taking incremental steps through the shadows cast about the living room, Megan put herself just around the corner of the kitchen to find Tony standing in the middle of the room with his hands up. Her mother lay twisted and broken at his feet while two police officers held him at gunpoint. A deep sob Megan could never have prepared for took her like a seizure. She held both hands to her mouth as her lungs gasped until they had deflated to capacity. Her vision clouded into a tunnel as it homed in on her mother's head snapped around just a few degrees shy of a half turn. Blood pooled up around her face on the floor and mirrored her reflection in the crimson puddle. Her muffled cries did not go unnoticed, as Tony looked over his shoulder at her with a smirk.

"ON YOUR KNEES!" The second cop barked at Tony.

"No. No, I think not," he replied while putting his hands back down at his sides. "You," he said, nodding to the cop standing closest to the door leading from the kitchen to the sunroom. "I want you to point that gun at your partner and blow his brains out."

Both cops scowled at him with murderous intent until beads of sweat bubbled up around the forehead of the policeman in question. He held his gun on Tony, but not without a struggle.

"I said, point that gun at his head and blow his fucking brains out."

"Noooooo," he responded through clenched teeth.

As the silence between them hung low in the kitchen, the officer's arms twitched and contorted. With a strenuous labor, he fought against an invisible hand pushing his outstretched forearms to his right. Breathing under duress like a first-time mother in labor, he exhaled in erratic bursts through clenched teeth.

"Do it," Tony said one last time.

In a bright flash, the officer trained his service revolver on his partner and put the five pounds of pressure against the trigger needed to unleash itself through his partner's skull. Entering just behind the officer's left temple and exiting with a splash of cherry rivulets across dated mustard yellow wallpaper, the slug buried itself into the sheetrock.

"Now, put that barrel in your mouth," Tony added.

Tears flooded Megan's eyes to utter blindness as she choked back a sob and sidestepped behind Tony until she found her back to the basement door; the same basement door that always had a skeleton key stuck in the lock on the inside of the door. Without looking back, she flung it open and slammed it shut behind her. Her trembling fingers slipped and fumbled across the old iron key until it rolled over, engaging the lock inside. A single gunshot from the .357 rang out behind the door, almost sending her next series of steps off course. She steadied herself against the railing before continuing into the darkness.

POTTER'S FIELD BLUES

With nothing but a fifty-nine-year-old lock and a wooden door between her and Tony, Megan fled the stairs into the bowels of the home. The atmosphere plummeted into an unbearable frigid temperature. Her bare feet connected to the frozen floor with sharp pricks that made her think twice about her escape route. Darting through a labyrinth of mildewed cardboard boxes and trash bags overflowing with clothes intended for charity, she didn't bother wasting her effort on any of the downstairs lights that she knew were unlikely to respond. Instead, she followed the flashing red and blue lights streaking across the windowpanes of the basement's side door.

The silence that followed her approaching the door became more unnerving than the series of loud crashes against the basement door she expected to hear. *What was he waiting for?* she thought to herself. Like the last one before it, and most of the other mechanisms in this house, the deadbolt resisted her every advance. Wrenching it with both frostbitten hands, she slipped and labored to maintain a grip. After too many failed attempts, the lock released itself. Hinges starved for WD-40 contended with her for freedom. She tugged with her entire body behind it, only to have the door move a few inches each time. Finally, it cleared the obstructions holding it back, and she swung it wide with one hard pull.

Winds saturated with frost ripped through the threshold and crashed against her bare skin. The pajamas could not shield her from what came next as the March night wrapped its icy tendrils around her. With a deep breath, she leaped into the yard. Frost hardened soil and pebbles tore at the skin of her soles as she hobbled through the side yard toward her crimson and navy beacons of hope.

Halfway to the front yard Megan let out a cry for help. Somewhere between the first and second syllable of a sobbing whisper, something struck her across the shoulders, dropping

Megan facedown into the dirt. The blow almost knocked the wind from her lungs which left her scrambling to orient herself. A series of heavy footfalls pounded the earth to her right before turning in front of her. She pushed herself up with her elbows and forearms to find Tony squatting down in her way with a maniacal smile painted across his grizzled, blood splattered face.

"Where do you think you're sneaking off to after curfew?"

Cherry and sapphire washed over the neighborhood as police and EMS swarmed 6023 Walnut Street. Neighbors and friends all stood out on their porch stoops and in the street behind police blockades. People looked back and forth at one another with the same faux expression of astonishment. As if they all did not have some inkling of a clue what happened and what had been happening. No one said a word to one another, but they knew. They knew it was a matter of time. They looked on as men and women from the coroner's office wheeled out the first body wrapped in black plastic.

Hellen pushed her way through the crowd until she hit the wooden barricade. She found her way to the front just as the body of Patricia Moore was being wheeled out in a black bag. The front of Megan's house lay in chaotic disarray with police and crime scene investigators combing over the property. An adolescent boy about nine or ten slid past Hellen in a matching pair of Star Wars pajamas covered with a bright blue parka. His curiosity seemed insatiable as he squirmed back and forth between onlookers to find his place for the show.

"DAVEY! DAVEY!" came a concerned voice from behind Hellen. "David! I told you to stay beside me where I can see you," a middle-aged woman said with deep concern as she dropped to the boy's level to scold him.

"I'm sorry, mom," he responded as he took her hand and walked back away from the crowd.

"Has anyone seen Megan?" Hellen shouted at anyone and everyone in attendance on the street.

No one answered her inquiry, instead the spectators kept their attention drawn to the scene in front of them. Before Hellen could ask again, a loud commotion erupted from the house as several cops dragged Tony out in handcuffs. His filthy wife beater that may have once been white was now stained grey and crimson with arterial spray. Droplets of hardened blood still stuck in the stubble on his neck and face. When the flashing lights danced across his features, he looked out onto the crowd of neighbors with a wide toothy grin.

"HAS ANYONE SEEN MEG..." Hellen began shouting before she gazed up to the second-story window. There, Megan stood looking down at everyone gathered around her house.

Hellen looked up at her with relief as she gave a slight wave toward Megan to get her attention. Instead of returning the gesture, Megan just stood there with a solemn look as she stared right through Hellen and everyone else.

A sharp tingling sensation crept up Hellen's spine and settled at the base of her skull as she watched her friend from the street. She could not find the words to describe it as the feeling enveloped her like a blanket. It felt like a sequence of acupuncture needles running up her body before merging in her skull. The climax hit her as she looked away from the window and back to the front door as the coroners wheeled out another smaller body in a black bag.

"Who...who is that?" Hellen said.

"That must be Patricia's daughter," an onlooker replied.

"No...no, you're wrong. I just saw ..."

Hellen looked up once more to an empty window. The tingling settled into a numbing in her nerves as the body wheeled past her and into the ambulance.

"Jesus!" one neighbor shouted as Tony broke out of his handcuffs and began smashing his way through the surrounding police.

He broke the nose of one officer to his right and fractured the knee of another to his left. Before anyone could react, he grabbed an officer in front of him around the neck and unholstered his service revolver in one swift motion. Tony took a few steps back into the threshold of the house with the .357 held against the temple of his hostage.

With guns pointed at him, he cleared his throat for an announcement. "Well, this has been a blast guys, but it's time for me to get back to work. I'll catch you on the flip side," Tony said as he stayed behind his human shield.

In a matter of seconds, Tony pulled the handgun from the officer's temple and shoved it in his mouth, aiming the bore straight back. He squeezed hard and fast, sending the slug into the back of his head where it over penetrated and finished its trajectory in Tony's face. The single shot rang out through all the surrounding neighborhoods, waking up anyone else who had not already witnessed the carnage at 6023 Walnut Street. With the crack of the .357 still ringing in everyone's ears, the bodies of both men slumped over into a pile on the front steps.

"God! Are we there yet?" exclaimed Joey.

"Don't take the Lord's name in vain, young man!" replied Kathy.

"And no, for the ten thousandth time, we are not there yet," Richard interjected with a chuckle.

POTTER'S FIELD BLUES

The family's trek from Norfolk, Virginia, to upstate New York had been a long and arduous one. Richard was a man of structure and discipline, so when the day came for the Murdock clan to relocate to Albany, he prided himself on making this journey with minimal stops. His original plan was to arrive at the new house in just under ten hours. However, having two kids in tow, one of which owned the world's smallest bladder, that estimate exceeded almost eleven and a half hours. The Murdocks had called Norfolk home ever since their second child, Joey, had been born eight years ago. But now with the prospect of Kathy's new job at the hospital, they had to uproot once more and follow the Lord, wherever He was leading them.

The faded red digital clock on the radio read 7:15 PM when the Murdocks came to the end of their journey and pulled up to 6023 Walnut Street. The two story, 1920s style brick Tudor towered in front of the captivated Murdock family. It appeared as a mistreated Cinderella among the rest of the neighborhood; an architectural crown jewel left to the elements and awaiting a fairy godmother to breathe new life into her tattered façade. Even under the patchwork roof, dirty windows, and paint peeling from the shutters, her beauty still glimmered underneath. Richard picked up on it from the first photos he clicked on the realty website. He knew then it would be their new home once he had time to mend her gown for the ball. The feeling did not waiver upon seeing her in person. The house showed a different face to each member of the family. While Joey saw a strange house in a strange town, Stacey saw an atrocious dumpster fire that was embarrassing to live in. Kathy saw the best they could afford on an already stretched budget, but Richard alone saw perfection shrouded in neglect. The house was a geometrical exhibition erected in a distant time when craftsmanship meant something.

As the family exited the vehicle, Kathy noticed a couple peering out at them from a house across the street. Then another beside them.

"I wonder if they're gonna get out and say hello?" Kathy asked aloud to anyone still conscious after their journey.

All around them, blinds compressed from nosey fingertips while prying eyes hid behind parted curtains. Almost every house in peering distance noted the arrival of the Murdocks. The front door of the home to their right cracked open as a middle-aged man in blue jeans and a plain black shirt emerged. He said nothing nor even wave when prompted by Kathy and Richard. He only turned his head their way for a brief second before retrieving some junk mail from his box and returning to his home without acknowledging the new neighbors.

"Well, we'll have to introduce ourselves later once we're settled in. Maybe we'll have the neighbors over for dinner one night," Richard added.

Donnie, as he allowed others to call him, gave everything for the department. As far back as his memory served him, he had been a company guy. His first posting in intake and distribution gave him the tools to ascend the corporate ladder where one day he hoped to have his boss's job. After a brief period, Donnie went to work in the call center, following up on leads and obtaining the critical data needed for the agents on the ground, before becoming the top field agent in acquisitions himself. He was simply the best of the best. His boss knew it, the other agents knew it, his rivals knew it, but most importantly, he knew it. His closure rate broke old records and solidified new untouchable ones giving him certain liberties and perks not granted to others, such as working without a partner. Fledgling agents new to the department learned more from studying his work in obtaining contracts than their own training manuals.

With only a few minutes to spare, Donnie made his way down the corridor to his supervisor's office for a meeting that he assumed could have been an email instead. He rounded the left corner past a row of closed offices and picked up his pace in a life and death bid to not spill his coffee. At the end of the hall, Mr. Killian's receptionist, Vivian, guarded the closed door to her boss's office while a small group of employees sat around in the waiting area to seek an audience with the wizard. Knowing how his boss detested being disturbed more than anything else, Donnie sat down without saying a word and waited for his summons rather than burst in. Vivian, preoccupied with a stack of invoices, did not see him walk by or played the indifference card well.

A lanky, frail specimen sat across from him making awkward on again, off again eye contact as Donnie attempted to wait with patience. The employee across from him wore black high-water work slacks revealing faded black dress socks with a crimson polo shirt. The first unrestrained thought crossing through his mind was: *this guy looks like he's in the market for a gently used, windowless, paneled van.* Donnie studied every corner of the lobby from the hairline cracks in the floor to the poorly patched drywall, just so he could not commit to eye contact. A hastily repaired patch in the ceiling was all it took not to risk starting weird small talk with anyone. He examined the poorly sanded splotch of drywall with its humps and cracks in the white ceiling paint before assigning those features eyes and a twisted mouth. He imagined if those could be misconstrued for facial parts, then somewhere in there existed other anatomical pieces. Maybe, the greyish section with the thinnest strokes of paint could be an ear and eyebrows. He stared with only boredom and introverted tendencies guiding him through his interpretation, but before long he understood how people could see Jesus Christ in their morning toast.

Pausing her task, Vivian picked up the headset and pressed a single button to dial out. "Sir, he's here. Yes, I'll send him back now," she said before putting the phone back down. "Mr. Killian will see you now, Donnie," Vivian said with a smile.

He shot up quick with a spring in his step toward the office door. "Hey now, my eyes are up here, doll," Donnie replied to her with a wink.

He entered the office to find Mr. Killian scanning over the contents of a manilla folder. Shutting the door behind him, Donnie pulled up a chair in front of his boss's desk.

"You wanted to see me?"

"Yeah. We have a potential lead for you to follow up on," Mr. Kilian said while keeping his eyes trained on a stack of documents resting on his desk.

"Well, you could have told me that over the phone," Donnie replied as though he spoke to an equal and not his boss. "Is there something pressing about it?"

"No, not at all. If everything checks out it should be one and done," he finished eyeing the last paper before bringing his attention forward. Mr. Killian cleared his throat hard before beginning again. "The reason I needed to talk to you in person is because we are making some changes around the department."

"What do you mean *changes*?"

"Starting with your next assignment, you'll be working with a partner. A new transfer who'll be shadowing you from start to finish."

Donnie gritted his teeth hard with eyes narrowed in a tight, skeptical arrangement that would have sent any less impressive agent flying out of Mr. Killian's window in a heartbeat.

"You know I've always worked alone," Donnie added as he choked back his contempt.

"This isn't up for discussion. The department is changing the protocol with acquisitions, and we're all doubling up, including you. Unless you *want* to go back to work in *Intake*? I know how much you loved it down there on the first floor."

Donnie sunk back in his chair gnawing on his lip as he feigned a cool composure.

"So, who is he?" Donnie asked with a sigh.

Killian picked up the receiver and pressed a cherry red button on the phone to dial out.

"Viv, send Vaughn in."

A few seconds of silence passed by before the door creaked open again behind Donnie. He turned to see the same frail creature from the lobby he assumed wasn't allowed within five hundred feet of a school walk into the office.

"Ahh, here he is now. Your new partner," Mr. Killian said as he stood up from his desk and pointed his right hand out toward the doorway. "This is Vaughn," Mr. Killian stated as he continued holding his hand out to shake Vaughn's upon his entry into the office.

Vaughn reached out and shook Mr. Killian's hand until his new boss dictated when to let go.

"This guy? You want me to ride shotgun with the spokesman for Subway?"

"Vaughn, this is Donnie. He's an asshole, but if you're gonna learn from anyone it should be this particular asshole."

Vaughn looked to Donnie as an adolescent meeting his long-time idol. He stood still waiting for his new partner to say something, anything, just to acknowledge him. Donnie held back his initial response and instead searched his soul for something less spiteful.

"All right, I guess it's just you and me now," Donnie said while nodding at the new agent in semi-approval.

"Your travel paperwork is with Carl. And try to wrap this one up quick. We're getting behind on our quotas for the month," Mr. Killian added before ushering both to the door.

For the third time now, Stacey's parents threw her into the chaos of a new house in a new neighborhood, going to a new school with new people to either befriend or avoid. The anxious pit carving a stomach ulcer deep inside her frothed at the Déjá vu of her newfound loneliness. Once the heavier goods made their way from the last truck and into corners and closets where they may be opened and sorted or abandoned in an attic as a time capsule, Stacey snuck away into a corner of her new bedroom closest to the outlet. The fresh paint still exhaled fumes of latex and the new LED bulbs her father put in gave a crisp glow from the lavender paint. With her phone still hovering around the twenty percent mark, she remained tethered to the white cord resuscitating her only window to the real world. Somewhere around 7:00 PM she gave up on unpacking her belongings and instead left towers of carboard and mountains of trash bags for another day or another week for that matter. At this particular time in this specific universe, Stacey could not care less about this house, this neighborhood, or what she could only imagine the next house would be.

Amid a text to her friend, a sudden commotion erupted from behind the closet door. A series of tiny collisions and crashes reverberated around the room, as if everything stacked to the top toppled to the ground. The abruptness shook the phone from her hand, punctuating her last sentence to Emma with a nonsensical combination of consonants. Stacey held her breath as she stared at the sealed door imagining what the contents inside might look like.

"What the fuck," she muttered to herself after several deep breaths.

Laying the phone down on the floor, she begrudgingly got up and gripped the door handle.

An avalanche of boxes toppled down upon opening the closet. She looked down at the torn cardboard and lidless containers shaking her head at the abrupt mess. Orange and blue yearbooks broke the seal of one refurbished cardboard box, ripping it open for the remaining contents to spill. She muttered profanity under her breath deciding then that she would not deal with this anytime tonight.

One box remained on the shelf above her clothes rack, one she didn't recognize, one she didn't remember stacking in there with the rest. A thin rectangular container made of archaic white carboard sat untouched from the disaster. With a fresh curiosity settling in the back of her mind, she pulled the box down from the top of her closet. The box was about the size of a board game with decades of dust caked on its surface and no visible markings on the outside, Stacey set it down on the floor by the rubble. Even as her phone dinged with push notifications and messages, the intrigue crawled deeper inside, driving Stacey to pry open the container before doing anything else. She clawed at both sides until she found the seam separating the top half from the bottom and pulled them apart. It gave quickly without any effort almost as if it waited with anticipation for the moment Stacey or anyone else would arrive to liberate what lay inside. She put the lid to the side without looking where it landed, keeping her focus on only the contents within.

Buried inside was a single board with black text on an aged wooden surface. A small wooden teardrop shaped object rested on top. Even through her parents' sheltered defenses, Stacey still knew what this was. The word *Ouija* painted across the top center of the board in time-faded black ink confirmed her suspicions.

She had heard stories from friends at school about what happens when you lay your fingers across it. But like the forbidden fruit of knowledge, something in her brought temptation in droves.

"Hey! Everything ok?" Kathy said, breaking the silence of the room.

The sudden knockless entry startled her, making Stacey hide the open box with her own body. The involuntary decision came from somewhere deep inside where she knew she wanted more time to examine this contraband artifact, and she knew not to let her family see it.

"Yeah, I'm fine," she replied while returning the lid before her mother could see the contents. "I dunno, I guess I didn't stack the stuff in my closet right, and it all fell."

"Ok, just making sure you're ok. Your dad's going to get some take out for dinner. We're all tired and I don't feel like cooking."

"Yeah, that sounds good."

"We found a Chinese place down the road. What do you want him to pick you up?"

"Hmmmm. I dunno. Maybe some shrimp lo mein."

"Ok, well I'll come get you when it's ready."

"Okay."

Kathy exited without closing the door behind her. Like any other day in their previous homes, she never left them shut. Stacey's mother was never an advocate for kids (especially teenagers) having lockable doors. Even when she feigned discretion it remained obvious that she kept tabs on everything in her home.

Keeping with the promise she made to herself, Stacey bulldozed the pile of belongings back into the bottom of the closet. Every bag of clothes and plastic container except for the aged off-white box, was pushed inside. After looking one more time at the door, she decided to tuck the taboo relic under her bed.

If asked why she did it, Stacey would shrug, and maybe say *I'm not sure*. She couldn't find the words to encapsulate the driving impulse. In a home balanced with equal doses of love and protectionist rules, strange things were labeled as prohibited in the name of safety and fealty to their Lord. She didn't have to think about it before acting. A fabled taboo almost fell into her lap and the primal curiosity to explore it in secret won the majority vote.

Removing her phone from its lifeline, she plopped on the worn mattress with its broken springs and began a series of Google searches that would change her life forever. Lying on her back with the phone propped up on her chest, she sounded out the words phonetically as she typed them out. "How…to…use…a…Oui…ja…board?"

"Carl my man, what's happenin'?" Donnie asked the extradition clerk.

An enormous office worker was hunched over behind the desk in front of Donnie. Equally tall as he was thin, the lanky creature curled his back forward almost ninety degrees to bring his face level with the agent. Thin fingers like fattened earth worms danced across a keyboard hidden out of sight. He grumbled and moaned a response only an ear trained in his special dialect could decipher. A guttural, spittle laden collection of consonants stacked illiterately close together spilled from his mouth as he finished his document before sending it to a printer behind him.

"Well, you look like you've lost some weight," Donnie replied.

Carl reached out behind him with comically elongated arms only partially extended and pulled the papers from the top of the stack. He turned and handed the forms to Donnie with a pen chained to his counter.

"Soooo, don't tell anyone I said anything, but I heard a rumor through the grapevine today."

The clerk moved his pale eyes back to Donnie and nodded with a single grunt.

"I heard someone signed up Colin Farrell last week."

Carl let out a low grumble followed by a guttural exhalation.

"No, no, you're thinking of Ethan Hawke," Donnie replied as he ran his fingers over each form looking for the lines in need of his initials. "Colin Farrell played the guy with the target on his forehead in that movie. You know the one where Ben Affleck was a blind lawyer in spandex."

The clerk took the paperwork, shaking his head once more in confusion, before bringing out a stamp from his desk drawer. He muttered another string of saliva filled gibberish before stamping Donnie's travel paperwork as complete.

"And Ben Affleck moonlighted as an angry gymnast. He went around beating up mobsters with a baton until he fell in love with Jennifer Garner, but she was also a ninja. I dunno, the whole thing just fell apart after the second act."

The clerk turned away from Donnie and back to another pile of work behind him. A heaving exhalation followed by another guttural rattle in his throat trailed off as he shook his head at Donnie's gossip.

"Yeah, I know they all look alike," Donnie responded.

Donnie's gossip stopped abruptly as a quick series of footfalls landed behind him. He turned to see Vaughn sprinting down the corridor leading into the terminal. Without the grace needed to stop on a dime, the lanky subject almost toppled over before reaching the counter.

"You up for this, slugger? There's no turning back once we leave."

Vaughn caught himself before tripping any further. He stood upright with newfound confidence, like someone who was prepared to unleash a winded monologue he had been running through in his head for the last hour. He looked Donnie in the eyes with the same self-assured manner before answering.

"I'm ready."

"Because if you're not, now would be the-"

"I said, I'm ready. I'm not waiting anymore for my big break."

Dumbfounded at the sharp response from his new partner, Donnie only nodded his head and motioned him toward the exit.

"So, where do we start?"

Donnie paused for a moment before delivering a response. "Well, let's knock."

The planchette sat idle on the board as Stacey dwelled on what to ask. In the time waiting for her family to pass out from the long day, she took notes from internet videos and researched as many threads on the spirit board until she found the courage.

"Is there anyone here?" she asked just above a whisper.

Nothing moved. She sat in the floor with legs tucked under her, propped up by her shins waiting for something to happen. The clock paused as she lost track of how long she waited. Every thought that passed through her mind in that moment brought more conflict. Her initial knee jerk reaction morphed into how this isn't real, and how it is only a piece of wood with archaic ink. Then that idea went from disappointment into anger at the notion that people like her parents demonized something as trivial as this board game. Why was she sheltered from something so trite and what other harmless things exist on their blacklist? She shook her head at the ludicrous notions, deciding then that this was a stupid idea to begin with.

Stacey removed her right hand from the planchette when it shot out from under her, dragging her left hand with it until the pointed end reached out for the left corner where a single *Yes* rested in black ink. The action spurred every reactionary explanation as she held her fingers over the small tool; *It must have slipped, I moved my arm by accident, the floor is slanted.* Stacey paused before returning the fingers of her other hand to the planchette and bringing it back to the center of the board.

"How many ghosts are here in this house?" she inquired after releasing a deep breath.

Without a second of hesitation the pointer moved again, this time straight into the semi-circled arrangement of letters. It moved over each letter one by one until spelling out the answer. *M A N Y.*

"Did you all die here in this house?" she followed up quickly.

The marker vibrated under her fingertips before sliding up to the right corner before stopping in front of the *No.*

She thought hard for a few moments of cautious reserve before coming up with the next question.

"What do you want?"

Once more the marker sat idle before fidgeting under her tense fingertips. One by one it crept around each symbol of the alphabet before spelling out a reply.

F R I E N D S

"Can you give me a sign that you're real?"

The planchette remained still. Stacey held her breath, waiting. She looked over her shoulder at the darkness behind her, scanning for anything. Her ears strained for whatever came next. But despite her diligence, she could not have prepared herself for what followed. A single knock landed on the floor to her right sending a jerked spasm through her core. A second followed it, driving harder still into the floor to her left. This made her sink into herself, almost ready to curl up into a ball between the two dead blows against the hardwood. The third, final, and loudest came from the center of the board in front of her. Echoes of the reply shifted the planchette around a few degrees before settling back under her fingers. Clutched oxygen held in the base of her lungs burst forth after she teetered on the point of suffocation. She took in another deep breath, concentrating on the nerves running the length of her fingers. With tips firm against the marker, she asked one more question.

"What's your name?"

In tiny increments the planchette flirted with every letter one by one before settling on each individual letter of the answer she demanded.

D O N N I E

The following Wednesday brought an unforseen casualty within the Murdock household. The shrill banshee screams reverberating from down the the hall signaled the death of their water heater. Any plans Richard had that day died with those screams. After finishing half a plate of lukewarm pancakes, he set out for the basement.

Dim beams of natural light penetrated the grime covered windowpanes in the back of the basement as only one fixture responded to the light switch at the top of the staircase. A thick chill radiated within the recesses of the Tudor. Every step Richard descended brought the frost deeper into his body. By the time he reached the chipped floor, the frigid air almost sent him retreating in search of a long sleeve shirt. If it were not for the nagging drive to finish this job quickly, he might have considered it. A heavy musty odor hung in the air, which intensified as he delved deeper toward the unopened moving boxes. Cardboard containers and plastic totes lined the southernmost wall with the usual overflow of a new move: the excess of life that people take for granted until that same life forces them to compile it all into boxes.

Michael Tyree

Behind a mildew-ridden wooden door lay a walled off corner of the Tudor's bowels that contained a small room with just enough square footage for the washer, furnace, and hot water heater. Richard crept through the basement, letting his eyes adjust before opening another door on the other side of the room which led to the dryer and deep freezer. He noted the distance between the washer and dryer and hoped the laundry chore would not fall to him, muttering *not it* to himself in the dark. With both opposite doors thrown wide, a few more rays of light cut the shadows just shy of where he needed to work.

Like many of the skills he picked up over the years, Richard taught himself through tireless trial and error. At an age when memory and learning retention failed him, online tutorial videos pulled him from the maw of failure.

...The first thing you want to check is your heating element. More than likely this is your culprit. It's a pretty easy fix for most models, and not very expensive. Now you're gonna need to locate the drain valve and attach a hose in order to drain your tank before work can begin. You see how this one is down at the bottom of the tank...

"Well, I guess that's easy enough," Richard said to himself as the video trailed on in the background. "Where did we put our garden hose?"

Pausing his video and returning the phone to his pocket, he set out to find a hose and a better source of light. "It might be in the shed? Do we even have a flashlight with good batteries? Probably not."

Leave us alone!

His phone began playing once more from inside his pants pocket. However, the initial audio clip sounded completely different from the repair video he had just been watching.

"What is that?" he muttered to himself while pulling the cellphone from his pocket. Richard held it up expecting to see an unwanted ad playing but found something else he could not explain. Disorientating and heavily blurred, a shaky camera followed two people as they ran from some unknown aggressor. After a few sharp turns and tearful cries, he realized despite his rational skepticism, he was watching a video of Kathy and Stacey sprinting through the house.

The person holding the camera chased them through their living room toward the stairs. Unaware of his body's involuntary reaction, he held his breath before the next shrill scream began, listening to the garbled audio. His family looked horrified and drained of life. Both Kathy and Stacey had lost most of their color. Stacey turned around once to look directly in the camera after they began the ascent to the second floor. Her face brought the air being held hostage in Richard's lungs out of his body. Dark sleepless circles and fresh dried tears bordered her exhausted stare. The scene brought his heart crashing against his ribs as his oldest tripped only to be pulled from the maw of some unknown terror by her mother.

As the camera ascended to the second floor, he lost himself in terror as the two women dashed into the master bedroom and slammed the door shut. Within seconds of the door closing, a pair of fists came into view as they beat on the door without mercy. Both closed hands struck down one at a time until pausing for a brief moment. The camera panned over to the left until a decorative hallway mirror came into view. The clammy skin of his palms loosened the phone as he looked at himself in the reflection staring back at Richard through the phone. His doppelganger peered hard into his soul with deep, dilated, bloodshot eyes. The skin of his face and neck were all drained of color, almost favoring a corpse. The reflection moved its eyes back toward the bedroom door as more commotion came from the two women barricading themselves in, then they returned to the center of the screen. *Attaboy Richard*, it said to him before giving a tiny smirk and a wink.

The phone slid from his palm to the floor with a flat thud. Richard stumbled back into the doorframe, dinging his hip hard on the way through. Hurdling over everything in his way, he sprinted through the basement, until he rounded the corner for the steps so fast, he almost slipped on some spilled detergent on the concrete. Richard took two steps at a time climbing the flight on the way back up to the kitchen.

"Kathy?! Stacey?!" he screamed through the first floor.

No one answered his call, leaving his blood pressure soaring.

"KATHY?!" he screamed again as he came around the corner of the living room too fast and collided with his wife he so desperately searched for. The high-speed crash toppled them both to the ground, along with the overstuffed laundry basket she had been hauling from upstairs.

"What's wrong with you? Is everything ok downstairs?" she said while nursing a fresh bruise on her hip. "Why are you tearing all over the house?"

He paused for a moment while he pushed himself up and gave Kathy a helping hand to her feet. The combinations of answers running through his head made his blood pressure set a new high score. Somewhere in him he wanted to tell her what he thought he saw on the phone. But that notion died quickly as he voted to keep it to himself.

"Everything's fine. I just...I thought I heard some loud noises up here and just...just wanted to make sure everything's ok."

The tension inside the Murdocks' home bubbled and festered with no clear catalyst. Like a dense weight about the air of the Tudor, some invisible agent flooded through the halls, leaving an atmosphere of agitation and malice that evening. Stacey's parents had been known for their screaming competitions in the past, but tonight set a fierce new standard. The argument roared past the thin walls of the master bedroom, finding their way down the hall and into the kids' rooms. Blocking the verbal onslaught with earbuds and secular music, Stacey lounged back in a tattered pink beanbag chair that had been mended through the years with duct tape along broken seams.

Slow and timid at first, Joey cracked open his sister's bedroom door, sticking his face through the separation. The angry sentiment that Stacey usually threw at her younger brother when he barged into her space didn't register this time. In this moment they shared the same anxiety and the need to turn him away didn't occur to her.

"And maybe if you weren't such a bum we wouldn't have put our life savings into this!"

"Bum? My leg…"

"There's nothing wrong with your leg anymore. It's been twenty years since your discharge. You haven't even needed your cane since before Joey was born! You just convince yourself that you're still broken so you don't feel guilty from cashing the government's check. It's been up to me to carry the burden of this family while you're perfectly able to get a real job."

With more venom slung back and forth from behind layers of drywall, Joey crept over to his older sister and collapsed beside the beanbag chair. He didn't have to say a word. She knew how it wore him down as it did her.

"Hey Joey, you wanna go get some ice cream from downstairs?"

He nodded his head as he continued facing the wall that reverberated with profanity. Stacey took her little brother's hand, leading them both away from the brawl.

"Hey, I think I found it," Vaughn said as he flipped through a pile of papers on the kitchen table.

"Let me see," Donnie replied as he took the bill and examined it for himself. "No. We're looking for bank records and mortgage statements. That's a cable bill. And unholy shit! Are these monkeys really paying that much for a hundred channels? What a fuckin' rip off!" Donnie added.

The two infernal bureaucrats scattered the spam folder that was the Murdocks' weekly mail call all about the kitchen, hunting for any information on the adversary. Frustrated their search bore no fruit, Donnie took to the cupboards looking for some mortal pleasures to take his mind off their numbing task. Even under his cool composure, the demon remained a slave to his habitual eating.

"Does it go against their religion to shop from anywhere but Whole Foods?" He added while tearing box after box from the cabinets.

"Wait, this might be it!" Vaughn said.

After excavating a half-eaten box of crackers from above the stove he walked back over to their work in progress. Donnie skimmed over the documents with care as he chewed through a handful of Triscuits. "That's what we're looking for."

"So why go through all this nonsense? I mean, why do you care what they're paying for this shit hole?"

Donnie paused to finish an unappetizing mouthful of wheat crackers.

"Do you play chess?" he replied, leaving a small pause for his partner's reaction. "You always have to think five steps ahead of these primates. I want to know if this move put them in over their heads. The man isn't working, and the woman hasn't been at the new job awfully long, so depending on how much they gambled on this little endeavor should tell us how hard it will be to back them into a corner here. We certainly don't want them moving again."

"Yeah, they kept bringing that up in orientation. I just don't understand why that matters. If they move to another house, we can just follow them there."

"And that, you're gonna find out, is easier said than done," Donnie replied while dumping the remaining Triscuits on the floor, box, and all. "While we're here, we have to mind the boundaries and deal with these chimps around the house. The only way, and I mean the only way you can go outside the property, is to either already be walking around in their skin or attach a piece of yourself to something personal of theirs. And believe me, it is not pleasant or easy. It's basically the nuclear option for this kind of work," he continued while kicking the box across the floor. "Which is why we have to keep them here while we fill our quota."

"Have you ever seen anyone pull it off before?"

Donnie pulled a coupon circular from the pile of mail and flipped through it out of a mix of boredom and curiosity before dropping it to the garbage pile they had accumulated on the kitchen floor.

"Some get away with it, but it's not easy," he replied with a sigh. "It always costs something," Donnie carried the conversation with him as he walked back toward the fridge. He shuffled through the Murdocks' assortment of cereal by smacking each one he didn't like to the floor before grabbing a box of Froot Loops with marshmallows. "I remember back when I first transferred to the DOA, I was shadowing my mentor at the time, Belezame. He was assigned to this real hardass. I mean a real tough nut to crack. He tried everything to work this guy over. I'm talking, everything. Wore him down 'til the guy was so mentally exhausted Belezame just walked right into his body. Then he went to town trying to get that chimp to sign over his

199

soul. But before he could get the signature, something ejected him from the body as this guy was on his way to a jail cell. Belezame knew he couldn't go back to the bosses empty handed, so he did a desperate thing and put a piece of himself in the human's pocket watch."

Donnie paused his fireside chat for a moment as he dumped the box of processed sugar cereal down his throat.

"Well, did it work?" Vaughn said as the anticipation forced his task to a dead halt.

Donnie shot a sideways glance back at the demon and smiled. He held up his index finger as if to motion he would continue the next thrilling chapter when his mouth wasn't full. Leaning back against the fridge, he took a casual posture to finish his story like a troop leader telling a captivating story around the campfire.

"It worked. He stayed on that guy like shit on Velcro for weeks and when it was all said and done, he brought a contract back with him. But…he was never the same after that." Shaking his head at the regretful last chapter, he shoved another fistful of cereal in his mouth before tossing the box to the floor. "Last I heard they transferred him out of the department sometime after that and put him back in the pit. He was one of the most ruthless agents I had ever met. Now he's about as bright as a six pack of dollar store crayons."

The haunting trip down memory lane caught Vaughn off guard. Mulling over the new information, he went back to sifting through more junk mail as Donnie took to excavating the fridge.

"So, what happens if we don't get a signature on the contract? If they get away, well what happens then?" Vaughn asked with a cautious tone that implied he regretted his question as he finished it.

Donnie shut the refrigerator with such force, the remaining boxes of cereal toppled on to the floor in front of him.

"Then these monkeys will probably get their very own episode of some low budget paranormal show on Destination America. And for us, if we're lucky, we'll just get reassigned," Donnie replied as he peeked into the empty living room. "The bosses do not appreciate failure. Which is why we're gonna hit 'em hard and fast, because *I* am not going to the pit just so I can shove pinecones up Mussolini's dickhole for a millennium."

"Did you leave the door open?" Stacey asked as gooseflesh crawled along her muscles with every step closer to the threshold of the kitchen.

"No," Joey replied, shaking his head.

A rustling sound fluttered about ahead of them and just out of sight. With Joey hanging back behind her, Stacey took a cautious posture while approaching the next room. Pungent aromas lashed out at her nostrils from the kitchen ahead. Concentrated odors with aggressive tendencies pushed into her face, forcing her to cover her mouth and nose: cat urine, expired eggs violated with rot and decomposition. The nasal onslaught brought tears just outside the corners of her eyes as the ammonia rich vapor scraped her eyes.

Keeping her younger brother behind her, Stacey edged closer while regretting the decision to do so. She turned in shock and awe as an icy current blew through the kitchen in her direction, scattering papers and debris across the table and floor. Cabinet doors caught in the invisible wind slammed back against their hinges with violent intent. One hyperventilated deep breath inwards brought Stacey reeling back against the counter. As the concentrated stench of rot pushed past her nostrils and filled her lungs with the choking toxicity, the bile in her throat rose to its tipping point. Still shielding Joey, the stench landed blow after blow to her gut, buckling her in the middle. Joey grabbed onto

201

her waist tight burying his face in the back of her shirt as a swarm of cereal boxes took flight and propelled themselves toward the Murdock children. The first two missed their mark while the third crashed into Stacey's forehead with such malice it split the seam releasing off brand Cocoa Puffs all over the floor.

With blinding pain burning across her face, Stacey turned with one eye open and ran from the kitchen with Joey in tow. The calamity behind them continued through the kitchen while they bolted through the living room and out onto the front porch. Stacey and Joey kept running until they reached the front yard. The levee holding Joey's tears back burst open wide. Without the courage to look back at their home, Joey could only sob into his sister's embrace while the crashing of dinnerware and glasses fired off from inside.

Standing on the barren sidewalk still locked in terror, something soft crashed to the ground behind her, followed by a series of scratches on the concrete. Before she could turn around to investigate, another landed behind her followed by a soft plop smacking the top of her head and writhing around in her hair. She squirmed in disgust and swatted at her brown locks until whatever it was fell to the ground in front of her. There on the sidewalk lay a blue jay fluttering in its death throes. Looking as confused and frightened as its spectators, the fowl let out one more shallow winded chirp before resting its head on the pavement. Stacey looked all around her in horror as more plummeted to their deaths from the sky a dozen at a time.

Late night recaps of this week's baseball games played through the background as Richard negotiated with sleep on his throne. A dusty, sun-faded La-Z-Boy complete with unidentifiable stains from Joey's toddler years cradled him as he battled against his drooping eyelids.

"Help, Dad," Joey spoke in a low pitch from the kitchen.

The call peeled Richard's eyelids back with a sobering momentum, which brought a deep yawning breath into his lungs. Frustrated at the abrupt use of his muscles after being called from a numbing cat nap, Richard rolled himself forward in the chair.

"Son, what are you doing up out of bed so late? It is way past your bedtime," Richard responded as he stepped into the kitchen.

Joey stood at the top of the basement steps with his head down locked on the darkness laying ahead of him. With nothing radiating out of the pit at his feet, only the single lightbulb over the stovetop threw any light on his back. Somewhere between his bed and here Joey had slipped out of his Looney Tunes pajamas and replaced them with dirty jean shorts and a tee he had worn earlier that day.

"Son! What are you doing? I know your mom didn't put you to bed in that mess. Come on, you need to get back to sleep," Richard said.

"Dad. Dad, will you help me find my baseball glove?" Joey asked while maintaining his posture.

"No, Joey. It's too late for that right now. We'll look for it tomorrow, ok?"

Richard stepped over and put a hand on his shoulder to turn him around, but the boy wouldn't budge. Tugging a little harder, he pulled at Joey in frustration before releasing his futile hold.

"Son, I'm not playing around. We're not going down there, and you need to get to bed right-"

Joey interrupted his father's scolding by leaping down the abysmal stairway, melding with the void. A quick pitter patter of footfalls sounded off in the darkness before resonating against cold concrete.

Michael Tyree

"JOEY! Come back here!" Richard yelled as he followed behind.

Fixtures ignored the commands of their switches as Richard struggled to find a source of light in the basement. Stepping with care through the murk, he reached into his pocket for a phone that was not there, bringing the desperation bubbling to the surface. His echolocation failed him once his feet hit the concrete. The din of children's feet ceased, leaving him wandering blind with arms outstretched ahead of him.

"Joey? Son, this isn't funny. Come on out now."

Nothing answered him but the faint echo of his own voice bouncing back against the hardened walls. Obstacles that brought Richard to his knees became landmarks in the darkness. A plastic tote stopped him in his tracks somewhere near the archaic floral pattern sofa Kathy wanted him to throw out before they moved. A stack of boxes to his left threw him off course where his hip collided with a ping pong table that should have also found a new home in a donation center.

"Dad. Dad, help me. Help me find it," Joey cried out from deeper in the bowels of the home.

"Joey, come back here right now!"

After several pleas, Richard ran the maze of the downstairs from the largest room being taken up with boxes and junk, all the way through the washroom and back around to a nonfunctioning shower stall that served as low-income housing for several species of arachnids. A feral prepubescent scream bellowed out from the base of the stairs before carrying back up into the kitchen. He rounded the corner to the base of the steps just in time to see Joey land at the top of the flight. Vague light from the kitchen backlit the young boy leaving a dark silhouette towering down over Richard. Without turning back, he darted out of sight into the kitchen as the door slammed shut behind him and entombed his father in total darkness. The abrupt loss of light handicapped Richard's eyes even further. In his miscalculated haste to follow Joey, the bottom three steps tripped him, sending Richard flying to his palms and knees.

"Damnit!" he screamed.

He jumped back up with bruised shins pulsing down his legs. He raced back up the stairs, but as he did, the air became more frigid with each step. As he reached the top, he could see his breath forming in front of his face while the prick of frost nipped at his skin. He reached out for the handle just to find it ice cold and frozen shut. The unforgiving temperature of the doorknob bit at the skin of his palm. He could only hold his grip on it for a few seconds at most before retracting it in pain. He resorted to using part of his shirt as a buffer between his skin and the handle, but even still the pin pricks found their way through the cotton and stung him. He wrestled with the cold steel solidified in place as the frost emanating from its core seared his palms.

"Joey! Open this door right now!"

Richard screamed and commanded as he wrenched the knob in futility. Ice nipped his skin until he could hold the door no longer. In another frustrated attempt, he slammed both fists in unison. As he connected both blows, the door finally gave up its ghost, flying open against its hinges and sending him tumbling to the beige linoleum. From his hands and knees, an amber light danced across the floor ahead of him. He lurched his head upwards until his gaze fell on the scene set on his behalf. Kathy, Stacey, and Joey all stood side by side with their arms hung low in a relaxed comatose posture. A roaring conflagration soared up past the kitchen windows casting orange light in an explosion all around the room from the outside. Deep backlit shadows from the flames wrapped around the faces of his family as they all grimaced at him. A low hiss sounded off to his left while a burst of flames shot up from the stovetop licking the cabinets above with fire. The blaze took off around the counters and cabinets like a stock car starting beside him and soaring around the room until the inferno surrounded the Murdock clan.

Kathy took a few steps forward and stopped in front of her husband, who was still wrenched over on his palms and knees. He mustered what little courage he still had and stood on his feet. The mandarin light exploded through the house, blanketing everything in the kitchen, and leaving his family with hellish accents painted across their skin.

"You did this," she said, looking through him with an emotionless stare.

"What?"

"You did this, Richard."

Without a precursor, Joey burst into flames screaming behind Kathy, followed by Stacey. The incineration ate the flesh from muscle in seconds and lit the subsequent tissue and organs melting under the hellfire. Stacey's eyes liquified from the searing heat, seeping from her sockets and down her cheekbones. The inner workings designed by her Creator were now undone as flame peeled back layers of vital organs now. Joey's legs buckled against his own weight as the cataclysm tearing his form apart devoured him alive. The boy dropped to his knees in forfeit as the incineration ran through every orifice.

While Richard's spine locked rigid as a steel cord at the horror show playing out before his eyes, Kathy moved out of his line of sight over to the kitchen island where she retrieved a small, curved paring knife from the block. Stepping back in front of her husband, she leaned over and rested her forehead against his with eyes clenched shut in a simple gesture of affection.

"You did this," she said again before plunging the knife under her left ear and dragging it through the flesh of her neck all the way to her right ear, spilling her life from the gaping laceration stretched across her throat.

"NOOOOO!" Richard screamed as he placed his hands around her throat in futility.

With no more words able to escape her lips, Kathy's mouth hung open as her release painted his hands a warm cherry tone. Blood ran between his calloused fingers until it trickled down his wrists and forearms. Her body gave up the high ground as her lifeless form slipped through his outstretched palms down to the floor.

Taking several steps back from the shock, Richard reached back to find the wall. But instead, the wall took in a deep breath and released hot, putrid air down the back of his neck. Whatever stood behind him placed a tattered leathery hand on the back of his neck and anchored his head in place. The other found his right arm as it brought his hand up in front of his face. A large shadow stepped out of his peripheral and stopped just in front of him. It blotted out the multiple raging fires, leaving Richard frozen in its presence. A mass of smoke loomed over seven feet tall, draped in a shawl of darkness with only two burning embers where its eyes should be. The figure held out its arm and snapped its fingers as a tattered scroll materialized in front of him. Smoky lines of illegible text formed from left to right all the way down the page where a thin black line dashed across the bottom with a small X at the end. The immovable force behind Richard twisted his arm at the elbow until it brought his hand just in front of the scroll. He fought against it but gained no ground as the beast held him in place without mercy. The figure draped in backlit shadow turned its head to the side revealing a pair of blackened ram horns. It continued looking off to the side until someone else joined him before Richard. Suddenly, Kathy was reanimated and walked out in front of her husband with the paring knife still in her hand and blood cascading down her blouse. She reached out to grasp his palm in hers. With her left-hand, Kathy pressed her thumb into his palm and wrapped her fingers around the top of

207

it holding his fingers up to the ceiling. She produced the knife and brought it up to his index finger.

"Nooo!"

She raised the curved talon blade above his nail and pulled it down to the underside of his second knuckle in tiny increments. Size meant nothing here as the small blade lacerating his finger almost brought him to the ground with pain. Still holding his hand, which was now gushing from his index finger, Kathy pulled it over to the piece of paper floating in front of them both.

"No," he cried out again in protest.

With otherworldly strength, she contorted his finger until the tip pointed toward the line seared in the contract. With manageable resistance from her husband, she took hold of the twisted pointer finger and began signing his name with the crimson fountain pen.

Richard K. Murd…

Cold sweat poured over clammy skin as Richard shot up out of bed. He looked over to his left to find Kathy still lying beside him in bed. His heart pounded against his ribcage like a heavyweight contender.

"Bad dream?" a deep voice whispered in his direction.

Richard pressed his sweaty back against the headboard as he held his breath in terror and anticipation. Pale moonlight seeped into the bedroom through sheer curtains. The shadows at the foot of the bed swirled about the room with two fluttering shapes stretched up to the ceiling, tattered and flailing like shredded black flags flying in all directions over rolling black water. Nothing in the void just inches from his feet stood still. Somewhere in the sloshing shadows lay two sets of small tangerine-colored lights. The two tiny pairs of lights floated with several feet between them. Taking a hyperventilated breath in, Richard closed his eyes under outstretched palms. He removed them to find the shadows melted away, leaving the nighttime atmosphere as he knew it until something blocked the light from his window. He turned his head as one pair of lights glowed above him before floating down to eye level. Layers of yellow and deep red had encircled the orange lights. They extinguished themselves and then reignited before he realized that something just blinked at him. Two razor tipped fingernails snagged his top lids before pulling them down over his eyes. He winced as the scraping drew blood which ran to his nose.

"Night night, sweet prince," the voice hissed at him after loosening the two fingertips from his eyelids.

Richard kept them shut as a fluttering sound took off around the room before falling silent once more.

"THIS DIDN'T HAPPEN ON ITS OWN!" Kathy screamed as she took in the chaos scattered across the kitchen. "All this wasted food. All this trash."

"Mom, I'm telling you we didn't do this! Joey and I-"

"Joey and you what? Do you hear yourself? Do you hear how crazy that sounds?"

Stacey didn't reply. Instead, she waited in silence as she put together her already failing counter argument. She pleaded with her mother to believe her, but even with her brother's alibi, nothing could prove they didn't trash the house.

"I can help clean it up…" Stacey added as she bent down around the largest pile of bills, scooping them up in her arms.

"You've *helped* enough," Kathy blurted out. "Just go take your brother out of here. I'll deal with this before your father sees it."

She didn't argue with the absurd command. With bubbling animosity held tight under her skin, she turned and walked away before countering with something that she might regret later. The fire roaring in her face turned into a blaze of blushed pink skin and unblinking eyes. Joey caught sight of the look on his sister's face as she passed through the living room and hunkered beside the recliner.

"Come on, Joey. Let's get out of here before she starts up again," she murmured while passing him.

"KEEP TALKING BACK AND SEE WHERE THAT GETS YOU! YOU'RE ALREADY IN ENOUGH TROUBLE!" Kathy bellowed out from the kitchen.

Kathy let out a frustrated exhalation before tightening her fingers around the broom handle until her knuckles whitened like the finger bones beneath. Muttering angry nonsense under her breath, she picked a corner of the room and began sweeping everything into the center.

"That really didn't take much to wind them up," Vaughn added as he took a seat at the table facing the matriarch of the Murdock family.

"It never does," Donnie replied while leaning against a counter covered in broken crackers and cereal. "You just have to get that first domino to tip." He wrapped his fingers around the stained brass drawer handle and teased it with a slight pull. Not enough to open it, but enough to make a tiny audible noise from the steel track inside. "Now, I'm about to teach you something you won't learn in orientation," Donnie added.

Vaughn raised his eyebrows at his partner's baited statement. "Ok, I'm all ears."

Donnie smiled wide at his response, leaving a few teeth showing through his parted lips.

"I like to call this one: *These are not the droids you're looking for.*"

Kathy sunk to her knees and scooped up what she could into neat piles. She painstakingly sifted through the debris for common denominators. The silverware lay scattered all about the

210

floor, mixed in with emptied cereal boxes, mail shredded like confetti, and the contents of their trash can. She piled the bills and other mail in a stack to be sorted through later, and then put together the knives, forks, and spoons in fistfuls, dumping them into the sink. Kathy pawed at the few things she could consolidate, but every time she looked around her the task became more daunting.

"Why would they do this?" she asked herself.

A shuffling noise from behind her drew Kathy's attention to the reflection in the window just above the sink. She looked up to see a silhouette in the glass standing just within the threshold of the door leading into the living room.

"I know what you're gonna say...I already yelled at them for it," she said. She hung her head in exhaustion, propping herself up over the counter. Kathy could only imagine the argument spawned from this morning's mess. After last night's run through the Thunderdome she wished to avoid another. Preparing herself for whatever response he had, Kathy gritted her teeth and turned around to face him. "Look, I..."

Richard had vanished from the doorway. "Richard?" she asked before walking to the edge of the kitchen. She peeked around the corner to find the living room completely empty. "Richard?" she belted out again.

Before she could attempt to summon him once more, a soft thud landed behind her and broke Kathy's concentration with a startling jolt. She turned to find every single cabinet flung wide open, every drawer pulled out to its limit, and even the fridge doors flung open against their hinges. Her breath stalled out somewhere in the middle of her chest. It hung there not moving between inhalation or exhalation. Her heart ramped up at the illusionist trick before her eyes. All this transformed with inhuman speed and stealth which left her looking over her shoulder multiple times before stepping back into the room in order to see it closer.

"How did…what…" she whispered to herself. With every query another hyperventilated breath formed and edged her toward a breakdown.

The eerie silence broke once more as a single ping fired off behind Kathy and made her jump and spin around. A single butter knife rested on the floor, one of many she had scooped up earlier and placed into the sink.

"But how did…" her statement was cut short as several pointed tips struck her in the back of the skull. "OOOOWWW."

Grabbing the back of her head, she sidestepped to the left. Kathy looked up to find every knife, fork, and spoon lodged into the ceiling above her.

"That…can't be," she whispered to herself before backing up toward the sink. Through every movement her eyes never left the collection of stainless cutlery embedded in the ceiling. The early morning light dancing across the steel left a hypnotizing aura. Still watching the display above her, Kathy reached back into the sink behind her with her right hand only to find it cleared out to the strainer. A few fluttered beats fired off before the bass drum in her chest accelerated into pounding thumps against her ribcage. She turned to see what her fingertips discovered first: the sink lay bare.

A few weeks went by since Stacey and Joey failed to convince their parents that they were not responsible for the kitchen catastrophe. The kids never talked about the evening in the kitchen or the dozens of dead birds plummeting from the heavens. They did their best to let that memory wither and die with other unwanted knowledge, but that experience, however strange, would be a mild encounter compared to what their unwanted guests had in mind.

Everyone in the house gained experiences they dare not discuss with others for fear they would not be believed. Missing items were written off as absent-mindedness, abnormal shadows in the twilight were justified as optical illusion, fatigue, and anything between. Everyone assumed the same thing: *if I tell Mom…Dad won't believe me…Richard will think I'm just losing my mind.* The truth is no one member of the Murdock clan knew who had the worst experience. They would not arrive at that realization until the coming days when a darkness all too familiar to 6023 Walnut Street would show its true face.

Joey lay awake in his bed for the fourth time that week. Sleep was a luxury in the Murdock home as night terrors and cold sweat became a cornerstone. The worst heat wave of the summer had reared its sweltering head over the last week and today it led into an overcast shroud throbbing for release. The afternoon sat on the cusp of a torrential downpour and thunderstorm. Small flashes of light came to life every few minutes through Joey's bedroom window. The crack of thunder crashing in the distance accompanied them, growing closer in repetition every time. The dusk to dawn light in the side yard molded visceral shadow puppets against the carpet and wall with the help of a lone Sycamore tree. As Joey lay there hypnotized in dread of the branches that sent skittering shadows across his floor, he almost made out the silhouette of a person swinging from one near the bottom.

As the digital clock taunted him throughout the night, Joey began to doze off; however, every time he came close, another clap of thunder shook the boy awake. In his drowsy state he suddenly became aware of a small, motorized din coming from the other side of the room. Somewhere in the darkness the low whirring continued its revolutions while Joey held his breath from fear. After a few more moments, he reached over and rolled the switch to his nightstand lamp without taking his eyes from where the noise in question originated. The incandescent bulb threw a warm yellow light on a tall bookshelf crammed with pop up books, Bibles, stuffed animals, and other knickknacks. Joey didn't flinch. He remained frozen with his eyes fixated on the shelf, and still no more clues as to the origin of the sound. Another thunderclap crashed closer to the house, shaking his concentration, and instilling more dread.

The sound came from the tape deck inside Joey's Buddy Wellington toy. He had begged his parents all year for one when he was five. He couldn't contain the excitement when he found him propped up underneath the Christmas tree that year. He was a stuffed bear in blue and yellow overalls with a cassette player in his back. The toy had interactive tapes that when played would ask questions about science, math, and history. However, Kathy never purchased anymore of the tapes other than the one that came with him. Joey only ever had kiddy hymnals and other Christian music to entertain him and Buddy.

The sound continued winding faster and faster until it came to a stop at the beginning. Then after a few seconds, a second click was heard as the cassette began playing.

Jesus loves me...

The song started in grinding intervals, like a record played on an RPM a third of what it needed to be audible. The verses screeched into each other with a low guttural rumble.

Thiiis I knoow, fooooor theee Biiiiiblllle teellls mee sooo. Liiiiiittlllleee oooonneees toooo hiiimm beeeloooong.

Thheee aaaaarrrrrre WEEEEEEEAAAAAAAKK.

The stanza crawled to a halt as the vowels clawed and pierced his eardrums.

"STOP IT! LEAVE ME ALONE!" Joey screamed at his favorite childhood toy.

The Buddy Wellington began shaking back and forth on the shelf, knocking over other toys and books until it toppled to the floor and continued to seize face down on the carpet.

"I'm not scared of you!" Joey dared to say aloud. "I'm...not...scared of you," he said once more at almost a whisper.

Another clap of thunder hit and the lights in the house fizzled out for a few seconds, flooding everything in darkness once more. When they came to life again, the toy sat upright at the foot of his bed. Positioned toward the window, it began inching around until it faced him. The tape engaged again, or at least it made the sound of the tape mechanism starting back up.

Yeeeeeeeessss youuuuuuu aaaarrrrrrrre.

The bear responded in a low growl. Every mechanism in the toy sounded as if it were at the point of complete failure. A grinding, screeching, whirring commotion arose from the bowels of Buddy Wellington following the drawn-out taunt. Then once again it began seizing. Its arms and legs flailed about while its head contorted, while it held the last syllable for almost a minute. Then a burst of flames shot from the center of its chest as a plume of smoke rose from the cotton toy.

"MOOOOOOOM! DAAAAAAD!" he screamed while leaping from the bed and to the door.

No sooner than he had put his hand around the handle, both parents burst into the room.

"JESUS!" Richard screamed as he jumped over to the bed and smothered the toy with a blanket.

He wrapped it tight and took it to the floor, stomping the flames that were now tearing at the fabric of Joey's comforter. Without being prompted to, Kathy had acted alone and retrieved the fire extinguisher from the kitchen.

"STAND BACK," she commanded so she could get a clean shot of the toy's funeral pyre.

It went out just as quickly as it had ignited, leaving a blackened circle on Joey's area rug.

The last straw split down its center as Kathy dragged her child's charred area rug to the trash can. She fought what she had seen and felt with her ingrained skepticism over the last few weeks. But on that day the latter lost. Despite Richard's blind denial of the house's quirks, Kathy accepted the things she could not explain. For the first time she feared for her family at the hands of things she could not define. Breaking with her husband, she began calling churches for help. Going through everybody within a hundred miles belonging to her own faith, she branched out and sought the help of Catholics, Lutherans, and even Spiritualists. Several hours passed as phone book and Google search resources began drying up. With nothing to show for her efforts, Kathy almost gave up before contacting a priest by the name of Sandoval, the only holy man to take her problem with the utmost urgency. He listened to every detail offered before suggesting she meet with some colleagues of his that had *experience with these things*. He took her name and number and said that he would put her in touch with the right people as soon as possible.

The next hurdle came the following day when Kathy informed her cynical husband, who was still trying to rationalize the incinerated children's toy, that she had taken matters into her own hands. The usual spat ensued, and Richard was left feeling emasculated, walling himself up in his own anger. As far as he concerned himself, if there was a problem here, it was up to him to find the cure with his own will. After hours of screaming and a few internally reflective moments taking in the smoke damage to his son's room, he conceded and accepted the help offered to them by the priest.

Hellen leaned back against the driver side door of her Buick and took another deep inhalation of nicotine as the Marlboro burned near its filter. The good folk of Chesterfield came out in their Sunday best to mingle with their fellow believers. Some were here for the fellowship and worship, some just for appearance, while others did what they needed to secure their fire insurance. As the congregation funneled into the big double doors, a few older patrons would sometimes look over to her finishing the cigarette with what she interpreted as calculated judgement. Hellen never associated with any of them in any real sense of the term. If she were honest with herself for a change, she would admit that the only reason she came to service anymore was to see Mateo Sandoval, or as anyone with a shred of respect for the church hierarchy called him, Father Sandoval. Her faith in the church had deteriorated over the ages leaving her in a loveless relationship with theology. Like a failed marriage well past its expiration date, coasting along, waiting to die of natural causes, Hellen continued going through the motions of a regular believer. She believed (or at least wanted to believe) that if she faked it long enough, one day she would find the fire in her heart one more time.

The early morning rays danced along the stained-glass windows of St. Florence leaving ruby and sapphire shimmers about the face of the grand cathedral. The fresh manicured grass was still wet with dew. A bell rang out with ten reverberating dins back-to-back, overpowering the ambient noise of good Christians flocking down the sidewalk and alerting those in earshot that service would begin soon.

Michael Tyree

As was tradition, Hellen found herself a nice seat in the back of the sanctuary away from most of the other regulars. Somewhere she could hear the sermon without a child kicking the back of the pew. Hellen once loved the God of the people with all her heart, but the people of God were another matter altogether. After the seats began filling up and the doors closed, the music minister, Thomas O'Neil, began leading the congregation in several hymns that Hellen halfway mouthed the words to while she daydreamed of just about anything else. The half-hearted sing along took almost twenty minutes to power through before Father Sandoval began this week's sermon, which was not lacking the hellfire and brimstone.

"Good morning, everyone," Father Sandoval addressed his flock. "I hope everyone has had a good week." He took a pause to clear his throat and open up a binder across his podium before beginning this week's sermon.

"My friends…the Devil's agents walk among us." He took in another deep breath before continuing. "They hide in plain sight waiting with bated breath for the opportunity to strike us down. They are the fallen ones, those who loyally followed Satan in his insurrection against the throne. And their determination to follow their master's will is unrivaled. They seek to destroy mankind at any cost. They cheat, steal, lie, and kill. They use any tools at their disposal to deceive us from the one true path. But we must never fear evil, for the Lord our God is with us always. He is our sword and our shield. He is our champion in the shadow of death!" Father Sandoval exclaimed to fanfare and amens.

After an intense sermon full of theatrics, the good folk found their way to the exit and back to their clockwork sin. A small line of the more devout spoke with Father Sandoval on their way out the door. Hellen observed them all at a safe distance while she brought another cigarette up to her lips. Occasionally the priest would break eye contact with those seeking rapport with the man upstairs and gaze over at his old lover. After he waved off the last straggler, Father Sandoval quickly strode toward her with a wide smile across his face.

"Hellen, how has your week been?"

"Just fine. I went back to Dr. Pond on Tuesday about my knee. Even after the therapy, the damn thing still doesn't feel right. I'm afraid they're going to say I need another surgery," Hellen replied as she shook her head.

"Well, you remember what I had to go through with my shoulder. I honestly believed it would never heal. To be honest it still bothers me from time to time."

Mateo turned so he could rest his back up against Hellen's car while standing beside her. He pulled a soft pack of Camels from inside his pants pocket and slid one out.

"I actually need to talk to you," he said while lighting the cigarette. "I spoke with a woman earlier this week that is having some...problems."

"What kind of problems?"

"The kind that you and your colleagues might want to look into."

Hellen looked at him with a piqued curiosity as she took a heavy drag.

"Well, it can't be as bad as Charleston."

With the mid-day sun glaring on his features, Mateo squinted as he knocked off a lump of ash from the end of his cancer stick. He shrugged and looked concerned as he prepared his response.

"Honestly...I think it might be worse than that."

Hellen didn't know how to respond to that as she imagined a situation that dire. She just finished her cigarette in silence and put it out with the bottom of her Value Barn dress shoes.

"Here," he said as he handed her a folded piece of paper. "You should call them as soon as you can. I think they're going to need your help."

Mateo grimaced as he ran the mental gambit of his vocabulary searching for the right way to start the next sentence. Hellen noticed his hesitation immediately.

"You look pale. Are you feeling all right?"

"No. Actually I'm not. I haven't felt right all week. I wanted to call you as soon as I had spoken with this person, but I just couldn't find the words. I didn't think it was something to talk about over the phone. Then I thought I would see you today, and well...it would be better left in person."

Hellen tucked the paper into her purse and turned to face him with a look of concern.

"What is it?"

"It's just...the lady I spoke with. She told me what was going on and how long it had been going on for. Then I asked her for their address..."

Hellen crossed her arms in impatience and shook her head at him. "What is it? Just tell me."

"It's...the family that called me...they moved into Megan's old house on Walnut."

She crushed another cigarette butt into a maroon porcelain ash tray as an abrupt series of coughs erupted from her chest. She had spent the last few hours chain smoking since setting to her task of researching 6023 Walnut Street. The face of the Tudor brought a frigid shiver down her back as newspaper articles and obituaries flooded her monitor. Even in the last months of her senior year and that following summer, she avoided that part of the street at all costs. Flashbacks of Megan standing in the window followed by her cold body being wheeled out in a black bag wormed into her present thoughts. PTSD flashes came and went when the subject came around (which she avoided as well). But now another family was living there. Hellen summoned up every ounce of courage in her bones to do something she had not dared attempt in thirty-seven years. With a breath held tight in her chest and a catch in her throat, she searched for information surrounding the night Megan and her mother passed away. Every article and paper came back with the same headline: *Double Murder/Suicide*. That's how the media presented it. Megan had refrained from discussing Tony if she could help it. She only brought up his name a few times in passing while he lived with her mom. Hellen always had her suspicions, but never knew where to go with the information. She said nothing, then when Megan and Patricia rode away from the house the last time in a coroner's van, everyone suddenly wanted to put in their two cents.

With bloodshot eyes, Hellen stepped away from the computer with as much information as she could retain for the evening. Despite her anxiety, she knew she had to make the call before it was too late in the evening; however, nervous procrastination twisted her arm every time she worked up the nerve. Instead, she distracted herself with something else. Stepping over her two fur babies, Patches and Silk, she stopped herself in front of an antique bookcase of her mother's. The bottom had ornate built-in cabinets with decades of forgotten treasures and junk piled to the front. She pulled a box from it and unearthed two scrap books, a snow globe, a cookbook of her grandmother's she had forgotten about, and three yearbooks with over thirty years of dust on the covers. Retrieving a gold and purple book with *Class of 1981* embossed on the front in black, she retired to the couch. Hesitation delayed her, making her question if what she set out for was the right choice. Staring at the cover and running her hands across it, she wondered if she should just put it back into her forgotten box of goodies. But she couldn't do that, she wouldn't. Putting another cigarette to her lips she cracked open the pandora's box laying across her lap. Flipping through black and white memories of old friends and lovers, acquaintances and enemies, mentors and tutors, she skimmed through the senior photos from that year. There on page eighty-seven Megan Moore smiled at her with a toothy grin wrapped in corrective braces. Hellen smiled back with a Marlboro hanging from her lips.

"Oh, that sweater," she said, remarking at the ugly cardigan her mother made her wear for picture day.

The walk down memory lane took its toll on her in increments. As tears began welling up in the corners of her eyes, she shut the book and set it aside. After enough time went by for Hellen to compose herself, she retrieved the folded scrap of notebook paper and her phone. Under normal circumstances this call wouldn't give her anxiety, but this was different. This house was different. The phone cycled through so many rings that she began to wonder if anyone would pick up. Before she could end the call, an out of breath woman picked up the other end.

"...I'm sorry. Hello?"

"Hi, is this Kathy?"

"Yes. May I ask who's calling?"

"This is Hellen. Mateo Sandoval gave me your number. He told me you and your family are having some strange things going on in your home and thought I could help you."

"Oh! Yes, I was wondering when I would hear from you."

"Yeah, sorry it took so long to get back with you. Can you tell me about the strange things going on in your house?"

"Umm...I think everyone in the house has seen something strange here, but I can only really tell you about what I've seen. Umm..."

"It's ok. Just take your time."

"Right. Well, it all started off with odd things here and there. Stuff went missing, doors would shut on their own, weird sounds in the *night. But the other week…" Kathy trailed off for a moment before finishing her sentence. "Whatever this is tried to attack my youngest child while he slept."*

"Is he ok?"

"Yes, he's just shaken up. But I didn't know what else to do, so I just started calling everyone until I reached your friend."

"Look, it's going to be ok. My friends and I will help you get through this. It'll take a few days to get everyone together, but will your family be free this weekend for us to come by and look at the house?"

"Yes! Yes, we'll be here. The sooner you can come by the better."

Orange and red light flashed through the windows of the Department of Acquisitions break room with the rise and fall of magma. The mini cafeteria's insulation left the usual cries of the damned at a minimum acoustic level. Donnie and Vaughn sat next to a window overlooking Pandemonium's largest river. The living flames carried countless punished souls downstream as they drowned perpetually in the fire.

"Mmmm. These are great ribs today," Donnie said.

"Yeah, we never had grub like this in the call center cafeteria," Vaughn replied.

Donnie picked up his plate and waltzed back to the other side of the room. There a bruised, naked human hung from the ceiling by his ankles with his wrists chained together. Donnie laid his plate down on the counter and picked up a pair of stainless tongs encrusted with blood and bile. He opened them up and brought them together with a clamp around what remained of the person's ribcage. With a snap he broke the last four ribs loose from his right side.

The tortured soul screamed in agony.

"I know. Mondays, am I right?" Donnie asked.

"Hey, while you're over there can you grab me a little more?" Vaughn inquired.

"Sure."

Donnie laid down the tongs and picked up an eight-inch kitchen knife. He then inserted the blade sideways at the man's hip and sliced down to his shoulders, peeling back a sheet of flesh and muscle. He folded it up onto his plate and brought it back to the table.

"Where were you assigned before this?" Donnie asked

"Oh, I was in the call center before the transfer. That's all I've ever done," replied Vaughn. "I used to hear stories about demons like you. I thought, well maybe one day I'd get my shot."

"I worked there, too, for a little while," replied Donnie.

"Really?"

"Oh yeah. Everyone starts there at first. But it's not like it was back in the day. When they dropped me in there, it was a whole different ball game," Donnie paused for a moment to shovel a forkful of barbecue in his mouth before continuing. "See humans used to take it seriously. Very seriously. When you got a call from someone, they did it with respect and reverence. They paid tribute to our Lord Lucifer and never hesitated with sacrifice. And usually all they wanted in exchange for loyalty was some trite tokens to their own vanity: eternal beauty, dominance over the opposite sex, long life, blah, blah, blah. Sometimes you might get a Druid, or some other pagan that dialed the wrong person, but usually it was an easy gig," Donnie replied.

"I've never had to deal with any of those," Vaughn interjected with an envious tone. "Nothing but spirit boards."

Donnie's eyes widened as he passionately nodded his head in agreement for the first time with his new partner. "I know, right? Fuckin' spirit boards." Donnie dropped his fork on the table in disgust. "Ever since the first Ouija board, all we ever get anymore are these entitled little shits that wanna talk to their meemaw or Kurt fuckin' Cobain," Donnie exclaimed as he shook his head in disgust. "It just takes the fun out of it, ya know." The demon got up from his chair, walked over to the window, and peered out over the burning river churning with lost souls. He let out a deep sigh from his fondest memories of nostalgia. "And it seems like every few years it gets worse and worse. Like thirty, forty years ago you'd crash a slumber party where kids just acted like kids. They weren't making themselves dumber than they already were with technology." He shook his head as a few particularly loud shrill cries made their way up to their floor. "Last month I was working a job in Vermont. I had been in the house for a few weeks, feelin' things out. Then the family's oldest kid decided to have a sleepover with some of the neighbor's kids. Do you know what those little shitheads were doing most of the night?"

Vaughn just shrugged his shoulders as he wished he had a witty response to further gain his mentor's approval.

"They all sat around on their phones taking Buzzfeed quizzes. One girl stared at her iPhone for fifteen fuckin' minutes just to figure out what kind of potato she was."

Donnie moved away from the window as the gurgled drowned screams ushered him back to his seat.

"I got to be honest with you. I've never been much on working with others. Just not my style. And you, well I thought I had you figured out before we started this gig. I thought you would just slow me down and fuck this all to pieces. But I...well I was wrong," he said reluctantly. Donnie went back to finishing the last of his plate before eating his own words about his new partner. "That thing with the stuffed animal, that was original.

This whole thing worked out better than I thought, and I haven't had this much fun on the job in a while."

"AWWW," Vaughn replied sarcastically. "Why don't you tell me how you really feel."

Instantly regretting his attempt at an apology, Donnie met the ridicule with eye rolls. He cleared his throat hard before adjusting his tone once more. "All that aside, what comes next is going to be a lot harder than what we've been doing. Everything up until now has been used to soften them up, divide and conquer if you will. The next steps we take are gonna call for some ingenuity, some quick thinking, and some ruthlessness. Today is the day your training wheels come off and the teeth come out."

Less than ten minutes away from the house, Hellen's nerves caught fire. The country had swapped out several two-term presidents since the last time she walked down Walnut Street. Before this morning, her understanding of it existed only as a distant memory. Now the old neighborhood stared her in the face, daring Hellen to come closer. She almost lost her direction in a new traffic circle splitting Winchester and Duncan, then found her true north once she recognized some older houses in the surrounding neighborhoods. Despite the new businesses moving in and the older houses going under reconstructive facelifts, a few others welcomed her back while some warned her to stay away. Even though it added another two minutes to the drive, she passed by Mateo's old house for nostalgia's sake.

Following close behind her silver Oldsmobile was a black van piloted by a team of paranormal investigators that partnered with her frequently. A decade after Hellen came to terms with her gift, she began using it whenever the need arose to help families deal with supernatural phenomena in their homes. Over the years she helped lost spirits move on to the other side, aided in cleansing homes of malevolence, and brought justice to those that could not speak for themselves. But today marked the first time she felt a sense of true dread in her craft. Deep down in her core she wanted to turn the car around and never come back. To put this whole neighborhood in her rearview again, and for the last time.

A week went by before the Murdocks heard anything back from the paranormal investigator team Father Sandoval endorsed. When they reached out the first time, it had been a general inquiry of the situation: how long had the activity in question been going on, had any harm come to anyone in the house, had any of the activity occurred outside of the property. After the first phone consultation, the team scheduled an appointment to come out with their equipment the following Saturday around noon to survey the property. The days leading up to that appointment crept by, and the Murdocks couldn't wait any longer for some form of help with the nightmare in their home. Chaos in the house began escalating around the clock in the days leading up to the investigators' arrival. So much so, that when they arrived, the Murdocks had only been able to sleep a few hours at a time with just enough energy to stay upright throughout the day.

Around ten minutes to twelve, a silver sedan pulled up the driveway followed by a black van. The two came to a halt in a single file line. The entire Murdock clan came out to greet their guests in the front yard, mostly for the sake of manners, but also because no one in the family liked to be in the house by themselves any more than they must be. An elderly woman with pearl white hair accented by splashes of gray stepped out of the sedan first. She was adorned in cherry red eyeglasses down near the front of her nose with a discolored, silver-plated, steel chain attached to the ends and wrapped around the back of her neck for retention. Two younger men exited the van behind her and took her lead to the house.

"Oh, hello. You must be Kathy. I think we spoke on the phone earlier this week. I'm Hellen," she said holding out her hand toward Kathy's.

"It's good to meet you," Kathy replied as she met her with a handshake.

"Likewise. These are my colleagues, Josh and Nick," she added while motioning to the paranormal investigators. "So, you're having some trouble, are you?"

Kathy turned to face her young son, who hadn't slept in his own room in over a week. His colorless face said more than she could sum up with small talk.

"That's one way of putting it," she added after a brief pause.

Hellen did her best to maintain the conversation, but the choir of disembodied chatter resonating from the Tudor buzzed in her head. She had to look away from the woman standing in front of her and gaze at the house in its full glory again. The two-story towered over her like a skyscraper. Even under the midday sun, its subtle darkness sprawled out unto her as a blackened welcome mat. Figures paced back and forth across the windowpanes, curious phantoms peeked around the hedges, and the giggle of children gave either a welcome or a taunt toward Hellen.

"Well hopefully we can give you some answers today."

"Thank you. We're just relieved that you're here. We…we just don't know what to do."

"That's ok. We're here to help," Hellen replied as her stare found itself pulled all around the property. "If you don't mind, I'd like to walk around the outside of the house before going in."

"Sure, whatever you need," Kathy replied.

Breaking off from the introductions, Hellen followed her intuition to the backyard. As she strolled through a manicured corridor of hedges, the unseen beacon called to her almost by name. Like so many other aspects of the world that revealed themselves to her and not unto others, the scant remnants of death filled her senses, sometimes to the point of nausea. Bodies left broken and forgotten in unmarked graves never let her forget who they once were. Old souls stranded without justice would whisper their pleas into her ear like a close friend confiding a secret.

Taking a few steps around the corner into the backyard almost brought Hellen to her knees. Bracing herself on an iron railing bordering the basement door, she paused at the horror before her. The stench of rot seeped up through the topsoil, lashing out at her nostrils. A putrid fragrance enveloped her as the half dozen bodies hidden in the earth called out to her in unison. As apparent by the corpses playing hide and seek under the swing set, death frequented the home as if he lived here himself.

The flurry of deceased voices left her searching for support. Hellen found respite against a Sycamore behind the swing set as she took a deep inhalation into her lungs. Her augmented senses would often leave Hellen not quite herself, but on occasion the shroud of death restrained nothing, leaving her tolerance in shambles. An abrupt thud sounded off behind her, followed by the groan of cord pulling against an immovable source. Hellen opened her eyes to a thin shadow cast in front of her by the late morning sun. Steeling her heart and mind, Hellen turned around with caution to find the spasming body of a middle-aged man hanging by his neck from a girthy branch just inches from her face. She took a step back just as the man opened both eyes with a blank stare. His rapid decomposition from someone she could have mistaken for the living into a putrid arrangement of bones and muscle sent her backwards to the ground. His head folded

229

to the side on a neck broken just above his collar. The man's tongue slipped from the corner of a mouth missing most of its lips while he swayed back and forth in the summer breeze as muscle mass fell away from his original design.

"Leave…now," the corpse whispered to Hellen as it continued falling apart.

Hellen pulled herself up to her feet with the swing set as a guide, steadying her resolve as well while averting her gaze from the dead man. She found more than what she expected before setting a foot inside the house. As she bolted across the yard toward the front of the home, the hanging man continued his advice that she leave the house now. Before facing the family or her colleagues, Hellen took a moment to compose herself as she couldn't imagine the shape she appeared to be in after that brief encounter. She took in a deep breath before emerging back around the front of the property to find the paranormal investigators assisting in the case conducting impromptu interviews of the family members as they finished unpacking their equipment. She found Kathy standing next to her family still guarding them as a vigilant mother bear.

"Our investigators need to set up some equipment in the house. Would someone be so kind as to show them around?" Hellen asked Kathy and Richard after another deep breath.

"Sure," Kathy replied as she motioned to Richard.

The two investigators followed him with armloads of hard-shell cases filled with infrared cameras, motion detectors, EMF readers, and a myriad of audio equipment. As the investigators set up shop all about the second floor, Hellen began her own exploration. Starting with the first floor, she noted at least a dozen spirits milling about the home. Some wandering phantoms took their time acknowledging her as she passed from one room to the next, keeping their distance, only peeking around corners, while more cavalier specters approached her like old friends and whispered their tales into her ear. Soon she had a few of the puzzle pieces assembled as the history of the property began weaving into a tapestry in front of her mind's eye. Stopping in the kitchen, Hellen took a moment to decompress from the otherworldly strain the home had placed on her.

"I've lost count of how many spirits are here right now. Some of them have been trapped since before the house even existed. But some terrible things happened here," Hellen said with an exhausted tone.

"Well, what happened here?" inquired Kathy.

Hellen stopped to brace herself against the kitchen table. She took several deep breaths as her inquiries into the other realm led her to further levels of exhaustion.

"I don't know exactly. It's dark. Dark and cloudy. I can't see it all. It's just…"

Hellen took another pause as she claimed a seat at the table. Concerned for her well-being, Kathy took a seat across from her.

"Violence. Spiteful, hate-filled malice. Sometimes death brought about from such brutality keeps the spirit locked in limbo. A never-ending state, where they replay their end over and over," Hellen added.

For the first time since her arrival, a stillness flooded the home. Spirits standing in congregation all around the family receded into the shadows and nooks with the caution of lesser creatures lying low from a nearby predator. In a few moments only the living occupied the kitchen. Dragging his feet across linoleum and toting his favorite action figure, Joey emerged around the corner thus breaking the silence. Beside him stood another boy of similar age in blue denim overalls and a red and yellow striped shirt. The boy ran over to Hellen and threw his arms around her waist, burying his face into her ribcage. His pale tone made her skin tan and alive by comparison. She returned the gesture and

231

put an arm around the child. She looked at him and then back from Joey to Kathy.

"You just have the one boy, right?"

Kathy looked dumbfounded at the remark. The answer fumbled around in her throat as she feared whatever brought up the question.

"Well, yes. Our son Joey right there," she said motioning to the living boy standing in silence. "And his older sister, Stacey."

"He's scared," Joey interrupted before Hellen could respond. "He said he's scared of the bad men. They all are."

Hellen looked down at the phantom child still clinging to her as she imagined he would with his own mother. "Do you know who the bad men are?" Hellen said to the boy.

He released his hold and looked up at her with pale eyes. Without saying a word, he just shook his head.

Hellen descended the staircase first, followed by Kathy, Richard, and then the two investigators. She stopped in the center of the basement and closed her eyes. Giving more concentration and dedication than ever before, she put her extra sense to the pulse of 6023 Walnut and listened. Through the whole property Hellen had hoped and even ventured to pray that she would bump into one spirit in particular, while simultaneously hoping she wouldn't. The war of wills in her heart tore at each other between wanting to say goodbye to Megan one more time, while her other half knew what torture lies in store for people stuck in this form. She knew deep down that Megan was better off not being stuck in this house like so many other poor souls. Regardless of what she wanted in her heart, there in front of her stood the agitated soul of Megan Moore pacing back and forth in the same dirt caked clothes she expired in.

The phantom milled about near the corner with her arms tensed and straightened down by her sides. Her fingers were sprawled open like talons. She made a few more laps before stopping. The girl stood with her shoulders raised up, facing the wall. As she halted, the phantom tilted her head to the side and rotated it around enough until Hellen became caught in her peripheral vison. Before Hellen could make a movement in any direction, the girl melted into a puff of black smoke and instantly stood to the left of Hellen, bringing her rotten, frigid breath to bare down on the psychic's neck.

"Megan? Megan, it's me, Hellen! Do you remember me?"

She took another step closer until what remained of her nose almost grazed Hellen's cheek. The ghost reached up with her bony fingers to touch Hellen's face but halted as something snapped in her.

"Megan! I'm not going to hurt you, ok?"

The outward husk of her corpse faded, and she appeared as a young girl. The hatred that swam in her pupils washed away and was replaced with that of innocence. Tears poured down her face as she embraced her friend once more. Hellen returned the sentiment, wrapping her arms around Megan. She pulled back from Hellen and looked up to meet her aged smile. The young spirit moved her right hand up to meet Hellen's cheek with an icy caress that the psychic didn't even register for the warmth she held in heart just then.

"It's ok. You don't have to be here. You're free to leave and be with your mom," Hellen said.

Just as the words left her lips, the calm on Megan's face melted as she cowered from something not on Hellen's radar. The spirit looked up above them before disappearing into the darkened corner again. A relentless weight of hopelessness burrowed into Hellen from her shoulders to her feet. Her muscles stiffened as she watched her friend disappear once more.

Michael Tyree

"Megan? We're just here to help you. I want to help you find your way to the light. We're not going to hurt you," Hellen reiterated with a compassionate tone to her voice.

Nothing Hellen could say would coax Megan from where she hid. Hellen could still feel her presence there just as if the two of them were back in high school again, sitting together on that ugly yellow plaid couch in Hellen's living room.

"Please, I just want to help you."

The back of the room began flooding with a liquid darkness. Slow at first, the onyx void rolled in across the floor like high tide. As it did, pitch stretched over the walls and ceiling, taking all perceived definition of depth and space. The blackness soon overtook everything in the basement in front of Hellen. Both investigators pulled out their phones and equipped the flashlights; however, neither one lasted more than a few seconds. As they aimed the beams into the abyss, it became clear how futile they would be. The torches didn't even scratch the surface of the murk. It was as if the void had swallowed over half of the Murdocks' basement. The light went nowhere, and after a few moments the phones fizzled out and died.

"Why hasn't she gone one way or the other? What's keeping her here?" Vaughn said.

Donnie squinted hard at the young specter. He could halfway recall someone somewhere in his past…if only his recollection weren't clouded with millions of other faces. He took a few more steps toward the ghost and looked harder before the wheels fell into place.

"Ooooooooh, well, I may have had something to do with that," he replied. "Either way, we can't afford to have any loose cannons on deck while we're working," Donnie moved within the blink of an eye. One second, he stood by Vaughn, the very next he rematerialized with his left hand on Megan's throat and his right hand sprawled out across her forehead. "I remember

234

you. You know, I saw Tony the other day. The other side hasn't agreed with him, but let's be honest, he wasn't doing too much when he was still breathing anyway. Well anyway, full disclosure, this is gonna hurt a little."

An electrical hum rang out as Donnie held his palm over her forehead. The ghost appeared to be in unbridled agony, yet no sound escaped her lips. She stood frozen as he maintained his hold on her. A bright orange circle formed around the ghost's feet. The diameter was just large enough to encapsulate her form. Lines started squirming around the perimeter, forming letters and symbols of some ancient forgotten alphabet that, once complete, glowed a deep cherry red. Then after those formed, two more circles emerged around the runes which began to move in opposite directions. The sacred geometry began burning like a newborn star, and with each pulse the radiance grew brighter as the revolutions moved faster. As the movement and luminescence became almost blinding, dozens of torn and tattered hands and arms reached up through the floor and latched onto the girl's legs. They squirmed over her body like a legion of serpents. The fingertips of the disembodied hands dug into her legs, dragging her downwards into the floor. Once she began her descent, Donnie released his grasp and watched as the girl sank into the undertow of corpse appendages. When the floor swallowed her up, the circle disappeared, leaving the dirty concrete exactly as it was.

"There, that takes care of that," Donnie said.

A filth-ridden odor poured into the basement as if a mass of rotten animal carcasses had been crammed into every air duct or the fresh exhumation of a septic tank.

"Lord...do you smell that?" Kathy inquired.

"It smells like...sulfur," Hellen replied.

They all held their hands over their mouths to block out the odor from penetrating their nostrils any further.

Michael Tyree

"There is something else here. Something much darker," Hellen added.

"You see the one standing over there channeling her inner Angela Lansbury?" Donnie said.

"That one?" Vaughn replied as he pointed toward Hellen.

"She talks to the dead. Which means they've already started bringing in outsiders. And we can't have that."

Hellen fell to her knees and palms gasping for air. She clutched her left hand into a fist over her breasts as she struggled to take a breath like a fish out of water. The investigators both leaned down to help her back up to her feet as the darkness soon washed over the entire basement leaving no traces of light. Both investigators clung to Hellen in the pitch as they lifted her back to her feet. Collectively, the three of them took Kathy and Richard's cue, and moved backwards through the void to the stairs, cramming into a clumsy single file column.

Richard breached the door to the kitchen first, followed by Kathy. The investigators pulled the rear as they still labored to assist Hellen up the flight. Finally, as they ascended the last step, she toppled again. This time she heaved violently until she lost her breakfast all over the kitchen floor. Kathy had disappeared to make sure she found the children before escaping the house. Richard halted until he knew Hellen and her colleagues had emerged from the basement in one piece. Even the daylight that pierced the windows of the kitchen could not penetrate the darkness swallowing the bowels of the house.

"There is something...very, very dark in this house," Hellen said between deep breaths. She scooted over to the middle of the floor and rested her back against the kitchen island. Laying her head back with eyes closed she continued to repeat the same statement over and over. "Something evil. Something very, very evil!"

She opened her eyes again to see the younger investigator, Josh, standing at the top of the stairs. Behind him the shadows began swirling and shifting, forming disproportional body parts out of thin air. After a few seconds, a tall shadowy silhouette stepped out of the black and lurched over Josh. Like two small embers bursting to life under a starless sky, a pair of fiery eyes opened wide in the shadow's face and peered down at the still unaware investigator.

"JOSH! Move...away...move away now," Hellen blurted out amid more bile filled coughs.

But he couldn't comprehend what she had been trying to convey. Not until he saw it with his own eyes. The shadow sprouted long, gangly arms which shot up over Josh, connecting around his neck, spinning him around, and bringing his face just underneath that of the shadow. It peered down at him, and even though it lacked any facial feature other than eyes and the smoky outline of a head and neck, Josh could feel the hate burning in the pupils. He could feel its contempt for his soul.

The shadow grabbed Josh once more. It latched onto his shoulders and pulled him off the ground as it threw itself back into the void. The specter launched him off the top step like a springboard and vaulted his body face first over every step in the flight straight into the concrete floor at the bottom. Out of sight, Richard, Hellen, and Nick froze in terror as Josh disappeared. The first couple of seconds lost their place in time as a deafening silence overtook them. Then a blood curdling crunch rang out as the thud of Josh's body collided with the floor. Richard and Nick both raced to the top of the stairs to find the darkness had subsided and everything had returned to normal. The daylight breaching the kitchen windows left a macabre vignette around the investigator's crumpled remains. He had flown over the entire staircase and landed on the top of his head, with his back up against the basement wall. The fall had snapped his neck and cracked the back of his skull across the concrete. His arms lay extended out away from his shoulders with his legs crossed over each other at the ankle running up the wall. His fractured body was splayed out like a bloody inverse crucifixion.

Hellen sat sideways in the driver seat of her sedan with the door opened wide. She lounged against the seat, gazing off into the distance as the paramedics rolled Josh's corpse out of the house inside a black bag. She pulled another drag from her cigarette while men and women from the coroner's office brought the dark reality out into the light of day. She had experienced violence from the other side before, but never like this.

"What…in the fuck…was that?" Nick exclaimed as he moved over to Hellen's car. His hands still trembled as he lifted a Bic up to the cigarette hanging from his lips and cupped his other hand to shield the flame from the wind. He pulled his hand away and took a heavy drag before expanding on his question further. "Seriously, what was that?"

"I saw her," she replied just above a whisper. "I felt her as soon as I walked downstairs. I felt her breath on my face. It was Megan," Hellen changed the subject without a pause for Nick's question.

Nick remained silent as he let out another puff of smoke from his nostrils. He shot her a curious look like someone who walked into the back end of an inside joke would appear, with confusion and intrigue.

was the first time I got to see the inside of her old house. We all knew something was going on in there. We all knew she never wanted to be in that house."

"Did she-" Nick started to ask.

"She died in there," she said cutting him off. "Her mother's boyfriend killed her and her mom before killing himself out here on the front porch in front of everyone. I was out here on the sidewalk with the whole neighborhood when they wheeled the bodies out," Hellen said as tears began welling up around her eyelids. "I thought maybe if she was here then I could help her move on. But when we were down there something happened. Something drew her away and I couldn't get to her. I tried getting through, but I just...I lost her again. She's gone, and I think whatever got to her is the same thing that took Josh." She took another drag from her cigarette and released the tobacco smoke through her nostrils. "Today is the second time I've watched people wheel corpses out of that front door. You and I need to help these people, so it is the last time."

Both Hellen and Nick let that statement hang in the air for a few minutes as they finished their cigarettes in silence.

"But are you ok?" Mateo anxiously responded into the phone.

"I'm fine. I'm fine. They're the ones who need help, Mateo. They need all the help they can get right now."

Silence fell as only the mild receiver static hummed in the background between dialogue.

"I...I've never done this...on my own,"

"I just don't know if I can..." Mateo trailed off as he glanced out of his kitchen window at the passing cars piercing the night with glaring high beams.

Deep down he knew he had to. He knew these people put their trust in him for help and they needed it more than he anticipated. But this, this was the tallest order ever asked of him in the name of faith.

"If you won't do it for them, then do it for Megan."

The last few syllables coming through his receiver took him back. As he heard her name again aloud, he thought of who she would be today if she had survived that house on Walnut Street.

"I'll be there as soon as I can."

"Thank you."

"I'll call you when I'm on the road. Bye, Hellen."

"Bye."

He laid the receiver back on the hook and took in the deepest breath ever held inside his blackened lungs. Knowing how idling by made his imagination run rampant, he set out at once to begin packing the tools for his coming hardship. Tucked away in the top of his bedroom closet behind suitcases he rarely filled and shoes he seldom put on sat a leather bag with brass handles and buckles. Mateo pulled it down and lay it open on his bed. It had been almost a decade since daylight found the contents inside. With reverence and anxiety, he removed each item and placed them on the comforter as he took an inventory of what he needed: a purple stole embroidered with golden alpha and omega letters across the front, a silver rosary, a leather-bound Bible, and a silver flask made for the sole purpose of containing blessed water. With each weapon in his arsenal set out before him, the fear crawled up his spine one vertebrae at a time until an anxious lightheaded spell came over him.

One last tool rested in the bottom of the bag, one never represented in fictious interpretations of the rite, one Mateo feared to ever use again. He reached into the deepest recesses of the leather bag and pulled out a bundled red cloth. Holding it in his left hand he unfolded the cloth one piece at a time until the relic buried underneath glimmered in the incandescent light. He held a pair of shackles forged before the priest had been conceived. The Damascus steel restraints were born in a time before Walnut Street and the Tudor, before Mateo's ancestors came to this country. They rested in his palm with an otherworldly denseness. With the weight of this artifact in his hand, the burden of needing them in the coming days weighed harder on his heart.

"God be with me."

The following day, Hellen and Nick returned to the house with Father Sandoval.

"Kathy, it's good to meet you in person," said the priest.

"It's good to meet you, too. I just wish it would have been under different circumstances."

"Well, I feel as though I underestimated your situation when we spoke before. But I assure you we will get to the bottom of it," Mateo responded as he placed his hand on Kathy's shoulder.

The family all huddled around in the living room along with Mateo, Hellen, and Nick.

"Now, you hear stories from time to time about violent poltergeists haunting the places where they died. That's not out of the ordinary. But sometimes, when a house or a piece of property has a long history of violence, it can wear a hole in the fabric between our world and that of the dead. When that happens, it's easier for more malevolent entities to cross over," Mateo added.

"We believe that some things came through the veil. Some very dark things," said Hellen.

"We think...we think you may have one or more demonic entities inside your home," Father Mateo added.

"Well, isn't that cute? Nancy Drew and the Hardy Boys are giving them the CliffsNotes," Donnie said as he and Vaughn eavesdropped on the Murdocks.

They kept to the shadows of the second-floor landing while observing the family meeting down below. Not that the two infernal bureaucrats needed to stay out of sight. They could pull up two chairs right in the middle of it without being noticed by the living.

"What can we do? I mean we can't afford to move again," Kathy inquired.

"No shit, after seeing that mortgage statement I'd be surprised if they could take out a loan for a cardboard box," Donnie added

"We would like to do a cleansing of the house. Hopefully, that will begin to exorcise the home," the priest replied.

"Will that work? I mean, have you done that before?" Stacey interjected.

"We have done this sort of thing before and it *will* work," Hellen added.

"Uh...yes Alex, I'll take *not so* famous last words for 500 please," Donnie said to himself while his prey drew their lines in the sand. After they began dispersing through the Tudor on their own tasks, he turned back to Vaughn with intent on igniting his own master plan. "Alright. You know what to do."

Richard, Kathy, and the kids stood together in the living room with Nick, Hellen, and Mateo. The priest began by reciting scripture and flinging Holy water from a flask all about the room. After a few minutes, the temperature in the house plummeted.

Mateo remained adamant about finishing every verse and stanza, despite the obvious distractions stirring in the home. With air diving toward the arctic, he recited the verses aloud as his breath formed clouds of steam out in front of his trembling lips.

"BE GONE, DEMON! YOU HAVE NO PLACE HERE!" Father Sandoval commanded.

No sooner had the taunt left his lips, the doors of a glass china cabinet flung open so hard the panes disintegrated upon impact. Dishes, saucers, teacups, and other fragile items began flying out in a violent procession toward the family members. Everyone ducked down onto the carpet except for Nick, who caught a gravy boat along his brow.

"FUCK...OFF!" Donnie roared as he toppled the cabinet to the floor, reducing the cherrywood to splinters.

The priest paused from his work as the din of the cabinet shattering reverberated in his brain, causing a sharp ringing in his ears. He propped himself up from the carpet where everyone else continued to take cover from the onslaught. Still clutching his Bible and rosary in his hands, he fought to find the courage he had possessed three minutes ago. Whatever he contended with right now understood malice and violence unlike anything he had ever seen before.

"We're not scared of your parlor tricks, demon! Begone! You are not welcome here!" He commanded again.

"IS THAT RIGHT?" replied Donnie as he crept around the group like a starved lion.

Father Sandoval stood again and picked back up where he left off with his scripture. This time he screamed the verses aloud, one after the other in a display of dominance over the evil in the home.

"IN THE NAME OF THE FATHER, THE SON, AND THE HOLY GHOST, I CAST YOU OUT OF THIS HOUSE!"

"FUCK YOU!" Donnie screamed.

Joey hit his breaking point and, unable to withstand it anymore, he jumped up and ran from the chaos toward the front door.

"Joey! Come back!" Richard screamed.

Richard made chase behind his youngest son but ran into invisible hurdles as an unexplainable wind roared through the hallway, knocking him to his haunches. He got back up again and made another mad dash to the front door, pushing as hard as possible to close the gap, but lost sight of Joey and found only the front door wide open. Richard hit the corner hard and darted outside to find nothing.

"JOOOOOEEEEY!" he screamed again.

Nothing. No sign of him. Just the humid air thrashing his skin. He screamed at the top of his lungs as he paced back and forth through the front yard looking for any clues. He stopped when he felt a bony finger tap him three times on his right shoulder. Richard spun around to a visual he would never comprehend.

"Well, hi there," Donnie said with a crooked smile.

Richard found himself on his knees in a cold dark room. The acoustic value left the erratic sound of his heartbeat pounding back and forth against the walls of his mind. A single light burst to life over his head. It illuminated a twelve-foot-wide section of the room leaving him at the epicenter. Even with the luminescence, the floor and surroundings remained black. The ground beneath as well as the walls around him existed somewhere inside pitch. His feet and knees rested on a surface so devoid of color, Richard's form appeared to teeter over the abyss.

A statuesque, well-manicured man stepped into view from the shadows. He was adorned in a black Armani suit paired with an even blacker shirt and tie. His golden blonde hair was slicked back tight.

"Where am I?"

"Richard, is it? Mind if I call you Dick?" Donnie inquired.

"Excuse me?" Richard replied.

"Well, I'm gonna call you Dick. See, it's like this, Dick. I'm in the driver seat now. And no matter how much you beg and plead; Jesus is most definitely not taking the wheel this time. It's just you and me, spending some quality time inside this primate brain of yours."

"What? You? You're the thing that's been scaring my kids?" Richard replied as he hunkered down prepared to strike.

"Well, I can only take partial credit for that."

Richard lunged at the demon just to crash through a dissipation of black smoke. His body collided with the frigid stone floor of his mind's prison. Donnie rematerialized somewhere behind him, grabbing Richard by the collar and hoisting him up to his feet again.

"Let me break this down for you like Sesame Street," Donnie replied with a sigh.

The demon snapped his fingers and a six-foot-long whiteboard appeared out of thin air on a slate black easel.

"This is you right here," Donnie said as he drew a malformed stick figure on the upper left side. Donnie had sketched the figure out with a drastic forward leaning hunch, which made the person in question appear as an eight-year-old's crayon interpretation of Quasimodo. Donnie followed up with a frowny face, and a single minimal dot of the marker in the figure's crotch to insinuate the person might be endowed like a small dog. He finished his drawing by scribbling the word "Dick" above the figure with a sharp underline.

"And this here, is yours truly," Donnie added. Donnie took his time and sketched out another figure on the upper right side of the board. This one was standing upright, at least three times as tall as the first. He accented the torso with an exaggerated set of six-pack abs and drew bulging round limbs to represent toned, muscular thighs, biceps, and triceps. Spending far more time than required, Donnie added a pair of sharp curved ram horns complete with tiny glimmer sparkles coming off the tips. He then committed at least a few minutes to drawing a cock hanging past the figure's knees and swollen larger than one of its legs. After finishing the last line in his magnum opus, Donnie stood back and sighed in approval. He then wrote the word "Donnie" above the drawing. Donnie snapped his fingers again and a matte black laser pointer appeared in his left hand. He directed the red laser dot over to the first figure.

"This is you. Nothing special, just one primate in an extensive line of Yahweh's failed simian experiments," He then moved the pointer over to exhibit B. "Now this, this is a fine example of infernal pedigree. I can trace my ancestry back all the way to the first fallen. Those that fought alongside our Lord Lucifer. Whereas even with all the DNA test kits on the market, you can't even follow your lineage to anyone that graduated community college," Donnie said with a frown.

Richard never budged from his posture. Remaining where the demon had picked him from the floor, a dumbfound look stretched across his face as he tried to make sense of what was in front of him. He just shook his head in disbelief.

Satisfied with the first part of his presentation, Donnie moved back to the whiteboard. This time in the middle he drew the first figure hunched over on all fours like a mule. The frowny face became one of duress, complete with large tear drop shaped beads of sweat falling to the ground. Then Donnie drew the second figure postured on the back of the first like a cowboy. The second had its arms stretched upwards to the sky with index and pinky fingers sticking up on both fists to form the universal sign language of devil horns. He completed his masterpiece with a toothy grin cast ear to ear.

"Still with me, Dick? Ok, here you can see Exhibit C. Notice how you're giving me a piggyback ride and how that brings me all the joy in the world? Well, that is very much like how I'm having the time of my existence riding around in your skin right now. You see, I'm in you right now. And not in an experimental phase in college way."

"I...I..." Richard stuttered.

"See, I need something from you, Dick."

Richard took a few steps back, putting distance between him and the demon.

"What the hell do you want?"

"What does any self-respecting demon want, Dick?"

"I, um...I don't know," Richard responded.

"Your Wi-Fi password."

The sometimes gullible and sarcasm illiterate Richard Murdock took a moment of silence as he examined the stone-cold serious face of the demon's human costume.

"Rea..."

"No, not really. I need your soul, Dick. Well, my boss's boss wants your soul. And you're going to sign it over to me, or you know...else."

Donnie snapped his fingers and a tattered white scroll appeared from thin air. The paper unraveled itself by several feet as the terms of the contract became legible one sentence at a time. The words did not appear as traditional ink, but as if an invisible hand had scorched each letter one by one with a red-hot soldering iron. With every punctuation of every clause, smoke began to rise from the scroll followed by the stench of burnt leaves. Finally, at the bottom of the contract lay a single line with a Romanesque X beside it.

"Just sign your widdle name here and you can go back to what's left of your old life. Easy peasy."

Michael Tyree

"This isn't real. This is just a dream. I fell down somewhere outside and I'm unconscious. That's it," Richard bargained with himself out loud as Donnie's impatience became more visible with every crease of the human facial features.

"Oh, I wouldn't count on that, buckaroo. Now really, you should sign this before things become far more perilous for you."

"What? No, I'm not selling you my soul."

"Oh no, not selling. This isn't a transaction. No, I'm not giving you anything for it. You're going to surrender it to me or else I'm going to turn your family into ground chuck."

"I cannot and will not give you my soul. I am saved by the Blood of the Lamb, my Lord Jesus!"

Donnie rolled his eyes at every syllable of Richard's protest, and in further mocking him, made little hand puppet illustrations to mime his words.

"Listen, Sally, I enjoy being the bearer of bad news, and maybe when this is over, we can sit down and talk about Santa, the Easter Bunny, the tooth fairy, or *real* Communism, but I have to tell you…the only thing you've been *saved* from, is the desire to think critically."

"No. Absolutely not!"

"You know what, Dick? I think you need something to put this in perspective for you. A motivator if you will," Donnie said as he laid his hand on Richard's forehead.

Richard snapped out of his trance and returned to the front lawn. A cloudy vignette masked his vision only allowing him a hazy tunnel to the scene straight ahead of him. Joey stood facing him with his back just a few feet from the road. Every few seconds a car or truck would cruise by bringing a rush of wind with it, throwing Joey's hair in all directions. The boy stared at his father with an expression he had never seen before. Not one of childhood innocence or fear, but more of a blatant taunt. Richard summoned everything in him to move forward, but

248

every part of his atrophied form remained where it was. Even his mouth muscles disobeyed his commands to form a simple protest.

"My partner and I need to illustrate a point for you," Donnie's voice echoed inside his head.

Joey looked to his right before extending his arms out to his sides like a crucifixion. He then began tilting himself backwards to the road just as a pickup came cruising down Walnut Street. The whole spectacle taunted his father in slow motion before Richard's vision blacked out again with the image of his son flying backwards burnt into the short-term memory of his retinas. He blinked to find himself back in the same room with Donnie.

"Now look, you still have one out of two living kids plus your old lady. I mean, that's not half bad."

Richard lunged from where he stood and threw himself at Donnie with a wild haymaker. Before he could connect, the demon dematerialized into a puff of black smoke and reappeared behind Richard, leaving him to fall flat on the ground once more.

"Now keep this in mind. You can stop this at any time as soon as you play ball. Just give me what I came here for, and the rest of your family might make it out alive."

"I'm gonna fuckin' kill you!"

"With what, Dick? Your thoughts and prayers?"

Richard picked himself up and, in a vain attempt to prove himself right about his own plight and ignore what the demon said about his own head, he took off running in the darkness looking for anything to release him from this hell. The overhead light that had once reflected on the whiteboard was swallowed in the black behind him.

"That's not a very good idea, Dick," Donnie said with a significant distance between them.

Michael Tyree

As Richard kept pushing, he noticed a small light in the distance. He picked up his pace despite the grinding pain now clawing at the inside of his knee. The light continued growing larger as he sprinted along. After a few moments, he slowed down as he slowly realized that he was racing toward another light bulb with the demon standing underneath. The coldest of sobering feelings hit when he understood that it was the same light with the same whiteboard over the same floor where Donnie stood waiting.

"Well ok. Obviously, I failed to give you the proper visual aids to help put this into context. My bad."

Donnie snapped his fingers again and Richard became hoisted up in the air by four chains bound to his wrists and ankles. They pulled him off the ground and suspended him face up, with his back hovering four feet from the ground. Donnie made a sweeping motion with his outstretched palm in the air and a series of loud thumps went off in unison underneath Richard and just out of his line of sight. Donnie ignored Richard's blunt protests and began ripping the front of the human's shirt open, exposing his abdomen.

The demon began humming the chorus to "Camptown Races" as he worked with diligence on his project. He leaned over and picked up a five-and-a-half-pound tub of extra crunchy peanut butter, lathering it all over Richard's bare skin. After applying the entire vat, he paused for a few moments to prepare the next phase of his master plan while Richard began sweating at the potential outcome. Suddenly a chorus of squeaks and chirps filled the air as he lifted a rusted cage packed to maximum capacity with feral rats. The rodents fought and climbed over one another hoping to find a more comfortable position in the cage. Counting the sum of disease carriers became a moot point, as the animals were packed so tightly against the cage that the ones on the outermost perimeter were being squeezed into the grating like raw ground

250

beef pushed into a meat processer. Tufts of bloody fur and pieces of ears and tails hung on the outside of the cage.

"I'm not giving you my soul!"

"Shhhhh. Hush now. We'll get back to that in a little while. I said you needed a better visual aid," Donnie replied while staying on his current task. "Alexa. Play "Africa" by the band Toto."

After an electronic beep went off from somewhere in the darkness nearby, the drumline to "Africa" began playing around them.

"Do do, do do, da do do doooo," Donnie whispered as he extended four small prongs downward a few inches from each corner of the cage. With one confident push, he inserted the spikes all the way into Richard's chest so that the cage rested on his sternum with the prongs exiting out through his back.

"AAAAAAAHHHH," Richard belted out.

"...But she only hears whispers of some quiet conversation..." Donnie sang along while he worked on the cage.

"As the late, great Billie Mays used to say: *But wait, there's more!*" Donnie tugged on a small handle at the bottom of the cage a few times until it gave way. The bottom panel of the cage slid out from under the rats, leaving nothing between them and Richard's abdomen. In the span of two breaths, the vermin began burrowing into his flesh like one hundred and seventeen impatient adolescents all looking for the same prize at the bottom of the same box of Froot Loops.

"Well, I'll just leave you to get acquainted with your new friends. Ta ta."

Several agonizing minutes had come and gone since Mateo ran out after Joey and his father. The silence that followed the initial chaos running through the house seared the nerves of everyone inside, still reeling from what they just experienced.

"Richard? Where's Richard and Joey?" exclaimed Kathy.

A stillness washed over the house as if they had not escaped the storm, but instead sat in the eye of the hurricane waiting for the next round of chaos and violence. Kathy continued calling out for her husband and youngest when Richard returned to them without Joey. He carried himself not as a man tormented by phantom assailants, but as one who almost had a new lease on life. His gait was more of a casual strut than the limp that had accompanied him earlier. The beginnings of a tiny smirk began to form in the corners of his mouth as he approached the family and guests.

"Where's Joey?" Kathy exclaimed

"Oh, he said he wanted to run away and join the circus and I was like, who am I to stand in the way of his dreams. I said, son, you go be the best carnie you can be."

"WHAT?????" Kathy screamed shaking her head. "Have you lost your mind? What part of this is funny to you?" Kathy screamed at him.

"Hmmmm, well pretty much all of it," Richard replied with a chuckle.

Kathy returned the gesture by slapping him across the face so hard, it almost knocked him backwards.

"What...the...hell...is wrong with you, Richard!" Kathy exclaimed as she punctuated each word with a hard strike across his face.

After seven blows, Richard reached up and grabbed both of her wrists spreading her arms out away from her shoulders and bringing his face close to hers.

"Richard can't come to the phone right now, but if you'd like to leave a message just state your name, number, and petty bullshit after the beep."

He held her arms tight, giving her no room to wiggle free. Richard then leaned in and brought his lips just to the edge of her right ear and held it there for a few moments.

"Beeeeeeeeeeeeeeeeeeeep" he whispered into her ear.

He released her wrists and shoved her backwards off her feet simultaneously turning to face the rest of the onlookers.

"Now, where were we? Ahhhh, you were saying something about how I was not welcome here and then I sincerely told you to FUCK...OFF!" Richard belted out.

"The demon, it's inside of him," Hellen muttered to herself.

"Ding ding ding! Let's all give a warm round of applause to Jessica Fletcher! Now let me make this perfectly clear, YOU are the ones who are not welcome here!" Richard screamed at Hellen as she hovered over Nick like a mother hen.

He closed the distance between them in just three short strides. In one swift motion, he struck Hellen with the back of his right hand. The blow hit her with an unseen inertia. The force that knocked her several feet across the room came, not from the raw power of Richard's biceps and triceps, but from some hellish kinetic energy born of Donnie's hatred for the living. In bypassing Hellen, nothing stopped him from bringing himself on top of Nick.

"Your buddy sends his regards. That was a hell of a dive he took! I mean his form was a little sloppy, but I still gave him an eight and a half out of ten on the overall execution," he said with a smile.

Before Nick could respond to the demon's taunt, Richard punctuated his previous statement with a hard-right cross straight into Nick's septum. He followed with a left and then another right as he struck without mercy or impunity. Richard reduced Nick's face to a bloody pulp in just a few moments of abuse. Nick clinged to a small shred of consciousness as his eyelids began swelling shut.

Richard paused with his right arm cocked back at his shoulder ready to strike again as a nonchalant pitter patter of shuffling feet skittered across the floor behind him toward the front door. He spun around to find Kathy leading Stacey out of the house by the hand. Richard left Nick in a puddle of his own blood and leaped up to intercept his family's escape. He quickly gave chase to the duo and overtook them in seconds, spinning around in front of Kathy as he stood between her and the door.

"Now, now, where are you guys running off to? Hmmm?" Richard said with a faux expression of concern.

The three of them stood there locked in a stalemate for what felt like an eternity. Then ever so slowly Stacey, who had been hiding behind Kathy, started taking a few steps back away from her dad.

"Now hold on a minute. I think we need to sit down and have a family meeting about this," he taunted.

They didn't listen to his request and soon Kathy took Stacey's lead. With arms outstretched at her sides to shield her, she began stepping back until they both turned and sprinted to the back of the house away from Richard.

"COME BACK HERE...NOW!"

The two ran for the kitchen to escape through the sunroom. Before they hit the threshold of the kitchen, a thundering crash went off in front of them. Stacey made it in first to see the dining room table had flipped onto its side and soared up against the door connecting the kitchen to the sunroom. An invisible force held it off the floor and pinned the table tight against the exit. Kathy didn't stand around debating the improbability; she reached out and grabbed onto Stacey's shoulder to redirect her up the stairs to the second floor. They raced up the flight and down the hall to the master bedroom.

A bloodied and swollen Nick met Mateo as he crossed through the living room with an unconscious Joey straddled in his arms.

"What happened?" Mateo belted out.

"It's the dad. It's in the dad!" Nick murmured before stumbling to the floor.

Mateo laid Joey on the couch before running to Nick's side. His eyes were all but swollen shut leaving one tiny slit around his right pupil to navigate with. With fractured and missing teeth, Nick spat out wads of blood with every coughing exhalation. Mateo assisted in reclining Nick into a less strenuous pose on the cleanest section of carpet available.

"Where is Hellen? Where is Hellen?!" Mateo asked with a panicked tone.

Nick only pointed behind his head to a spot across the room littered with broken china and glassware. Mateo set him down easy and dashed over to the pile of rubble. Hellen lay crumpled under a broken board that was once part of the Murdocks' china cabinet. A faint murmur emanated from the pile as Mateo rushed to her side while she fought a losing battle with consciousness.

"Hellen? Hellen? Are you alright?" Mateo blurted out as he flung pieces of broken furniture from her body.

"I'm fine," she replied rolling over to take a knee.

"Here," he said holding out his hand to assist her.

"I got it," Hellen replied turning down his help. "Come on, they ran upstairs."

Stacey tripped over herself as she burst into the room after Kathy. With mere seconds between them and the demon, the duo slammed the door shut and threw themselves upon it in a vain attempt to lock him out.

"Really? Really?" Richard inquired as he beat on the closed door with both fists.

He swung away with hands and elbows. At the height of his frustration, he resorted to taking several steps back and ramming the door with his shoulder. Richard worked away until blood leaked from between his knuckles. He stopped the physical advances and for a few brief moments Kathy couldn't figure out if he had given up or not.

"It's gonna take a lot to drag me away from youuuu. There's nothing that a hundred men or more could ever do. I bless the rains down…"

Kathy's nightstand lamp began scooting back and forth next to the bed. The movement escalated as the light vibrated in place before launching itself across the room on a course through her and to the door. It missed them by inches as she took a dive to the floor, pulling Stacey down with her. Soon the nightstand itself launched toward them followed by jewelry boxes, a watch case, dresser drawers, and everything in between. The entire room cannibalized itself in a wild haymaker play to maul the family. All the flying debris kept them face down on the carpet as Kathy lay on top of her daughter, shielding her from the onslaught as best she could. Then all at once, it stopped. Everything remained still for a few seconds in the room. The silence was finally broken by Richard kicking the door in. The force not only broke it free at the handle but also separated it from the top hinge, leaving the corner stuck into the accompanying drywall.

Richard stood in the doorway staring down at Kathy and Stacey. His chest was heaving from exhaustion while his eyes remained wide open with anticipation. Bloodshot outer rims encompassed his dilated pupils. The vessels branched off the centers of his eyes like diseased yellowish orange tendrils, flaring with every pulse.

"Now what's with the long faces? I just want to spend some quality time with my family!"

Richard grabbed Kathy by the hair and hauled her back up to his level. She clawed at his grip with futility as he held her in place.

"Is that too much to ask? Hmmmm?"

Before Kathy could answer his question, Mateo cut their conversation short with Holy water breaking against the side of Richard's face, causing an immediate series of blisters. The splash left swelling burns all along the left side of his face and neck. Before Richard could calm himself, another stream struck him between the eyes.

"AAAAAAHH...Fuck!"

Mateo summoned the ingenuity of his ten-year-old self who grew up on professional wrestling, leaping out to buckle Richard at the waist and grounding him to the bed. Running at Mateo's heels, Hellen rifled through the priest's duffel bag until she produced the pair of steel restraints from the bottom. With one swift motion she flung the bag away and landed next to the priest as he wrestled Richard down on the mattress and pinned his arms behind his back. Hellen snapped the antique shackles on Richard seconds before Mateo's grip began to fail. A sizzling hiss erupted from Richard's wrists as the Damascus steel seared his flesh into blistering pockets. Father Sandoval followed his assault with more prayers and scripture as the demon inside Richard writhed and recoiled. Donnie's moment of vanity left him wide open for one of the few things his adversaries could use against him.

"BE GONE, DEMON!" Father Sandoval screamed at the top of his lungs.

The priest took full advantage of the opportunity given him and threw his right palm over Richard's forehead as he continued to pray.

"No, no take your fucking hand off of me, you filthy cocksucker!" Richard bellowed out at the priest.

His protests fell on silent ears this time as Donnie's vision blurred and contorted. First his peripheral disappeared, then everything else went into a tunnel until that dissolved to nothing.

Mateo felt his age in every joint and tendon of his body as they approached the fourth hour of Richard's exorcism. A darkness swelled in the bedroom that evening. Despite the remaining daylight spilling through the blinds, the room absorbed it into its epicenter, extinguishing all. The center of the blackness congregated around Richard as he remained tied to the bed with wrists still shackled by the ancient steel. Like a black hole, no light touched him as the demon inside rested in a blanket of shadow.

"I mean really. This is nice and all, but I would have appreciated it if you had at least bought me dinner first," Donnie said egging on the priest.

"Be gone! I command you out of this servant of the Lord. Leave NOW!"

"And let's be honest. I'm probably a little too old for you anyway. Am I right?"

Mateo answered the demon's taunt with another hard splash of Holy water across Richard's face. The demon recoiled in agony as steam rolled from every drop of Holy water resting on his skin. After a few seconds, Donnie regained his composure.

"You're never gonna save him. But you know that, right? I mean I appreciate the theatrics and everything, we all do. It makes our jobs interesting," Donnie added before cracking his neck from side to side. "But this guy isn't walking out of here."

"BE GONE! I COMMAND YOU OUT!" Mateo screamed over Donnie's taunts. The priest paced back and forth through the bedroom losing steam with every exertion. Crinkles and lines began to show in Mateo's poker face as he pushed forward with his counter attacks. "I CAST YOU OUT! LEAVE THIS CHILD OF THE LORD NOW!"

"Hey bud, just wanted to let you know that you're doing a bang-up job. I know you don't have a lot of experience with it, but you're doing great. Five out of five stars would be exorcised by you again," Donnie added.

Donnie returned to find Richard still suspended with an empty cage embedded in his upper torso and a gaping hole the size of a bowling ball punched through his chest. Donnie pried the cage off with no effort and tossed it into the shadows engulfing the room. The only remaining signs of the rodents were dozens of bloody trails all leading off into different directions.

"Wow, would you look at that? Wait, hold on. I have something just for this occasion."

Donnie crouched down beside Richard and held up a cell phone high above them to take a quick picture.

"Now, on the count of three, I want you to give me your best John Hurt impression and go AAAAHHH!"

"Ready? One…two…three! AAAAAAHHHHH."

Donnie pushed a black monster hand puppet up through the hole in Richard as if it were bursting out of his chest.

"Annnnnnd. Got it."

Donnie stopped to revel in the picture he captured. He snapped his fingers again and Richard became free of the chains, back on his feet, and missing the crater in his chest.

"What the hell is THIS?"

had a chance to meet your lovely family face-to-face so to say. And I gotta tell ya, that Kathy is a feisty one."

"Son of a…bitch!"

"Whoa, whoa there, Dick. Such language. Is this where you want to be when Jesus comes back? Throwing fifth grade reading level profanity at the adversary?"

A low ringing noise from Donnie's pocket interrupted the brief silence between their insults. Donnie pulled his phone back out and swiped it open.

"Oh, Slovath liked my picture!"

He smirked as he typed a short message and returned it to his pocket.

"So, Dick, have you had enough time to reconsider? Are you ready to give me what I came here for?"

"FUCK YOU!" Richard belted out, sending spit flying through the air.

"Now, now, Dick, don't be a dick."

"I'm not giving you my soul. My God is a god of vengeance. Do your worst, but your day is coming, and He will protect me."

"If by vengeance you mean the kind of cosmic level temper tantrum that would give creatures free will and then go nuclear on two cities because those creatures wanted to try butt stuff, then yeah he's a god of vengeance. But as far as swooping in and saving you, well I have some bad news for you. The truth is he doesn't give a wet donkey shit about you, any of you."

"That's a lie! You're nothing but a liar and your day will come!"

"I may have underestimated you, Dick," Donnie replied with a sigh. "I thought you would be a tad more reasonable. But I can see now that you and I need to take a little field trip."

Donnie snapped his fingers and the two of them found themselves in a small desert village surrounded by shanty huts.

"Now normally I don't like to pull the *"It's a wonderful life"* card, but you are an exquisitely unique brand of ignorant so, here we are."

Richard followed Donnie down a beaten dirt path into the middle of a tiny desert village. Forty or fifty people were all hunkered down between exhaustion and starvation, taking shelter from the sun in any way available. Along the edge of a muddy body of water lay a young boy on his back. His head rested against a tattered pile of cloth with his hands crossed over his stomach. His belly was swollen and sunken down past his waist. An even younger girl kneeled by his side and held an IV bag over him with the needle inserted into his left forearm. Both children had almost zero muscle mass and looked like tiny skeletons biding their time while the carrion birds circled overhead.

"Where are we?" Richard asked.

"Somalia." Donnie turned around just enough to look Richard in the face while continuing his monologue. "Now, not that I care at all about your collective pain and suffering, because honestly it's my job to instill some of that said pain and suffering, but I want to show you something here."

Donnie motioned to the two children on the ground.

"Do you see that one laying in a puddle of his own feces? He'll be dead by Thursday. And the little one giving him the medicine? She has maybe another week."

Donnie turned back to face Richard.

"Now tell me, how arrogant do you have to be to think your all loving, all caring Jehovah can look at this every fucking day of the week and do nothing. Yet He will drop what He *is* doing at this moment and come rescue a candyass nobody like yourself? No, Dick, he isn't. Because he couldn't give a shit about anything but himself. In fact, in the grand scheme of things, he is nothing but a spoiled toddler amongst the rest of the pantheon.

An angry brat upset that his favorite toy isn't behaving the way he wants it to. And you are nothing but a flea on his back."

Donnie snapped his fingers again, and they returned to the dark room inside Richard's mind.

"What I'm getting at, Dick, is that no one is coming to save you. It's just you and me in here. So, take some personal responsibility and give me what I came here for, or I'll leave you locked in here with a much, much bigger box. And you'll stay in here until your body starves to death. Meanwhile I'll be making this same pitch to the rest of your family until someone decides to be a team player."

Donnie let the monologue hang on his tongue for a moment while he watched Richard mull the actions and consequences over in his head.

"So, what will it be, huh?"

Kathy occupied the same seat at the dining table she had claimed last night. She had been waiting in the kitchen ever since Father Sandoval and Hellen restrained Richard in their bedroom. Terror held Kathy in place as it ran its course through her new home. While her husband battled forces unseen for his very soul, Joey remained passed out in bed under the guard of his older sister. The unspeakable, undefinable, and unforgivable had torn her home to pieces over the last few weeks. Her hopes of a fresh start had never made it out its honeymoon phase. Wild dreams conjured by old souls and young hearts were stripped naked and dragged through the valley of death. Her family, much like her home, lay in pieces this morning. Anxiety and nerves kept her deadlocked from any other routine that day. She wouldn't eat unless someone took the liberty of reminding her she should. She stayed downstairs away from everyone else, waiting with bated breath for some relief. But every time Mateo came downstairs, he only hung his head in solemn defeat.

The creak of the front door hinges startled Kathy from her daydreams as Hellen emerged from the tattered foyer. Despite Kathy's natural skill at reading a poker face, she missed something with Hellen. Unsure what emotion and thought hid behind the psychic's expression, she waited for her to make the first move. Hellen pulled up a chair and took a seat next to Kathy.

"How is your friend Nick?" Kathy asked after rubbing her fatigued eyes.

"He's going to be ok. He needed some stitches but he's resting back at the hotel room," Hellen replied. She took Kathy's cue and rubbed her tired eyes as the long night caught up with her. "How is your son?"

"He's resting." Kathy paused to contend with the tears welling up behind her eyes. "I just…I just don't know what to do," Kathy said with exhaustion at her heels.

"Honestly? You should pack," Hellen responded with a hand placed on Kathy's shoulder.

"But we can't."

"You have to. Look, this house…this house is no good for your family. This place has taken too much from too many people," Hellen said with tears welling up in her eyes. "I lost someone to this house, and I don't want to see you lose anyone to it, either."

Hellen pulled open her purse and retrieved a roll of cash from inside. Taking the money in her hand she planted it in Kathy's palm and rolled her fingers over it to signify its importance.

"Take this. It's not much, but it's a start. Take it and start packing your family up today. Take whatever you can and as soon as your husband and son can walk you need to put them in the car and go."

"But we…"

Kathy opened up the wad of one hundred-dollar bills and counted them out. The reasoning for her protests dissolved as she came back to her senses again. She folded them back up and look back at Hellen with tears rippling down her cheeks.

"Thank you!"

"It's ok," Hellen responded while wrapping her arms around Mrs. Murdock in sympathy. "You just do what you need to do and get them out of this God forsaken house."

A grindingly slow succession of footfalls down the stairs interrupted their solemn moment. Father Sandoval rounded the corner like a pitiful beaten dog. Loosened clothing saggy with perspiration from his task hung heavily on him. Pale and teetering on the cusp of unconsciousness, he stood in the doorway, leaning against the frame with all his weight.

"I'm not one hundred percent sure yet," Mateo let out just above a whisper. "But I think he might be out of the woods."

Kathy held her breath for a moment before replying to the priest. She searched inside for the words but only found the first few,

"Is he…"

"He's in and out, just trying to rest right now," he added. Mateo ran his palms over his face and took in a deep breath. "Would you like to talk to him?"

Kathy said nothing back. She just nodded her head and followed the two of them into the bedroom. Richard lay asleep on the queen size bed, his hands restrained to the headboard with tattered rope acquired from the shed. The sheets he rested on had more color than his own skin. If not for the brief rise and fall of his chest, he could almost pass for a corpse. Caution still lingered in her gait as she walked to his side.

"Richard? Sweetie, can you hear me? It's Kathy," she whispered.

After a night battling a demon and his own faith, the sound of his wife's voice called out as a beacon from his nightmare. Richard's eyelids moved in tiny increments until they pried open enough to meet Kathy's gaze. Even the act of blinking drained his energy reserves, causing Richard to take several deep breaths.

"We're getting out of here. Ok?" She said while kneeling down by the bed. "As soon as you and Joey are ok, we are leaving this place behind."

The last sentence stirred something in her husband. Whatever fatigue held his eyelids down low diminished after hearing those words. His eyes stretched wide open, and his brow arched up in anxiety. The color that had remained in Richard's skin at that point washed out with the news. He worked his mouth muscles around in a test run before speaking again.

"Joey is ok? He's...all right?"

"Yes, he's ok. Mateo saved his life. I'm not sure what happened exactly. Father Sandoval can tell you exactly what happened," she replied while sharing a glance with the priest. "But he was there to stop Joey from falling in the road."

Richard's eyes darted around the room refusing to make eye contact with either Kathy, Hellen, or the priest, just rolling back and forth as he fought with something internally.

"Are you ok, Richard?" Mateo asked.

"Yes...I'm fine. And...thank you."

In the three weeks that followed that night of violence and Holy intervention in their home, a calm fell over the house. Father Sandoval and Hellen both came through for the family and, with the charity of others, they put a plan in motion to begin their exodus of Walnut Street forever. Kathy took Hellen's advice and made arrangements to move her family out of the house. An uncle on her mother's side who lived just outside of Albany agreed to help them out while they figured out a more permanent residence. Kathy and Stacey worked tirelessly through the days repacking their belongings and discarding junk they could live without.

Joey came around first after a few days of being confined to his bed. He didn't budge from his Batman sheet and comforter for the first thirty-six hours, leaving them drenched in sweat. When he did finally wake, any doubt Kathy had about Hellen's advice fell to pieces. Hearing her young son retell the story of that night in his own words set the wheels in motion.

Richard, however, was not present for the decisions made about the near future. He never recovered to full capacity. The PTSD alone handicapped his attention to detail, as well hobbling him with a deficit of energy. Kathy understood that what happened to him could have also plagued her or Stacey, so she recognized that he needed space and time to heal. The rest of the family left him alone over those next few weeks.

Time faded in and out without a touchstone for the day or hour. The next Tuesday he woke up to Stacey bringing him some toast and a glass of grapefruit juice. His memory remained competent up until he had almost finished eating. Somewhere before the last bite he closed his eyes and opened them once more while staring at a pale, clammy doppelganger in the bathroom mirror. Night had fallen by then and darkness overtook the mid-morning daylight seeping through the blinds just a moment ago. Pale, shaking hands he didn't recognize went up to his face and massaged the skin of his cheek bones. The looking glass showed him the fingers and arms of someone else. The person before him wore hard lines across his face, like a stretch of desert dying of thirst, the premature aging of his skin showed off cracks around his expression. The disbelief surrounding his appearance muddied his perception of time further. The brief glimpses of his husk came and went with hours and sometimes days between,

leaving any progress his body made in healing impossible to decipher.

After a few minutes of quiet examination, a hazy vignette formed around his vision, followed by another familiar fit of lightheaded nausea. He stumbled through a pitch-black bedroom that he recalled being full of sunlight not long ago. In the few moments after his weathered cheek connected with the pillow, the projector of his mind's eye stopped rolling. The blacked-out hours took him again until sometime after lunch the next day.

Richard stood alone in the back yard, underneath the shade of a Sycamore tree he guessed was older than the house itself, if not remarkably close. The cool shadow and solace came as a welcome change of scenery from the bedroom.

"There you are," Kathy said as she walked across the yard towards him. "I just got off the phone with Father Sandoval. He called to ask how you were getting along."

Richard didn't respond at first. Instead, his attention became drawn to a particularly girthy branch of the Sycamore. One just a few feet above his head. For whatever reason, his mind wandered to the tree while his wife continued on about the priest's wellness checkup.

"So, how do you feel today?"

He looked down from the tree and towards the dirt beneath. He decided not to use up any energy making eye contact as he responded. "I'm fine. I just wanted to get out of the house," he responded while rubbing his eyes from fatigue.

"Well, are you hungry? I made grilled cheese and…"

Kathy's voice slowly cut out. The next thing Richard knew, he was towering over the remaining utensils not already packed up for their journey tomorrow. With the daylight he sought out just moments ago now replaced with the amber streetlamp spilling into the kitchen window, he sulked alone in the void. Without a reference of when or where he was in his blackout, he glanced to the digital clock on the stove. The clock pulsed 3:01 AM in cherry numerals on the top of the range. *Did I talk to Kathy outside today? Yesterday? When is...?* His thoughts trailed off as something drove his attention to the counter by the sink. Deep inside his gut a nameless master instructed him on what his attention should be spent on. Like an invisible leash tugging on his collar, an unseen hand pulled him along until he stood in front of it. The knife block.

Stacey awoke that night to a burnt aroma wafting through the house. The smell of overcooked food breached the threshold of her bedroom door with an odor that welcomed her from her sleep at first, like the nostalgia of late-night popcorn or toast. But after a few moments reality begged to differ, and she realized the true dread of the situation. She turned on her bedroom light to see a thin haze of smoke rolling into the room. Upon opening the door, Stacey found several dozen trails of towels, laundry, toilet paper, and paper towels strewn about the hallway like party ribbons. Shredded paper was soaked in rubbing alcohol and piles of laundry lay next to a couple empty bottles of nail polish remover. Everything in the house even remotely flammable had been dragged out and let loose in a master plan of arson yet to be unleashed.

As Stacey cautiously went down the hall, the murderous intent put into this act became clearer. The epicenter resided in the kitchen. All the burners had been left wide open with pots full of boiling leftovers. Black smoke rolled from around the door of the oven as the hellish orange light from whatever had ignited inside glowed through the glass.

"MOOOOOOOOOM!" Stacey shouted as she started up the stairs to wake the rest of the family.

Why aren't the rest of them awake? she thought to herself.

She stopped on the third step. Stacey's emotional response to what stood at the top of the staircase ran the gamut from desperate relief, to confusion, then, finally crippling horror. Richard waited at the top, staring blankly ahead of him. He didn't make eye contact with his daughter, instead his vision glared through the flesh and blood of the Tudor, and into a deep nothing beyond.

"Dad?" Stacey asked cautiously.

The call didn't persuade Richard either way. He remained stiff and unresponsive as he blocked the way to the second floor. Stacey waited for him to give her anything in the way of a response. A glimmer from something wet in his right hand caught the light, bringing Stacey's attention away from her father's dead gaze. A tiny, curved blade glistened under the halogen light.

Before she could step away, the oven door blew off the hinges as the payload of burning pork loin catapulted across the kitchen into the opposite wall, followed by three casserole dishes loaded with burning ham and produce. The domino effect that began to destroy the Murdocks' home was as beautifully constructed as it was visceral and without mercy. Flaming chunks scattered across the room like napalm as they stuck to chemical-soaked paper towels and toilet tissue, which spread the fire along the floor, walls, and ceiling in every direction.

Donnie and Vaughn stood on the front lawn, in awe of the blaze roaring room by room through the Tudor, silently taking in the violent majesty of 6023 Walnut Street's funeral pyre. The choir of screams bellowed out from the home in unison as the second-floor windows blew out from the cataclysm tearing it apart.

"Not everything lives forever," Donnie said as flames devoured the façade of his most infamous repeat customer. "Maybe one day someone will rebuild, and we'll get assigned something with a nice open concept design." The infernal bureaucrat dwelled on the notion for a moment before pulling out his newest trophy. Donnie snapped his fingers, and the contract appeared in the middle of the air. It unrolled revealing a bloody signature at the bottom. *Richard K. Murdock.* Vaughn shot an awe-struck glance towards his partner and then the archaic scroll.

"I always get my mark," Donnie added.

Vaughn just nodded without saying a word. He turned back to the inferno as it took off around the roof sending flaming chunks of the ancient architecture down to the ground. The shrill banshee call of first responders cried out from a few blocks away, sending a tiny shred of hope to those who prayed for their neighbors' safety. A tiny chuckle started in Vaughn's core. He shook his head a little as the demon guffawed internally at an inside joke only he was privy to. Soon the joke mutated and evolved until the chuckle erupted from his lips. Vaughn burst out with laughter at nothing in particular.

"What's so funny?" Donnie asked.

"It's just that, somewhere in all of this," Vaughn said while motioning towards the Tudor as it now collapsed under the weight of its charred roof, "is a very important PSA about checking the batteries in your smoke detectors."

POTTER'S FIELD BLUES

Michael Tyree

About the Author

    Michael Tyree is a writer of dark fiction, machinist, and cat whisperer. He lives in Virginia with his wife Morgan, their four cats, and two dogs. He can be found online at the following.

Instagram @Michael_tyree13
Twitter @MSTyree1
Facebook @ Facebook.com/bedtimestoriesforheathens

Michael Tyree

ACKNOWLEDGEMENTS

First is honoring the dead. For obvious reasons, I wouldn't be here now typing this if it hadn't been for my mom. She was the catalyst for my love of horror, and all things spooky. Some of my best memories of her involve collecting and binge watching all of the Universal monster movies on VHS. She introduced me to the greats like Lugosi and Karloff. I know I wouldn't be the person I am today if not for her.

The person I initially confided in about this book was my wife, Morgan. She took me seriously from the first terrible pitch, till I placed the last punctuation on the final draft. Morgan was the first person to believe in me crossing the finish line and I owe her everything for it.

Big thanks to Jon "Craig" Young for taking time out of his schedule to design the artwork. Also, thank you to Kevin Massie for laying out and formatting the cover for me.

A cabal of the best friends anyone could ask for came together as alpha readers for this project. Specifically, Joleen Boelter and Beth Jennings for painstakingly going through this book with me cover to cover before anyone else.

Lastly thank you! Thank you for picking up this book and I hope you found something in these pages just for you.

Michael Tyree

COMING SOON

THE PALE HORSE

By

Michael Tyree

Preview section from the story
The Psalm of Saint Jackie

She was there, but not in the literal sense or any other senses measurable with science or reason. No, Jackie Diggs existed inside of her old skin like a dated outfit that didn't quite hang across the shoulders or fasten around her waist the same way. She was here, looking through her cold, glassy eyes at the examination room light overhead. The coroners had not shut her eyelids yet, but even if they had Jackie could still see without them. Her senses of the world around her existed in a new plane where arteries and muscle tissue were not a prerequisite.

Everything either was or was not. Jackie Diggs, in her next evolution, did not dictate any effort towards where she may go from here. If she found herself in front of pearly gates or not, she could not dwell on that now. She simply existed like the wind that carries pollen across spring fields, or the freshwater flowing downstream, carving rock in any way it saw fit. She was calm.

She remained there for days that meant nothing to her new form. Days for the medical examiner to write up his report and prepare her for the trip to the funeral home chosen by her family.

On an evening after she had been stitched back together, she received some visitors. At first it appeared as a ball of light descending from the ceiling, then a second after that. They both pulsed like the heartbeat she no longer needed and glowed with a bright gold that shamed the condition of the room she had been stored in. They stopped in mid-air and hovered for a minute before metamorphosing like two tiny suns bursting into supernovas. They expanded and contracted until the light they expelled came to term and let out a blinding flash about that room. Even in her nonexistent state of Zen, the performance made her ethereal heart heavy with what she may have considered joy once before.

When the light dimmed, two figures adorned in the same gold and light-born attire of the orbs appeared at the end of the room. A male and a female pair stood and smiled at her lifeless form. They were covered in white robes that expelled the glorious luminescence from between every crease when they moved. The woman glided closer to Jackie's body without ever touching the floor, as if parting every atom in the air around her. She tilted her head to the side and smiled at the slain doctor like a comforting parent, here to kiss scraped knees and bruised shins. If Jackie could force a smile through those corporeal lips now governed by rigor mortis, she would indeed.

Suddenly something changed in the face of the male being. It contorted in displeasure, somewhere between dread and disgust. He opened his mouth, but the words were not of any human language. They came out as one long distorted chord like a steam engine horn screaming its obscene howl in the night. If Jackie had ownership of her mortal ears they would have most likely pooled up with blood and liquified brain matter at the holy exclamation. It pointed to her body and when the second being looked down and saw it, she averted her now shut eyes at the perversion. She stumbled back, returning her gaze to Jackie's corpse with her hands over her mouth.

For the first time since she was tethered to her former body, she began to feel stings of the flesh. She understood what it meant to be cold once more. It was slow at first, but eventually a shiver ran up her nonexistent spine, sending goosebumps across phantom flesh. A charcoal-colored smoke crept around her right side, just in her peripheral. The more that lurched into view, the more distance grew between Jackie and the golden beings. Soon the female figure had receded back to where her partner stood against.

The smoke grew in volume as it began wrapping around the exam table on every side. It split apart and took three forms throughout the morgue, each floating through the air like tattered black flags, spilling wildfire fumes through their flailing ribbons. The black smog gave the shredded, charred cloth masses what resembled heads, and shoulders. Just like the one she saw in the hall that day, they had long gangly arms that remained upright in a posture to grapple with whatever crossed them.

The one closest to her floated over Jackie's corpse and moved its head around, scanning with eyes hidden deep in the shadow of its hood. It reached down with care and placed its fingers upon a dark outline of a hand the same size directly over her left breast. It looked back towards its compatriots then to the holy beings. The angels tried to protest, stepping forward in unspoken disagreement, but the other two beings of vapor and shadow stepped in their way, forcing them back to their corner.

It removed its hand from her chest and brought its bony tar-tinted fingers to the side of her face. Its articulation of fume and ripped linen lacked the ability to appear as anything but erratic and twitchy, but Jackie knew the gesture was meant as a caress. She felt its thoughts the second it's charred skin slid across her cheek and temple.

Cries of anguish rang through her head, but not of the damned, or any preview of infernal constitution. No, the screams and pleas of those long overdue justice. Millions of voices filled her mind. Like a symphony of sorrow, those disembodied declarations yelling to the sky to their merciful deity somehow found her ear instead. She lay there, soul on the cusp of a sadness Jackie thought she was now immune from in her most recent state.

It did not need to speak in a sense meant for her former ears. She could feel its thoughts unfolding in her own mind. She knew what it asked, what it offered, and the choice that only she had a say in. The golden beings shook their heads at the fellowship displayed in front of them. But she did not pay attention to them. Her choice was made, here side by side with her feral angel.

It removed its hand from her face and brought it down near her torso. With their offer accepted it pierced her chest cavity in one swift push of its hand. Flesh and muscle receded around the phantom limb like hot, pink candle wax. With a snap of its fingers, ribs gave up their ghost with a wet crunch before falling to the side. It pulled back revealing the heart of Jackie Diggs in its coal-colored palm.

Jackie watched as the other two who held her golden visitors at bay now surrounded her former body as well. They did not need to stand guard any longer as the holy ones had already retreated in disgust. Suddenly she was no longer tethered to that corporeal form riddled with bullet holes and the witness marks of morgue technicians. She was standing side by side with her new companions.

The one holding her deceased core organ put it up to its cowl and consumed a piece of it with its nonexistent teeth. It pulled the heart away and handed it to the black phantom hovering near the body's feet. Suddenly sensations returned to Jackie. She was no longer numb to the world, but instead she felt the air move around and then through her. She was not standing barefoot on the cold tile as her once rotting avatar, but instead she floated above the ground like a buoyant child living amongst rippling ocean current. The molecules and particles of the world around her flowed in and out of Jackie's form, as she became one with it all.

The second phantom continued their visceral communion with her heart and as it removed another third of it into its gullet, she heard the voices again. But this time she did not feel the cusp of sorrow as before. Only an understanding of purpose crossed her mind in the reaches that still belonged to her alone. The cries, the screams, the death bed pleas, she heard them all one by one. She did not need any instruction or explanation as to what it meant, what they showed her. Her old life of student debt and torn ligaments died with her former flesh as the last morsel of muscle was consumed.

All she knew now were the voices.

Made in the USA
Middletown, DE
11 January 2022

57826149R00166